"Marriage is a big commitment."

"It isn't like we love each other." Abby held her breath, not sure what she hoped to hear from John.

"We like each other," he said slowly. "Isn't that enough?"

"Are you planning on this being a real marriage?" she asked, her voice barely above a whisper.

"Yes."

The flat answer made her shiver, but she couldn't have said whether it was with anticipation or uncertainty. She jumped when John's hand cupped her chin, turning her face to his. Her eyes met his reluctantly.

"Would it be such a hardship to have a real marriage with me, Abby?" There was tenderness and a certain humor in the gentle question.

She remembered the kisses they'd shared, the kisses that had haunted her dreams. She shook her head, a delicate flush coming up in her cheeks. *A hardship?* she thought. *Actually, it'd be anything but.*

Dear Reader,

For all the hundreds of you who wrote in to tell us how much you loved Dallas Schulze's *Together Always* (Harlequin American Romance #291) and who expressed concern at the character of John Lonigan being left alone at the end of that book, Dallas has written *A Practical Marriage*.

You'll meet up with John once again, a few years after *Together Always*. He's still sexy, still a bit of the "bad boy"—but his time he's met his match in Abby Taylor.

"John is too nice a guy to be left unattached," Dallas says. "I think Abby is the perfect woman for him."

We hope you agree.

Sincerely,

Debra Matteucci
Senior Editor & Editorial Coordinator

DALLAS SCHULZE

A PRACTICAL MARRIAGE

Harlequin Books

TORONTO • NEW YORK • LONDON
AMSTERDAM • PARIS • SYDNEY • HAMBURG
STOCKHOLM • ATHENS • TOKYO • MILAN

Published October 1991

ISBN 0-373-16409-2

A PRACTICAL MARRIAGE

Chapter One

Today was his fortieth birthday.

John Michael Lonigan frowned at his reflection in the mirror over the sink. Forty. Four-Oh. His thirties gone forever. Middle age staring him straight in the face.

Were the lines around his eyes just a little deeper today than they had been yesterday? Maybe there was just a little more gray sprinkled through his dark hair?

Stepping back from the mirror, he studied his body for signs of incipient decay. He'd pulled on a pair of jeans before going out to get the paper but he hadn't bothered with a shirt. Were the muscles in his arms just a little too soft? And was there just a hint of a bulge around his waistline? Not much, certainly, but he had to face the fact that he'd gotten soft.

Scowling, he picked up the brush and slathered shaving soap over his jaw. The lather formed a white beard, as if predicting what he'd look like in another forty years.

"Remind me not to grow a beard," he muttered, picking up a straight razor.

He applied the honed edge to his jawline. Forty wasn't so bad, he told himself, drawing the blade across the stubble on his chin. The prime of life, really. He wasn't ready for a rocking chair yet.

But the small pep talk did little to relieve his gloomy mood. The fact was, half his life was gone—and what did he have to show for it?

A rented room over the liquor store where he worked. Some money in the bank and a Mercedes Gullwing parked in a shed behind the store. He'd bought the car with the proceeds from selling his father's liquor store in Los Angeles. It was a substantial piece of property but hardly an impressive list for a forty-year-old man.

He had no real home. No family to speak of. No one who'd miss him if he disappeared tomorrow. That was the way it had been most of his life. He'd drifted from place to place, seen quite a bit of the world, but he'd never set down any roots.

John rinsed away the last of the shaving cream and patted his face dry. Over the towel, he met his reflected eyes, seeing a deep weariness in them. His eyes revealed his age. They were eyes that had seen too much of the world's frailties, witnessed too much of its cruelties.

It wasn't the numbers on a calendar that made him feel old. It was the look in those gray eyes staring back at him from the mirror.

With a grunt of disgust, he tossed the towel down and turned away from his reflection. Staring into mirrors and debating about the meaning of his life—he *was* getting old.

TURNING FORTY was hardly the best way to start the day. Unfortunately it was beginning to look as if that might have been the high point. Before lunch, John managed to drop a six-pack of beer on his foot, to the detriment of both bottles and foot.

Limping out to take care of a customer, he bumped into a stack of cases and sent them tumbling to the floor. The crash of breaking glass served to muffle a particularly pungent curse. One delivery came in late. Another came a day early but wasn't what had been ordered.

He had three calls from an elderly woman who insisted that this was the number for her cousin Millie and seemed to feel that John might be guilty of having done away with the woman in order to purloin her phone number.

All in all, it was not one of his better days. By three in the afternoon, he was ready to go home. The store's owner, Bill Davis, was due to arrive at four o'clock. The minute Bill arrived, he was leaving.

John leaned against the counter. Maybe he'd stayed in this town long enough. Maybe it was time to move on. When he'd arrived in Beaumont, Washington, he hadn't really planned on staying. Actually he hadn't *planned* much of anything for the past couple of years.

Driving down the main road of the small town, he'd seen a Help Wanted sign in the window of Bill's Liquor. Without giving it much thought, he'd parked the Mercedes in front of the store and gone in to apply for the job.

That was four months ago, and he was still here. He liked Bill, liked the sleepy little farming town. Days had drifted into weeks. With not much behind him and nothing in particular ahead, there hadn't seemed any reason to leave.

But when he woke up this morning and realized it was his birthday, he'd felt a wave of the old restlessness. He'd stayed here longer than he'd stayed anywhere in years. Maybe it was time to move on, see what lay over the next hill.

It was three forty-five when the bell over the door rang. John looked up, hoping it was Bill coming in early.

But the figure stepping into the store was considerably smaller than Bill. And younger. Probably not much more than ten or eleven. He backed through the door, his head bent over something he held. It wasn't until he straightened and turned that John realized that this wasn't just a kid wanting to buy a candy bar.

The faded jeans and T-shirt were practically a uniform these days. But unless fashions had taken a radical turn, John doubted that the ski mask was typical attire.

Nor was the .38 held between both fists and pointed in his direction.

John had been leaning against the counter, contemplating his future. Now he straightened slowly. There was nothing like looking down the barrel of a gun to sharpen your interest in the present.

His hand dropped casually to the counter. On a shelf just under his fingers was the gun Bill kept in the store in case of burglary. Not that there was much worry about that in a town the size of Beaumont. John had cleaned and oiled the gun a couple of weeks ago, more for something to do than anything else.

"Stick 'em up." The words were right out of a bad western. The voice was right out of the *Muppet Babies*.

If this kid was more than ten, he'd be surprised. Ten and scared to death, John thought, hearing the tremor in the voice.

He wasn't the only one.

"This isn't a real good idea," John offered quietly.

"I've got a gun," the boy said, as if John might not have noticed. He came a step closer and then had to stop. The ski mask was too big and it was threatening to slip down over his eyes. Clenching one hand around the grips of the gun, the boy tugged the mask back up. The weight of the gun dragged his hand down, but he was too far away for John to make a grab for the weapon.

"Look, this is no way to solve your problems." John edged his fingers lower. He didn't doubt that he could reach his gun before the boy could get up the courage to pull the trigger but he sure as hell didn't want to shoot the kid. On the other hand, the boy might be new at this game but the gun wasn't going to make allowances for that. He could end up just as dead being shot by an amateur as he could by a professional.

"I want all your money."

It wasn't hard to guess that the lines had been carefully rehearsed with no room for innovation.

"There isn't all that much here, boy. Believe me, it's not worth it. The police will be after you in a matter of minutes. Why don't you put down the gun and we'll talk about this."

Blue eyes blinked at him from the holes in the mask. It was clear that, in planning this robbery, the boy hadn't expected there to be any discussion. He'd obviously had a certain dialogue in mind and John wasn't reading his lines properly.

"Put...put the money in this." His voice shook so badly he had to start the sentence twice before he could get it out. He took a step closer and thrust a blue backpack in John's direction. Written in neat white letters across it was the name Jason Taylor.

John was caught by an unexpected urge to laugh. If it hadn't been for the look of terrified determination in the boy's eyes, he would have begun to suspect this was some sort of joke. But the gun didn't look very funny. On the other hand, up close, it didn't look as threatening as it had from a distance. For one thing, he could see light through the cylinder that indicated that most, if not all of the chambers, were empty. And the important ones were empty. Whichever direction the cylinder turned before firing, there wasn't a bullet to be fired.

John reached for the backpack, deliberately not extending his arm, forcing the boy to come a step closer. Uneasy, the boy edged forward, struggling to keep the gun pointed in the right direction as the weight strained his thin wrist.

John took hold of the backpack with one hand, getting a good grip on it. With a quick, hard jerk, he pulled the boy forward, throwing him off balance. His free hand closed over the gun, wrenching it out of the boy's hand.

With a speed borne of fear, the boy released the pack and darted for the door. Cursing, John stuffed the gun in the waistband of his jeans. Putting one hand on the counter, he vaulted over it. He caught the would-be thief before he reached the door, his hand closing over a handful of T-shirt and jerking him to an abrupt halt.

"Lemme go! Lemme go!" The boy writhed wildly, threatening to make his getaway yet. John solved the problem by jerking him off his feet and hoisting him under one arm like a sack of laundry. He carried his struggling captive into the storeroom behind the counter and set him on the floor.

The ski mask had slipped to one side and now completely covered the boy's eyes. John reached out and plucked it off, dropping it to the floor. Frightened blue eyes stared at him out of a stark white face. Sun-bleached brown hair stuck up in wild disarray. The boy looked like an advertisement for the Average American Boy, aged ten. He should be in school or playing sandlot baseball. Or maybe he should be dipping some little girl's pigtails into an inkwell.

What he shouldn't have been doing on a bright spring afternoon was attempting to rob a liquor store.

John pulled the gun out of his waistband, turning his attention to it. A few seconds of silence in which to contemplate what he'd just attempted to do could do the kid no harm.

The gun was far from new, though it had been cared for. A Colt Police Special, showing a fair amount of wear. The cylinder flipped out with a click. Empty, just as he'd thought.

"Where did you get this?" He let his eyes settle on his captive.

"None of your business." The defiance would have been more effective if the boy's voice hadn't shaken so badly.

"Fine. But I think the sheriff is going to consider it his business."

"The sheriff?" The words were choked.

"Sure. What did you think would happen when you tried to rob a store? The police are usually involved in things like this."

"But I didn't rob you," he protested, his voice trembling.

"You tried." John set the gun on top of a stack of liquor cases and folded his arms across his chest. His cool eyes studied the would-be felon in front of him.

"Where'd you get the gun, Jason?"

"How'd you know my name?"

"It's on your backpack," John told him, gesturing to the nylon heap on the floor. "Jason Taylor. Next time you go to rob a store, I'd suggest you find something else to put the money in."

"I won't do it again. Honest I won't."

Those blue eyes shone with sincerity. John didn't doubt that it was genuine. He hadn't spent much time around kids but he'd spent a lot of time analyzing people, often enough with his life depending on the accuracy of his judgment. Jason Taylor wasn't likely to try anything this stupid again. Still, he couldn't just turn the boy loose.

"Does the gun belong to your parents?"

"It was my dad's," Jason offered reluctantly.

"Was?"

"He's dead. So's my mom." For an instant, his lower lip showed a hint of a tremor before he tightened it. He glared up at John. "I don't need no sympathy."

"I wasn't going to give you any," John told him coolly. Surprise flickered in the boy's eyes. John wondered if he'd been secretly hoping that his orphaned state would soften John's attitude.

"Who's taking care of you?"

"I'm not going to tell you."

John sighed. "Look, I know your name. I wouldn't be surprised if you've got your address in that backpack." The way Jason's eyes flickered uneasily told John his guess had struck a nerve. "It wouldn't take me long to find out where you live, even if you don't tell me. But if you make me go to all that trouble, I'm going to have to go through the sheriff. I doubt if you want that."

"You said you were going to call him, anyway."

"I could be persuaded otherwise if you'd show a little cooperation."

"I said I wouldn't ever do it again." He gave John an earnest look. "Really I won't. I swear it. Couldn't you just let me go?"

"No."

The blunt refusal made Jason drop his eyes to the floor, but not before John had caught the sheen of tears in them. He hardened his heart. If he'd been a more nervous type, the sheriff could have been trying to find the boy's next of kin, and Jason could have ended up as a feature on the evening's news.

"Who do you live with, Jason? Your grandparents?"

"Ain't got none."

"So who do you live with?" When there was no answer, John heaved a loud sigh and straightened away from the crates he'd been leaning against. "Have it your way. It won't take the sheriff long to find out."

"Wait!"

John turned back at the panicked cry, raising one dark brow in question. Jason gave him a pleading look but John's expression remained implacable. The boy's eyes dropped to the floor.

"I live with my Aunt Abby," he said sullenly. "She's been taking care of us since Mom and Dad died."

"Us?"

"Me and my little sister."

"Would your aunt approve of what you did today?"

"No," Jason mumbled to the floor. "She'd be real upset, if she knew." He threw a quick glance upward.

John was surprised to discover that he wasn't entirely immune to the hopeful look in those eyes. But he hardened his heart against the urge to tell the boy that his aunt didn't have to know.

It took a few more minutes to pry Jason's address loose. By then, John was feeling like a first cousin to Atilla the Hun. Never in his life had he expected to have to interrogate a ten-year-old boy. Given a choice, he'd rather be tortured himself than have to do it again. By the time he had the address, he was beginning to think it would have been much simpler just to let the kid rob the store.

Especially since now he was going to have to go talk to the boy's aunt. Aunt Abby was probably seventy-five and deaf. She probably thought her nephew was a saint. John wasn't looking forward to disabusing her of the idea.

ABIGAIL TAYLOR was not having a good day. It had started when she put a run in her last pair of panty hose and it hadn't gotten any better since. Working as a checker at Dale's Supermarket was hardly one of life's more exciting jobs but it was generally tolerable. Today, it had been anything but.

By the time her shift ended at four o'clock, she felt as if she'd spent the day participating in a contest no one had told her about. This had to have been the preliminary round in the Customer From Hell Sweepstakes, she thought as she slipped into her car and shut the door behind her.

Leaning her head back against the cracked vinyl upholstery, she closed her eyes. The car was hot from sitting in the sun all day. There were only a few parking spaces with any pretense to shade and they were claimed by the first to arrive. Abby was never among them. By the time she'd managed to get her niece and nephew settled for the day, she felt as if she were doing pretty well just to make it to work at all.

Today, she didn't care about the heat. She didn't care about anything but the fact that she was alone. For a few precious moments there was no one arguing about whether she should accept an expired coupon; no one suggesting that her I.Q. was something less than normal since any fool would know that the mayonnaise was not in aisle eight.

The stuffy car felt like a haven. But she couldn't sit here for long. She was supposed to pick up Mara at preschool at four-fifteen. With a sigh, Abby sat up and slid the key into the ignition, muttering a prayer that the tired old engine would start one more time. It turned over sullenly before catching but it was welcome to be as sullen as it wanted, just as long as it started.

Pulling out of the parking lot, Abby put the unpleasant day behind her. It wouldn't do for Mara to sense that she was upset. As always, thoughts of her niece brought a mixture of love and worry.

But only the love was allowed to show when Mara came out to greet her aunt. Around her, the other children ran to greet their parents, waving pictures they'd colored or books they'd borrowed from the school library, full of eager chatter, their voices sometimes painfully shrill.

Mara was like a quiet pool in the midst of a bubbling stream. Her tiny jeans and T-shirt were as tidy and clean as when Abby had put them on her this morning. No grubby knees or grass stains to show that she'd spent the day running and playing. Her hair, paler blond than her aunt's, was still neatly braided.

Abby blinked back tears, her smile extra bright as Mara approached. She bent to hug her, feeling Mara lean into the embrace.

"How was your day, sweetie? Is that a picture you drew? Oh, it's beautiful." Abby rambled on without waiting for the answers she knew wouldn't come. Mara hadn't spoken in a year, not since the day her parents were killed.

Taking the small hand in hers, Abby led the child to the car, keeping up a light patter as she settled Mara into her seat and latched the safety belt around her.

Jason would be home by now. She hated the fact that he came to an empty house. Steve and Diane would have hated their son being a latchkey child.. But Abby didn't have much choice. She had to earn a living. She'd managed to work out her hours so that Jason was only alone for an hour or two. It was the best she could do but she still felt consumed by guilt.

Guilt had become an all too familiar emotion in the past year. Guilt that she couldn't possibly take the place of both parents. Guilt that her niece—her bright, beautiful niece—didn't speak. Guilt that Jason seemed to feel he was now the man of the house and tried to take on the responsibilities that went with it. Guilt that she didn't ever have enough time or money to do the things she needed to do.

Her hands tightened on the wheel as she slowed to avoid the pothole at the corner of Maple and Ivy. The pothole had been there since before she got her driver's license. The town council kept saying they didn't have the money to fix it but the real truth was that it was an easy way to slow traffic. Simpler than putting in a stop sign.

Money. So many of her problems came down to money. The estimate for the new roof had been higher than she'd expected. If she put a new roof on the house, it would wipe out her savings. On the other hand, if she didn't put a new roof on, she was going to have to buy scuba gear for the three of them before next winter's rains hit.

But she didn't have to worry about that right now, she reminded herself. It was spring. Summer stretched ahead. If they could make it through summer's lighter rains, maybe she'd have come up with a way to pay for a roof by autumn.

Of course, summer meant school would be out, which meant she'd have to worry about Jason being home alone all day instead of just for a couple of hours between his leaving school and her getting home.

Of course, Jason would be offended by the suggestion that she might worry about him. Nearly eleven, he was so sure he could take care of himself. And most of the time he could. But what about in an emergency?

He could always go to Mrs. Childers, Abby reminded herself. Mrs. Childers lived next door, but she was nearly eighty and likely to be in need of help herself.

Abby rubbed her fingers over the ache starting to build across her forehead. Sometimes she wondered if Steve and Diane hadn't misplaced their confidence in her when they'd left the children in her care.

She was a twenty-six-year-old single woman with a degree in botany. Hardly the best qualifications for raising two children. But Jason and Mara were her family and she was determined to keep the three of them together.

She chewed on her lower lip as she flipped on the signal and turned the car onto the tree-lined street where they lived. Glancing sideways at Mara, she caught the little girl's eyes on her, wide and solemn as if she sensed her aunt's mood.

"We're almost home, sweetie." Abby pushed her worries aside and smiled at Mara.

Whenever she began to feel like throwing in the towel and admitting that she couldn't handle her sudden parenthood, she had only to look at Mara or Jason to know it was all worthwhile.

"I bet George has missed you." Mention of the dog brought a smile to Mara's eyes. George had followed Jason home from school a few months before and had proceeded to move in with the small family, despite Abby's halfhearted protests. George was the size of a Shetland pony but he had the brain of a flea. He was shaggy, untrainable, affectionate and completely devoted to the children. For Abby, he held a casual affection. An affection she suspected was due more to the fact that she provided his kibble than anything else.

Approaching their house, she felt her spirits rise. The house was the shabbiest one on the block but it was home. And she and Mara and Jason were a family. Things were bound to start looking up, she told herself.

But perhaps not immediately.

Abby's smile faded as she turned the big old sedan into the driveway. Parked at the curb was a sleek black car. She didn't recognize the make. Cars had never held much interest for her beyond their ability to get her from place to place. But she knew expensive when she saw it. It wasn't the kind of car a person expected to see in a town like Beaumont.

She would have assumed it was someone visiting one of the neighbors if it hadn't been for the rather large man sitting on her front steps. Jason stood next to him, his thin shoulders unnaturally squared as he watched his aunt's scruffy old Ford pull into the driveway.

Abby fought to keep her uneasiness from showing as she parked the car and leaned over to unfasten Mara's safety belt. Pushing open her door, she circled the car to open the passenger door.

There was nothing wrong, she told herself. The man had just given Jason a ride home. Or he was a coach or teacher at the school.

The stranger was now standing next to Jason, towering over the slender boy. Abby approached them slowly. One look at her nephew's face told her the gentleman was not here on a friendly visit.

Squaring her shoulders, she straightened her spine, wishing she were an imposing five foot nine instead of a measly inch over five feet. Whatever mischief Jason had gotten into, it couldn't be all that serious. He was a good boy. Maybe he'd broken a window or something.

She stopped in front of the stranger and looked up—a long way up—into a pair of cool gray eyes.

"Aunt Abby, I didn't—"

A glance from the stranger cut Jason off. At another time, Abby might have felt a twinge of admiration. She'd certainly never managed to shut Jason up so quickly. At the moment all she felt was indignation. How dare he give Jason such a look.

"I'm Abigail Taylor." She thrust out her hand, trying to look calm and authoritative. If Jason had to break a window, couldn't it have been in some nice little old lady's house? Did he have to offend a man with eyes that seemed to be weighing her and finding her wanting?

"John Lonigan." His voice was deep and slow. His hand swallowed hers. She felt the faint roughness of calluses. And a surprising tingle of awareness. "I gather you're Jason's guardian," he said as he released her hand.

"That's right." She lifted her chin. "Is there a problem?"

"You might say that," he said slowly.

"If Jason's broken a window or gotten into some mischief, I'm sure we can work out an arrangement for him to pay you back . . ." A glance at Jason made her words trail off. Her heart gave a faint, unpleasant bump of panic. The boy looked positively terrified. And guilty. Whatever he'd done, it was something more than a broken window.

"Aunt Abby, I—" Jason broke off at a glance from the tall stranger.

"Actually it's a bit more serious than that," he said.

He reached into the familiar blue backpack he was holding—Jason's backpack. "Does this look familiar?"

Lying in his hand was a gun. Abby remembered it quite well. It had been Steve's. She'd put it in the back of her closet, out of reach, she'd thought.

"What happened?" she whispered, dragging her eyes from the gun to his face—his hard, unforgiving face.

"Jason used this to try to rob a liquor store this afternoon."

He went on, but Abby heard nothing beyond the first sentence. For the first time in her life, she wished she were the sort of woman who fainted. She would have welcomed oblivion.

But Abby never fainted. And she never, ever cried.

She promptly burst into tears.

Chapter Two

"I'm sorry. I'm sorry." The apology was gulped out between sobs. "I never cry," she added fiercely, denying the evidence before him.

John returned the gun to the backpack, looking away from Abby to give her a chance to regain her control. His eyes met those of the little girl at her side. He guessed she was about four—a pretty child, with flaxen blond hair and wide blue eyes. Wide blue eyes that were fixed on him with that solemn attention that seems peculiar to the young of most species. John reached up to smooth his fingers over his jaw, uneasy under that steady regard.

It wasn't his fault her aunt was crying.

"I'm sorry." Abby was digging through a purse of truly mammoth proportions, sniffing and gulping. "I never cry. Where is a damn tissue when you need one?" she asked despairingly.

John pulled a handkerchief out of his back pocket and silently extended it. She hesitated, sniffing, and then snatched it out of his hand.

"Thank you." She wiped her eyes and then blew her nose. "I never cry," she muttered into the soggy linen square. "Never." She seemed to think that repetition might deny the tears still trickling down her cheeks.

"It's okay," John said.

"No, it's not. This is not the way I handle things like this. Not that Jason has ever... has ever robbed..." Her voice disappeared again and she buried her nose in the hankie, mumbling apologies.

John was beginning to wish he'd just let the kid rob the place. He shifted uneasily, glancing around in hopes that someone was going to do something to get them all out of this awkward scene. But no one appeared. There was just him, alone with a sobbing woman, a four-year-old with accusing eyes and a would-be bank robber who looked as if he might burst into tears himself.

"Look, why don't we move this all indoors," he said, noticing the curtains moving in the house across the street.

It took only a moment to shepherd the little group onto the porch, which was badly in need of paint. Abby fumbled in her purse and came up with a key ring. As she was unlocking the door, John wondered why she'd bothered to lock it in the first place. The cheap lock was badly set in the frame; the door itself was warped. A solid kick would have sprung the door open.

He frowned. A woman living alone with two children really ought to have better protection. Even in a town this size, crime was a possibility. Not that it was any concern of his. All he wanted was to impress the seriousness of her nephew's crime on Ms. Abigail Taylor. Make sure the kid was scared out of any future urges toward felonious behavior and then get out of there. Weeping women and children were way out of his line.

Once in the little hall, Abby stopped, still sniffing and dabbing at her eyes with the handkerchief. The little girl stood next to her, one small hand wrapped around the hem of her aunt's skirt, her accusing eyes fixed on John. Jason hovered behind the two of them, his thin young face pale and distressed.

John waited, but no one made any suggestions. He'd have liked nothing better than to walk out and forget this whole mess. He didn't want to get involved any further than he already was. But he'd started this thing and now he had to stick with it to the bitter end. Next time, he promised himself, he'd just call the police and wash his hands of the whole thing. What on earth had made him play Good Samaritan? He sighed.

"Where's the kitchen?"

While Abby struggled to stem a seemingly inexhaustible flow of tears, John took charge. Following his hostess's sniffed instructions, he put a pot of water on to boil for instant coffee.

"You shouldn't be doing this," Abby said, dabbing at her red nose with the handkerchief. She wasn't quite sure how she'd come to be sitting at her own kitchen table while the man Jason had tried to rob—God, what an incredible thought—made coffee.

Her guest glanced at her without answering and rinsed out a coffee mug. She spared a brief wish that she'd somehow found time to do the dishes before she left this morning but there wasn't much force behind the thought. The tears had left her drained. The headache that had been threatening all afternoon was rapidly becoming a painful reality. She wasn't sure she could have gotten out of the chair at that moment, let alone boiled water.

Dumping a heaping spoonful of instant coffee into the mug, John filled the cup with hot water, gave it a quick stir and set it in front of her.

"You look like you could use the caffeine," he said.

"I suppose I could." She took a grateful sip, trying to gather her thoughts, trying to ignore the pounding in her head.

Mara had come to stand next to her chair, leaning against Abby's knee, her eyes fixed on John's large and unaccustomed presence in the rather scruffy kitchen. Jason, the cause of the whole mess, was hanging back in a corner near the doorway, his young face so anxious that Abby wanted to put her arm around him and tell him not to worry.

But she couldn't tell him that. This was far more than a childish prank that could be brushed off with his promise not to do it again. Abby caught sight of the backpack her visitor had set on the counter and shuddered, feeling her eyes sting anew. She'd been so sure the gun was well hidden.

She straightened her shoulders, drawing a deep breath. It was too late to fully salvage the situation. She'd already made a complete and utter fool of herself. There was nothing she could do about that, but it was time she proved she wasn't a total nitwit.

Her guest was leaning against the counter, his arms folded across his chest, his gaze focused on nothing in particular, giving her the time she needed to pull herself together. Under other circumstances, she might have been grateful for his consideration. At the moment, she could only wish he didn't exist.

"Mara, honey, why don't you go play in your room," Abby suggested. Mara leaned closer against Abby's knee, reluctant to leave her aunt. "Go on, sweetheart. I'm fine. Mr. Lonigan and I need to talk."

Mara looked from her to John, her suspicion easily read.

"I'm not going to hurt your aunt," John told her.

Whether it was John's blunt reassurance or the gentle push Abby gave her, Mara left Abby's side and trailed to the door. She stopped in the doorway, giving one last, uncertain look over her shoulder before disappearing.

Abby rubbed her fingers over her temple, closing her eyes for an instant. Her stomach churned in time to the pounding in her temples in miserable choreography. She hadn't had a migraine headache since college but the symptoms were unmistakable.

She swallowed hard and forced her eyes open. She'd deal with this situation. She'd be firm, adult and prove to all of them that she was a suitable guardian. She'd see Mr. John Lonigan on his way and then go crawl into a corner somewhere and die.

He was watching her, those disconcerting gray eyes concerned. "Are you all right?"

Abby felt tears sting her eyes. She swallowed them back. No, she wasn't all right. Her head hurt. She was nearly broke. She had two children to raise and no clue how to do it. It had been a hellish day. And now, to top it off, her nephew had turned into a junior Pretty Boy Floyd. She was definitely not all right.

"Just a bit of a headache," she said, forcing a smile. She was starting to see stars. Wouldn't it just be a peachy end to a thoroughly rotten day if she fainted at his feet?

"Jason, would you like to tell me what happened today?"

She shifted slightly to bring her nephew into better view. The small motion sent a wave of nausea washing over her. She could feel dampness breaking out on her forehead though her skin felt icy cold.

"I'm sorry, Aunt Abby. I was trying to help. I know you're worried about money and everything, and you said I couldn't quit school and get a job."

He went on, but Abby caught only an occasional word. Something about wanting to help. His voice faded in and out as the pain in her temples expanded until it filled her head.

John listened to the boy's garbled explanation with half an ear. He'd pried most of the story out of him on the short drive here. Frankly, he was more concerned about Jason's aunt. She wasn't at all what he'd been expecting. She was younger, softer, prettier and much too vulnerable.

His gaze sharpened as she lifted her fingers to her temple again. Her hand was trembling. In the past few minutes, her face had lost all color so that her eyes—rather pretty eyes, he noticed—looked more black than brown. Her forehead was damp though the room was far from hot.

"Ms. Taylor." John cut into Jason's garbled explanation. Jason subsided into silence, looking grateful for the interruption.

Abby winced as his voice echoed in her aching head. It took a conscious effort to turn her eyes to his.

"Are you *sure* you're all right?"

"I'm . . . Actually I'm afraid I don't feel very well." She pressed her fingers against her forehead.

"Migraine?" John had once worked with a man who suffered from migraines, and Abby's pallor and the still way she held herself brought back old memories.

"I . . . never get migraines," she said faintly.

John felt himself grin. She never cried, either. He wondered what else Abigail Taylor "never" did. There was something touching about her stubborn denial of the obvious.

"Maybe you'd better go lie down," he suggested quietly.

"But we need to talk," she protested, looking as if a stiff breeze could carry her off.

"We'll talk later," he said soothingly. "You'd better lie down before you pass out. Jason, why don't you help your aunt to her room."

She frowned and then looked as if she profoundly regretted the small movement. Things weren't going at all well. She should have taken charge of this situation from the start.

"Maybe you're right." She eased herself to her feet, moving very carefully, as if she had serious doubts about the ability of her head to stay on her shoulders. "If you could come back tomorrow, Mr. Lonigan . . ."

"We'll talk later," he promised.

"Jason will see you out. I'm very sorry about everything." She gestured vaguely.

"Don't worry about it."

John watched her leave the room, Jason hovering nervously at her elbow. He should leave now. There was no reason to hang around here. He glanced around the rather shabby kitchen, noticing the cupboard doors that needed repair, the spot where the tile was coming loose.

While waiting for Abby to come home, he'd had plenty of time to notice the house's shabby appearance. It was the sort of place a real-estate agent would euphemistically call a "handyman's special." A more realistic term might be a "dump."

The place needed a lot of hours and several thousand dollars to put it into shape, as well as someone who knew a hammer from a screwdriver. He'd be willing to take a guess that Abby didn't have the first two and he had his doubts about her knowledge of carpentry.

But it was none of his concern. He'd done his good deed for the day by not having her nephew thrown in jail. That was as involved as he wanted to get.

Before he'd taken more than a step toward the door, Jason came back into the kitchen. John looked at him, wishing he didn't feel a certain tug at his emotions. The boy was so young. Wanting to help his aunt had been a noble motive, even if his method had been poorly chosen.

"Does she get headaches like this very often?" John asked when the boy showed no signs of saying anything.

Jason shrugged, his eyes darting to John and then away. "Not since she's been taking care of me and Mara. She hasn't been sick once. You think she's goin' to be all right?"

"Sure." John didn't need a degree in child psychology to read the fear underlying the question. Since his parents' death, Jason's aunt probably represented the only security in his small world. "After she's had a chance to rest for a while, she'll be as good as new."

John reached into his pocket for his keys. There was no sense in hanging around. Unless he missed his guess, Abby wouldn't be up for a discussion anytime this evening.

"Are you going?" Jason's question was sharp.

John would have thought that the boy would be doing handstands over the prospects of him leaving. But he didn't look particularly happy at the thought. Maybe it wasn't such a great idea to leave the kid alone with his little sister and an aunt who was down for the count.

Not that it was any of his concern.

He frowned at Jason. "You hungry?"

Jason shrugged. "Kinda."

"You think your sister might be hungry?"

"Maybe. Mara don't eat much."

"*Doesn't* eat much," John corrected absently. He reached for the phone book on the counter. "How do you feel about pizza?"

"Great!" Jason's face brightened. "With pepperoni?"

"Sure." John punched out the number of an Italian restaurant that promised to deliver. Wouldn't it be great to be Jason's age, when the promise of pizza was enough to put the world back on an even keel?

He was only hanging around because it was the responsible thing to do. As soon as "Aunt Abby" woke up, he'd be on his way. This whole mess had taken up enough of his time as it was. This was hardly how he'd imagined spending his fortieth birthday.

Not that he'd had any plans. Still, it was the principle of the thing. A man just didn't spend his fortieth birthday baby-sitting a ten-year-old burglar and a four-year-old with suspicious blue eyes. Not even if their aunt did have the biggest, brownest eyes he'd ever seen.

ABBY WOKE SLOWLY, aware that the house was quiet around her. She didn't attempt to move at first but lay still, taking a careful inventory. Her head actually felt as if it might stay in place. The blinding ache was gone, replaced by a faint, residual tenderness.

Moving slowly, she turned to look at the clock. *Eleven-fifteen.* Long past time for Jason and Mara to be in bed. She could hear the low murmur of the television, which meant Jason had probably taken the opportunity to stay up late.

Jason. She closed her eyes. Staying up late was the least of Jason's crimes today. Was it possible that she'd dreamed the whole mess when she got home from work? With a sigh, she abandoned the hope.

Abby forced herself to remember. John Lonigan. The name was etched in her mind, as was a picture of its owner. Tall, broad shouldered. Dark hair, with a dusting of silver at the temples. Not a classically handsome face but attractive. Gray eyes, a strong chin with a cleft in the center. Not a face that was easily forgotten.

At least *she* wasn't likely to forget it anytime soon. She pulled herself up and swung her legs over the side of the bed.

Jason had tried to rob a liquor store.

The thought simply wouldn't come into focus. Not Jason, who'd tried so hard to be strong when his parents were killed. Not Jason, who had been such a model of good behavior in those first months that she'd actually welcomed it when he began to show signs of occasional mischief.

Of course, he'd been trying to help. Abby groaned, remembering his garbled explanation. Her head had been pounding so hard, she'd missed half of what he was saying but she'd caught enough to know that he'd thought this was a way to help her.

He knew she was worried about money. Hadn't he suggested quitting school to get a job only a week or two ago? She'd vetoed that suggestion, knowing that the prospect of quitting school held at least as much appeal as contributing to the family finances. She'd assured him that they'd get by, though there were times when she had strong doubts. Other than being touched by his concern, she hadn't really given the conversation another thought.

She should have known he wouldn't let go of it that easily. He'd inherited all of his father's tenacity, as well as his sense of responsibility. If Steve were alive, he'd know what to do now. God, what she wouldn't give to have Steve to help her through this.

Abby blinked back the tears that thoughts of her brother invariably brought. Steve wasn't here. But his son was and it was her responsibility to see that he grew up strong, with a solid understanding of right and wrong. Even if she hadn't dearly loved Jason in his own right, she owed her brother that much.

She ran her fingers through the waist-length fall of dark blond hair, smoothing the worst of the tangles. She'd pulled the pins out before lying down, unable to bear the feel of them against her scalp. The blue-and-gray uniform she wore to work had been discarded across the foot of the bed. She briefly considered putting on clothes, but since her intention was only to see Jason off to bed, a robe would do.

The gold silk robe had been a birthday present from Steve and Diane the year before. Abby pulled it on over her underwear, enjoying the feel of the soft silk against her skin.

She'd send Jason off to bed and then heat up a can of soup for supper. She wasn't particularly hungry but she hadn't eaten anything since breakfast—her lunch hour was spent worrying about how to pay for the roof repairs.

The living room was dark except for the flickering light from the television screen. Abby clicked her tongue in exasperation.

"How many times have I told you not to watch television in a dark room?" she muttered as she crossed the room. Chances were he'd fallen asleep anyway.

"Actually, I believe this is the first time you've mentioned it."

The deep voice was definitely not her nephew's. And neither were the long legs stretched out in front of the one chair in the room that was big enough to hold a man of his size. Abby came to a dead stop next to the sofa as John Lonigan stood up.

"Mr. Lonigan!"

"In the flesh." He reached up one hand to rub the back of his neck. "I hope I didn't startle you too much."

"No, of course not. Well, actually, I wasn't expecting to see you." Abby found her hand creeping up to draw the collar of her robe closed. She was suddenly very aware of his size.

"I wasn't expecting to be here," he admitted ruefully. "I fell asleep."

Why hadn't she taken time to get properly dressed? Because she hadn't expected to find a large—very large—man in her living room, she thought with a spurt of defensive annoyance.

"Why are you here?" she asked bluntly.

John raised one eyebrow at the touch of belligerence in her tone. "Your nephew seemed a little reluctant to be left alone with you unconscious and the little girl to watch."

"Jason is perfectly capable of keeping an eye on Mara for the evening." Abby closed her eyes as she heard the edge to her voice. Heaven knew, this man had already put up with enough from her family today. All she had to do was snap at him to complete the impression that the Taylor family was comprised of criminals and shrews.

"My mistake," John said coolly. "I apologize for intruding." He turned to leave.

"Wait." For a moment, Abby thought he was going to ignore her and walk right out the door. But he hesitated and then turned slowly. He didn't say anything, only looked at her, his eyes chilly.

"Look, I'm sorry. I didn't mean to sound like a shrew. God knows, you've had enough trouble with this family for one day. It was nice of you to stay, especially after Jason caused you so much trouble."

"I didn't mind." Abby was relieved to see his eyes warm. His mouth relaxed in a half smile. "He seems like a good kid."

"He is. He's a terrific kid."

There was a short silence. He just stood there, looking at her. Abby tightened the belt of her robe, aware that beneath it was nothing but a few scraps of nylon and lace.

"Well, I—"

"Would you—"

They both broke off. He gestured toward her. "You first."

"I was just going to ask if you'd like something to eat. You must have missed your dinner, unless Jason fixed you a peanut butter and jelly sandwich.

"Actually we had a pizza. I hope you don't mind."

"No, of course not." Abby's teeth worried at her lower lip, wondering if she should offer to pay for the pizza. Would he be offended? Did she even have enough money in her purse to make such a gesture?

"I'd already ordered the pizza," he said casually. "I just called and asked them to deliver it here instead."

Abby eyed him doubtfully, wondering if he was just trying to make her feel better. But there was nothing to read in his bland expression. With a sigh, she gave up trying. She was just too tired to worry about it.

"Well, thank you. It was very kind of you to feed Jason and Mara, Mr. Lonigan. Especially after what Jason did today."

"Oh, he had good motives. And call me John."

"His motives may have been good but his methods stink," Abby said succinctly.

"I can't argue there." John thrust his hands into the pockets of his jeans. "I think he figured that out about halfway through the holdup. Only he couldn't figure out how to get out of it then."

"Did he actually point the gun at you?"

"Yeah. But I wouldn't bet on him in a shooting match. His aim is pretty shaky."

"I don't see how you can joke about it." Abby ran her fingers through her hair, her stomach tied in knots just thinking what could have happened.

"Well, I wasn't all that amused at the time," John admitted. "But distance makes it easier to see the humor in it. No insult intended, but as a criminal, your nephew has a long way to go. The gun wasn't even loaded."

"Thank heavens for that."

"And just in case I wanted to get in touch with him later, the backpack he handed me to put the money in had his name on it in big bold letters."

Abby had been studying the scuffed wooden floor at her feet, but his words made her lift her eyes to his.

"What?"

"His name was on the backpack. Jason Taylor. Big as life." John's voice was solemn, but there was a suspicious tuck in one cheek.

Abby felt her lips quiver. She sternly tightened them. "He gave you his name?"

"I guess he felt it would be rude not to," John suggested.

Abby bit her lower lip, picturing the scene. It wasn't funny. Not at all. Jason was lucky he'd picked this man to rob and not someone who might have shot first and looked to see if the gun was loaded later. He could have gotten himself killed.

Still, the image of him handing his victim the backpack with his name clearly visible was so absurd.

John saw the smile quivering at the corners of her mouth. It was sternly suppressed, but a moment later it peeked out again. He wanted to see her smile. The thought struck him suddenly. In their short acquaintance, he'd seen her wary, frightened, in pain and defensive. What would she look like when she smiled?

"He was wearing a ski mask, which I thought showed a certain amount of foresight," he said thoughtfully. "Unfortunately it was a bit large and kept slipping down over his eyes."

The image was too much for Abby. The smile she'd been trying so hard to contain simply refused to cooperate.

John felt the impact of her smile in his gut. It took her from pretty to something perilously close to beautiful. The anxious crease was smoothed from her forehead and the dark smudges under her eyes disappeared. She sparkled.

Her soft laugh washed over him on a wave of awareness. If his hands hadn't been safely tucked into his pockets, he might not have been able to resist the urge to reach out and draw her closer. He wanted to see if her mouth tasted as warm as it looked, if her skin was as soft as the silk of that damned robe she wore.

He glanced away, shocked by the sudden wave of desire that ran through him. He was no kid to be swept away by lust for every pretty woman who came down the pike. In fact, it had been months since he'd seen a woman who roused more than a twinge of interest. And this was considerably more than a twinge.

It had to have something to do with turning forty. One last burst of hormones before he settled into the doldrums of middle age.

"Poor Jason." Abby's voice drew his attention back to her. She was shaking her head, her mouth still curved in a soft smile. "He's tried so hard to be the man in the family since Steve died."

"His father?" John concentrated on the conversation, forcing himself to ignore the urge to taste the curves of her mouth.

"Yes." The word held remembered pain, and she was silent for a moment. "Would you like some coffee or something?"

John hesitated. Every instinct said that the sooner he got out of here, the better. He didn't want to get to know Abigail Taylor any better than he already did. He didn't want to get involved with her or her family. He'd managed to avoid entanglements for forty years. There was no sense in breaking a terrific record.

On the other hand, he hadn't met a woman who attracted him the way Abby Taylor did in a long, long time. He wanted to stay and talk to her, get to know her.

Why? So he'd know just what he was leaving behind when he drifted away from this town?

He cleared his throat, pulling his car keys from his pocket. "It's pretty late. I ought to be getting back to my place."

"Oh. Yes, of course." Was it his imagination or did she sound regretful?

"Well, it's been interesting," he said, when the silence threatened to become awkward.

"We haven't talked about Jason." Abby suddenly remembered the reason he was there in the first place.

"I don't think you have to worry about him pulling another stunt like this. I think he got a pretty thorough scare."

"I'll certainly have to talk to him about it." Abby followed him to the door.

She should have been glad to see him go, glad to have scraped through what could have been a disaster with so little damage. Instead she found herself wishing for an excuse to keep him a few minutes longer.

"You've been more than kind about this whole mess."

John turned in the doorway. "Well, it's been an interesting experience. And no one was hurt."

"Thank you for staying this evening. And for the pizza." Abby wrapped her arms around her waist.

"It was no problem. I didn't have any plans."

He lingered, wishing he had an excuse to stay, to talk to her some more.

"You know, the lock on this door isn't very sturdy," he said, fingering the pitted brass.

"I know. Steve was going to fix the place up."

The silence stretched.

"Well, so long," John said abruptly. If he didn't leave immediately, he wasn't sure he'd be able to resist the urge to pull her into his arms and find out just how soft her mouth was.

He lifted a hand in farewell and all but bolted off the porch. It was more than time that he began to think about leaving Beaumont, Washington. He hadn't realized just how much danger could lurk in such a little town.

Chapter Three

"Lord, it feels good to get off my feet." Abby slid into the booth with a sigh of pleasure.

"If you'd come to work at Bixby's, you wouldn't have to spend all day on your feet," Kate Bixby told her, her unsympathetic tone weakened by the concern in her dark eyes.

"I'm not yet to the point where I have to sponge on my friends." Abby wiggled her toes, wishing she dared to slip her feet out of her shoes.

"It wouldn't be sponging," Kate said indignantly.

"Right. I'm sure Bixby's is desperate for another secretary, especially at the outrageous salary your father offered me."

"You're the only person I know who would turn down a job because you were offered too *much* money. I don't see why you have to be so stubborn about this."

"It's important to me to make it on my own. I think it's important for the children. I want them to know that I can take care of them. I don't want them to see me taking charity from my friends."

"You are the most stubborn, pigheaded, irritating person." Kate snatched a menu out of the holder and thrust it at Abby like a weapon. "I don't know why I'm still friends with you."

"Because you're just as stubborn and pigheaded and even more irritating." Abby shot her friend a grin over the top of the menu.

She and Kate Bixby had been best friends since kindergarten. Kate, a whole six weeks older and two inches taller, had taken it into her head that little Abigail Taylor was in need of protection. By the time it had become clear that Abby's delicate build hardly made her helpless, the two of them were fast friends.

The friendship had lasted through all the stresses and strains of school, first boyfriends and adolescence. It had survived Abby going off to college while Kate stayed in Beaumont.

A year ago, when Abby came home to take up raising her brother's children, Kate had been there for her, helping her through the grief, making her laugh, reminding her that the pain would lessen with time.

"Look, I don't mean to be pushy but I can't help but worry about you." Kate began speaking as soon as the waitress had disappeared with their order.

"There's nothing to worry about. I'm managing just fine. The kids are doing great."

"I'm sure the kids are fine. *I'm* worried about you." Kate waved a bread stick for emphasis. "You've lost at least five pounds. Ordinarily I'd hate you for it but I can't be jealous when I know it's worry that's making you so skinny."

"You're the one who worries too much," Abby said lightly.

"Well, someone has to worry about you. You're too busy worrying about the kids to give yourself a thought. And you've managed to convince your family that everything is peachy keen. I don't see why you don't at least put some of those cousins of yours to work on that house. Honestly,

Abby, that place is going to fall down around your ears one of these days.''

"Steve wouldn't have asked for charity—''

"It's not charity when it's people who care about you,'' Kate cut in, her voice rising in exasperation. "Besides, Steve wasn't a single woman with a practically useless degree in botany. He was a contractor. *He* was perfectly capable of doing the work himself. You don't have the skills to do the work and you don't have the money to hire it done.''

There was no arguing with the truth. Kate was depressingly right. She was like a dog with a bone on this subject. She figured if she just kept poking at Abby, she'd get her to shift her position. The problem was, Abby knew she was right. Logically she couldn't do the work on the house. But she just couldn't bring herself to ask for help.

"Actually, Jason nearly solved our monetary problems for us yesterday.''

"Jason did?'' Kate raised her eyebrows.

"He came up with an interesting scheme for raising money.''

"What scheme?'' Kate reached for her water glass.

"He tried to rob a liquor store,'' Abby said in a conversational tone.

Kate choked on the water. The glass hit the table with a thump while she gasped for air. Abby reached for another bread stick, crunching into it while she waited for Kate to regain her breath.

"He did what?'' Kate got out at last, her eyes still watering.

"He tried to rob a liquor store,'' Abby repeated in a conversational tone. Twenty-four hours ago, she'd never have believed she'd find any humor in what Jason had done. Distance had put the whole thing into perspective. Distance and John Lonigan's attitude.

"You almost sound like you mean that."

"I do." Abby leaned back to let the waitress set a chef's salad in front of her. She could feel Kate's impatience as she waited for the woman to leave. Questions were nearly choking the other woman.

"I think they do a great chef's salad here, don't you?" Abby said in a chatty tone as the waitress left.

"Forget the salad." Kate shoved her own to the side and leaned toward Abby, her eyes stern. "Tell me what happened with Jason. Did he actually try to rob a liquor store?"

"That's what I said. Pass the salt, would you?"

"Abigail Taylor, I'm going to bludgeon you with the salt shaker if you don't tell me what happened."

"Did anyone ever tell you that you have a violent streak?" When Kate drew back her hand, the salt shaker poised to throw, Abby relented. "Okay, okay. I'll tell you."

It didn't take long to tell Kate the story. It seemed even more incredible in the telling. Getting up this morning, she'd had the feeling that it had all been a fantastic dream. Even knowing it wasn't, she still couldn't make it seem real.

"So this guy isn't going to press charges or anything?" Kate asked when Abby was through.

"No. He thinks Jason learned his lesson."

"Boy, are you lucky." Shaking her head, Kate leaned back against the booth.

"I know. He was really very nice about it. He even fed the kids a pizza while I was out of it."

"You know, maybe you coming down with a migraine made him feel sorry for you."

"Maybe. But I don't think he was going to drag the police into it, anyway. If he were going to do that, he wouldn't have brought Jason home and waited for me."

"Nice guy," Kate commented, poking at her neglected salad.

"I don't know that I'd call him 'nice' exactly." Abby nibbled on a sliver of ham, her eyes focused on nothing in particular. "Not that he wasn't. Nice, I mean. It's just that it sounds too...bland."

"Oh, really?" Kate's attention sharpened. "Just how would you describe this guy?"

Abby realized her mistake too late. Now she'd sparked Kate's interest.

"Oh, I don't know." She shrugged with elaborate unconcern. "Boy, this salad is great."

She might as well have tried to divert a Sherman tank with a water pistol.

"How old is he?"

"I have no idea."

"Take a guess." Kate could be relentless in pursuit of information.

"Mid- to late thirties, I guess. Maybe forty."

"Attractive?"

"I hardly noticed," Abby told her. Unfortunately, Kate had known her a long time.

"Liar. Is he short? Tall? Dark? What color are his eyes?"

"You sound like a health insurance questionnaire," Abby groused.

"It's not nice to lie to your friends."

"It's not nice to interrogate your friends like a cop in a gangster movie, either."

"You might as well tell me. You know I'm going to get it out of you eventually." Kate waved a forkful of lettuce for emphasis. She must have read resignation in Abby's expression. "How tall is he?"

"I don't know. He's taller than me."

"So were the Seven Dwarfs," Kate said dryly.

"He's a lot taller," Abby clarified, feeling cornered. Why hadn't she just let Kate's comment about John being nice go by? She knew that Kate worried about the nonexistent state of her love life more than she worried about her financial condition.

"Good-looking?" Kate pursued ruthlessly.

"No. Yes. Well, very masculine. Not pretty but strong. Like you could depend on him."

"Sounding better and better."

"It doesn't sound like anything," Abby protested vainly.

"When do you see him again?"

"I don't."

"Of course you do." Kate pushed aside her salad bowl and leaned toward Abby, her eyes sparkling. "It's obvious that the two of you were destined to meet. Fate swept you together."

"That's the first time I've ever thought of fate as a ten-year-old boy. Get that matchmaking look out of your eye, Kate Bixby. Tell me how you and Dillon are doing," she added hastily, when she saw that Kate was prepared to argue the point.

The diversion worked. Kate's eyes softened, her mouth taking on a gentle curve. "Dillon is fine. I saw him last night."

"And the night before. And the night before that," Abby teased.

"So we see each other a lot. There's no crime in that."

"Of course not. Tell that cousin of mine he'd better treat you right or he'll have me to answer to." Abby glanced at her watch and gave a squeak of dismay. "I've got to run or I'll be late."

"Lunch is on me," Kate said when she reached for her purse.

"That's not necessary."

"If you reach into that purse, I'm going to stab you with a butter knife," Kate said conversationally. "I asked you to lunch. I'm buying."

Abby hesitated, pride warring with common sense, which told her that she'd only look like an idiot if she argued. "Thanks. I'll buy next time."

"Agreed." Kate threw a handful of bills on the table and slid out of the booth. She gave Abby a stern look. "People who go against Fate inevitably regret it."

"People who matchmake generally come to a bad end." Abby headed for the door, anxious to drop the subject of John Lonigan.

"Don't you think you owe him a proper thank-you?" Kate switched tactics with treacherous ease, aiming for Abby's conscience.

"I am *not* going to track the poor man like some pathetic old maid in a Dickens novel, Kate. Besides, I'm the last person he'd want to see. Considering the trouble my family has caused him, he'd probably run for cover if he saw me coming. Thank you for the lunch."

She waggled her fingers at Kate and all but sprinted across the parking lot to her car. Shutting the door behind her, she heaved a sigh of relief.

Kate was her best friend and a wonderful person but she was like a dog with a bone once she got an idea in her head. And the idea that Abby should go looking for John with some flimsy excuse was a bad one.

Even if she'd wanted to, she couldn't see any reason why he'd have any desire to see more of her or her family. They'd been nothing but trouble to him.

JOHN WAS IN THE STOREROOM when he heard the bell over the front door jingle. Setting down the case of bourbon he'd been moving, he dusted his palms on the seat of his jeans. Bill was working out front today while John was in charge of reorganizing the storeroom.

He didn't mind the work. Hefting boxes around was a pleasant change from working the counter. The store didn't usually do all that much business during the day. He usually spent the time catching up on twenty years' worth of reading. But a man could only read so many hours a day. A little physical labor felt good.

He rotated his shoulder, grimacing at the twinge of discomfort. He'd let himself get out of shape, no doubt about it. Reading might be fine exercise for the mind but it didn't do much for the body. Two years of drifting around the country, picking up jobs here and there, weren't enough to keep a man in peak physical condition.

"John? There's somebody here to see you."

John frowned at Bill's call. He didn't know anyone in this town except his boss. And the only people who knew he was here were Trace and Lily Dushane, but they were in Los Angeles.

His right hand twitched uneasily toward the shoulder holster he hadn't worn in over two years. As far as he knew, there was no reason for anybody to be looking him up. He'd cut his ties with his old life quite thoroughly. Still, he'd spent a lot of years living in the shadows and old habits died hard.

Hardly aware of his actions, he picked up a length of two-by-four he'd found leaning in a corner, a remnant of some project Bill had probably never gotten around to. It wasn't much of a weapon, but he felt a little less vulnerable with it in his hand.

He stepped up the side of the door, careful not to expose himself in the doorway. As he glimpsed the front of the store, he felt all the adrenaline suddenly drain away. In fact, he felt more than a little foolish. Leaning the two-by-four against a stack of boxes, he stepped out to greet Jason Taylor.

"Hello, Jason."

"Hi." After getting out the word, Jason seemed suddenly struck dumb.

John glanced at Bill, but the older man shrugged. John hadn't told Bill about yesterday's excitement. The way he figured, the store may be Bill's but the decision on how to handle the boy was his.

"You're a ways from home, aren't you?" John asked when Jason showed no signs of speaking.

"Yeah." Jason shot him a look from under shaggy brown hair. He was wearing jeans and a T-shirt again, the familiar blue backpack dangling from one hand—this time full of books, John sincerely hoped.

"You wanted to see me..." John prompted.

"Yeah." Jason hesitated, as if doubting the wisdom of his decision now that he was here. John waited, aware of Bill's amused interest. Jason drew a deep breath and released it, shooting John another glance before fixing his gaze on a display of breath mints.

"I lost my key," he blurted out. "To the house, I mean. I can't get in and I didn't know where else to go. I thought maybe you'd...well, you could...you know..." He trailed off, his fair skin flushing.

John did know. It was obvious that the boy missed having a man in his life. Their meeting had been under unfortunate circumstances but, once he was convinced John wasn't going to have him drawn and quartered, Jason had become downright outgoing.

Over pepperoni pizza, John had learned the name of his best friend, how the extremely large dog sleeping on the back porch had followed him home, and about the cruelties of homework and a teacher who didn't understand how it could get misplaced. He'd shown John the model car he was building, soliciting his opinions as to the proper color for the interior.

John had done his best to keep up with the flow of conversation, offering opinions when called for but mostly just listening.

The little girl, Mara, hadn't spoken a word. Jason accepted this as normal, talking to her but not waiting for a reply. It was obvious that she could hear and equally obvious that she didn't speak, but John didn't ask whether her disability was physical.

He told himself it was none of his business, that it hardly mattered to him when he wasn't likely to ever see her again, anyway. When he'd left the little house last night he'd been glad to be out of an awkward situation.

So why did he feel something suspiciously like relief now that Jason had shown up?

"So, I suppose you want to leave early so you can take your young friend home." Bill's voice snapped John out of his thoughts, reminding him of where he was.

He looked at Jason. If he had any sense, he'd send the boy home. Chances were, he could stay with one of the neighbors until Abby got home. At the worst, he could hang out in the backyard, hardly a terrible fate on a nice spring day.

He didn't want to get involved with the Taylor family, for their sake as much as his. He'd already begun to think about moving on. It would be cruel and irresponsible to encourage the boy to develop any kind of attachment with him when he'd be leaving any day now.

The only responsible thing to do was to sever the tenuous connection right here and now.

"Yeah, I'll need to leave early, Bill. I'll give Jason a ride home."

He was rewarded by the grin that creased the boy's face. It was enough to enable him to push aside the doubts he had about the wisdom of his choice.

It was no big deal, really. He'd take the kid home, maybe wait with him until Abby got home, just to let her know what had happened. It was the responsible thing to do.

It had nothing at all to do with wanting to see her again.

IN AN ODD WAY, Abby felt no surprise when she saw the sleek black car parked at the curb in front of her house. All day, in odd moments, she'd found her thoughts jumping back to the day before. John Lonigan had been a big part of those thoughts.

He'd been so much in her thoughts that it seemed almost natural to see the car waiting for them. She'd been keeping up her usual patter to Mara, expecting and getting no response. But when she broke off abruptly, the child turned to look at her, her eyes questioning.

"It looks like Mr. Lonigan is here," Abby told her as she eased her car past the immaculate Mercedes and turned into the driveway.

She shut the car off, hardly noticing when it continued to rattle and groan before finally subsiding with a sullen mutter. Dillon had been after her to let him take a look at the old car. Maybe she should take him up on it.

But her thoughts weren't really on mechanical troubles. She fumbled with her seat belt, aware that her heart was beating a little faster than it should have been. It was just nerves, she told herself as she hurried around to Mara's door. It wasn't that she was excited about seeing John again. She was just worried about why he was here.

She lifted Mara out of the car and slammed the door. Pausing to draw a deep breath, she patted her hands over her hair, wishing she'd taken time to comb it before she picked up Mara.

Mara was already heading for the side gate, following the sound of her brother's laughter. Abby trailed after her niece, wishing she didn't feel quite such a sense of anticipation at the thought of seeing John again.

Mara had stopped at the corner of the house, one arm wrapped around her doll as she watched the scene in front of her. Abby stopped behind the child, resting one hand on her shoulder.

Jason, John and George were all in the middle of the lawn. The dog sat looking up at John, with every appearance of intelligence, a look Abby knew to be misleading.

"Stay, George," John commanded firmly. "Stay." He began backing off, keeping a stern eye on the dog. George waited all of five seconds before leaping to his feet and charging straight for John, his enormous body quivering with the fun of this new game. John dodged him easily, but George's momentum carried him forward several yards before he could get his paws to obey the command to turn around. Jason's laughter rang out as the big dog skidded into a lawn chair, sending it flying.

John was watching the dog, his mouth relaxed in a smile as Jason ran forward to throw his arms around George's sturdy neck. Abby didn't think she'd made any sound, but John stiffened before turning abruptly to look in her direction.

Abby felt her heart lurch in something close to fear. In the instant before their eyes met and the tension left his body, she'd been looking at someone very dangerous. Someone capable of violence.

She shook the thought away. Simply an overactive imagination.

"Aunt Abby!" Jason abandoned George, who flopped back in the grass with an exhausted groan. The boy came flying across the yard toward her. John followed at a more leisurely pace, arriving just as Jason was finishing his explanation about having lost his key and not knowing what to do.

"Hello again."

"Hi." Abby's eyes met John's over Jason's head. "I guess I owe you another thank-you for bringing Jason home."

"De nada," he said, shrugging.

"John speaks Spanish," Jason told her, glancing up at him with a look that was nothing short of worshipful. "He says it's a good idea to speak another language. Can I take Spanish lessons, Aunt Abby? Can I, huh?"

"We'll see. You shouldn't have bothered Mr. Lonigan, Jason."

"He says it's no bother. That's what *de nada* means, Aunt Abby."

Abby curled her fingers against the urge to reach out and smooth his hair into place. He was still young enough to tolerate a certain amount of fussing on her part, but not in front of another adult. Particularly not in front of someone he wanted to impress.

"You still shouldn't have bothered him. If you lost your key, why didn't you get the one we hid under the rock in front?"

Jason dropped his head to study the tips of his battered tennis shoes. He was going to need new ones soon, she noticed. Another expense.

"I guess I forgot about the key," Jason offered. He shot her a glance from under his lashes to see if the excuse was going to be accepted. After the riot act she'd read him over yesterday's escapades, he was well aware that he might be skating on thin ice.

"It's an easy thing to do," John said, taking pity on him.

Abby's eyes met his. He knew as well as she did that Jason hadn't forgotten about the key. She shook her head, her mouth softening in a smile. How could she be upset with Jason when she'd wished she could think up an excuse to contact John herself? Jason's ploy might be obvious but it had a child's honesty.

"See that you don't forget again," she told her nephew, risking a gentle cuff on the side of the head that wouldn't be misconstrued as anything mushy.

"I won't," Jason promised. "Look what we taught George to do." He dashed off across the lawn to where George lay contentedly chewing on the leg of the lawn chair.

"I hope he didn't cause you any inconvenience," Abby said to John, her eyes on the boy who was vainly commanding George to roll over.

"No problem. I didn't have any plans."

George wagged his shaggy tail, threatening to smash the delphiniums Abby had lovingly planted. Abby hardly noticed. She was watching the boy and dog, but all her senses were tuned to the man standing next to her.

"In that case, why don't you stay for dinner," she suggested.

Jason had switched to commanding George to stay. The huge animal promptly rolled over, waving his great paws in the air and generally showing both his affectionate nature and severe lack of brains.

"I... Sure. Why not? I appreciate the offer."

Abby had the distinct impression that he'd started to refuse and then changed his mind. She decided not to wonder why—why he'd refuse or why he'd changed his mind. Just like she wasn't going to think about why she'd wanted him to say yes.

"Let me change out of this uniform and then I'll get something started."

"No rush. Oh, I opened the lock on your back door so Jason could get in. It's worse than the one on the front," he said, his dark brows drawing together.

"I know. Thank heavens we don't have much by way of crime in Beaumont. I'll be right back. Make yourself at home."

Actually, "right back" wasn't exactly accurate. She threw off her uniform quick enough and ran a brush through her hair, but then she had to decide whether to leave it down, which made her look softer and younger—too young, maybe?—or tie it back. She finally settled on clipping it at her nape.

Then there was the matter of what to wear. Usually she put on a pair of old jeans and a baggy shirt. Would that look too sloppy? On the other hand, velvet lounging pajamas would look a trifle overdressed.

Why was she shilly-shallying like this? She barely knew the man, for heaven's sake. What difference did it make whether he thought she was a slob?

Impatient with her own foolishness, she pulled on a pair of relatively new jeans and a soft pink shirt that Kate swore made her look radiant. A glance at the clock told her she'd been waffling back and forth for nearly half an hour. John probably thought she'd died.

And *what* was she going to fix for dinner? When she'd blithely offered to feed him, she hadn't stopped to consider that the cupboards were practically bare. It was ridiculous that she worked in a supermarket yet she never seemed to find time to shop for groceries. She wondered how he felt about packaged macaroni and cheese.

The house was quiet when she left her bedroom. She could hear Jason outside, giving commands to George that George was undoubtedly ignoring. But there was no sign of John or Mara until she stepped into the kitchen and looked out the window.

John was sitting on the porch step, watching Jason's attempts to convince George that sitting was a fun game. Mara stood just outside the kitchen door, watching him with the same solemn attention she gave to most things in her life.

As Abby watched, the little girl started toward John. She held her breath as Mara stopped beside him. She approached so few people. John's face was at nearly Mara's level as he turned to look at her. They studied each other for a moment. John didn't make any overtures, allowing Mara to set the pace of the encounter.

Did he know Mara didn't speak? Would he have picked up on that over the pizza he'd shared with the children? Or maybe Jason had told him that his little sister hadn't said a word in nearly a year?

After a silent perusal, Mara thrust her hand out to him. Clutched in her short little fingers was a doll who'd lost an arm nearly a week ago. The plastic had resisted all Abby's efforts to restore the limb, and she'd intended to ask Dillon to perform first aid next time he came to visit.

Apparently Mara had decided not to wait that long.

John took the doll from Mara. His hands dwarfed it, making it seem even smaller than it was. Abby chewed on her lower lip, hoping he'd understand how important the inexpensive toy was to Mara. She needn't have worried. He studied the patient, treating the moment with the solemnity it deserved.

After careful consideration he set the arm against the socket. With a seemingly effortless twist of the wrist, he returned the arm to its rightful position and handed the doll back to its owner.

Mara studied the doll, confirming that the injury was now healed. She nodded her head, satisfied that the repair had been properly made, and then retreated back to the kitchen door.

Abby blinked back tears. If she'd been the sentimental sort, given to believing in such things, she'd have been inclined to fall madly in love with John Lonigan on the spot. But she was much too practical for nonsense like that.

Wiping the back of her hand over her eyes, she stepped out onto the porch, ruffling Mara's hair as she passed. John stood up, his eyes running over her in a quick, appreciative glance that made her glad she'd taken the time she had in getting ready.

"Hi. Sorry it took me so long."

"It was worth waiting for," he said without a trace of flirtation in his voice.

Abby hesitated, oddly off balance for a moment. She was out of practice when it came to dealing with the opposite sex. Since Steve and Diane's death, the children had been her sole concern. Then again, she had the feeling that no amount of practice would have prepared her for John Lonigan. There was something very different about him.

"Thank you," she said, hearing a breathlessness in her voice that she hoped he wouldn't notice. "It was very nice of you to fix Mara's doll," she added quickly, anxious for a new subject. "I'm afraid I didn't have the muscle to get the arm back in place."

"It was no big deal." He turned his head to watch as George tackled Jason, sending them both thudding to the ground. "Is that a dog or a horse?"

So he didn't want to be thanked. "I'm not sure." Abby followed his gaze. "Dillon thinks it may be a Shetland pony."

"Dillon?" His eyes slid back to her face, one brow raised in question.

"My cousin," Abby explained, telling herself she was an idiot to imagine that there'd been a note of jealousy in the question. "And my best friend's boyfriend," she added, just in case he might not understand the situation perfectly.

"I think he may be right." John returned his attention to George who was now sitting on Jason, happily wagging his tail as the boy tried to throw him off.

The doorbell chimed softly. Abby dragged her eyes away from the contemplation of his profile, a frown creasing her forehead. "I hope that's not Mr. Frickle again."

"Who's Mr. Frickle?" John asked, following her into the house.

"Our neighbor. He lives to complain about Jason and George. The least little bit of noise drives him into a frenzy." Abby stalked toward the door, mentally preparing a speech to put the gossipy old man in his place, even as she offered an explanation to John.

"I suspect it's not Mr. Frickle," John said.

"Well, I don't know who else it would be." Abby jerked open the door with a quick gesture that startled the youth on the other side so badly that the box he held wobbled dangerously. John reached over Abby's shoulder to steady the box.

"You're not Mr. Frickle." Abby couldn't think of anything else to say. She wasn't sure if it was finding a strange young man with a box full of Chinese takeout cartons or the fact that John was standing so close that she could actually feel the heat of his body, but every thought scampered out of her head, leaving her only with the accurate but absurd statement to offer.

"Should I be?" The boy looked uneasy.

"No, of course not." Abby felt her cheeks warm as she groped for what was left of her brain.

"Here." John handed the boy some money and took the box of food from him. "Keep the change."

"Thanks." He shot one last, uneasy glance at Abby before leaving.

"I hope you like Chinese. Jason said you did."

Abby pushed shut the door. "I love Chinese."

"Good." John started toward the kitchen, leaving her to follow.

"I was going to make you dinner," she protested, her stomach already grumbling as the scent of moo goo gai pan wafted back to her.

"I thought you might be tired." John set the box down on the kitchen table.

"This is the second time you've fed this family. I can't let you keep doing this." Abby tried to sound stern but it wasn't easy when her mouth was starting to water.

"I already had this ordered. It was no trouble to have it delivered here instead."

Abby looked at the array of boxes he was unloading. Not even Paul Bunyan would have ordered that much food only for himself.

"It looks like a lot of food for one person."

"I like leftovers."

"You said the same thing about the pizza. That you'd already had it ordered."

"That's right. I get a lot of take-out food." He turned to look at her, arching one eyebrow, his eyes holding a hint of amusement and the slightest touch of challenge. "Does that bother you?"

Abby's stomach waged a brief battle with her pride and won. She could offer to pay for the meal but she couldn't really afford it. Besides, she didn't doubt that he'd refuse.

"Not at all. But next time, dinner's on me."

She'd started for the cupboard to get plates when she realized that her words assumed there would *be* a next time.

"Fine."

She lifted the plates out, feeling a foolish warmth in the pit of her stomach.

Chapter Four

When Abby turned into her street and saw the black Mercedes at the curb, her heart gave a quick bump that she refused to acknowledge. It had been three days since John had shared Chinese food with them. She'd spent a good part of those three days wondering how to go about inviting him back for the dinner she'd promised.

He'd acted as if he expected to see her again, but maybe he was just being polite. Like she'd told Kate, his acquaintance with her small family had hardly been relaxing. Most people would have run in the opposite direction. Twice Jason had dragged him into their lives. Both times, John had been gracious, pleasant and understanding.

But that didn't mean that he wasn't secretly hoping to have seen the last of them. Abby had given Jason strict orders not to visit the liquor store again. Jason hadn't been able to understand her reasoning but he'd reluctantly promised not to disobey.

The presence of the Mercedes meant that unless Jason had gone back on his word, John must have chosen to make this visit. She'd given him an open invitation to drop in anytime but she hadn't expected him to take her up on it.

She pulled the car into the driveway and shut off the engine, taking a deep breath as it sputtered to a halt. Glancing at Mara, she saw the little girl watching her with those extraordinary eyes that always seemed to see too much.

"It looks like John has come to visit again," Abby said too brightly. She helped Mara out of the car before opening the back door and pulling out a bag of groceries. She was reaching for a second bag when the first was taken out of her hands.

"I'll get that."

She turned. "Hi."

"Hi." His mouth quirked in a half smile. "I took you at your word when you said I could show up anytime. I hope you meant it."

"Of course." He leaned past her to grab two more bags, and Abby held her breath as his chest crowded her back against the open door. Her fingers were unsteady as she picked up the last bag and followed his tall figure to the house.

"Jason let me in," he said over his shoulder, pushing open the door and holding it so that she could go in first. "I hope you don't mind. I got off work and I found myself wandering in this direction."

"I'm glad you did."

She watched him set the bags down on the counter before her mind registered what she'd seen on the way in. She headed back to the front door. But it wasn't the front door she'd come to know and despise this past year. In place of the scarred, warped panel she'd cursed was a straight, solid door with a shiny new brass lock.

"I realize it's pretty intrusive of me," John said, coming to stand in the entryway. "I should have talked to you about it but I had the feeling you'd argue me out of doing it. I actually did it for selfish reasons," he added when Abby only looked from him to the door and back again.

"You put a new door up on my house for selfish reasons?"

"Well, I've lain awake the past couple of nights thinking about you and the kids alone here with nothing but that flimsy lock. I wasn't getting any sleep."

"I bet." She recognized the exaggeration and knew it was designed solely to forestall her protests. The problem was, it was an effective ploy. "You'll have to let me pay you for it," she said firmly.

"The door was already in the garage," he told her. "I just put it up."

Abby stared at the door, realizing now why it had looked vaguely familiar. It had been sitting in the back of the garage. Steve had probably purchased it for just this purpose, only he'd died before he had a chance to get it into place.

"The lock wasn't in the garage," she said, her eyes daring him to argue.

"Oh, that."

"Yes, that. You have to let me pay you for the lock."

"Well, actually, I'd already ordered it. It was no trouble to have it delivered here instead." He gave her a bland look that dared her to argue.

"You don't order locks like you do take-out food."

"Sure you do. There's a terrific take-out lock place over on Fifteenth. They deliver all over town."

"They do not." Abby knew she was losing the argument, though she wasn't quite sure how. She'd made a perfectly reasonable demand. How was it he'd managed to turn it around so that she felt vaguely foolish for pursuing the issue?

"Sure they do," John said, raising his brows as if surprised that she didn't know all about it.

"You're not going to let me pay for it, are you?" There was more resignation than annoyance in the question. How could she be angry with him for doing something so nice?

"No." The look in his eyes told her that he recognized and appreciated her dilemma. It also said that he wasn't backing off an inch.

"Well, the least you can let me do is make you dinner," she said, a trace of belligerence that made the invitation sound like a threat.

"I'd like that."

Abby couldn't decide what she liked most about him—the way his eyes smiled before his mouth or the interesting dimple that appeared in his cheek.

JASON DOMINATED the conversation over dinner just as he had the night John had ordered Chinese food. Abby hadn't realized just how starved he'd been for masculine attention until she saw him with John.

Maybe it was foolish of her not to have known it before. Jason had been very close to his father. The two of them had spent a lot of time together. With Steve's death, he'd lost a friend as well as a father.

She'd never realized how much he might crave someone with whom to discuss baseball statistics, or to talk, endlessly it seemed, of cars. The fact that John owned such a spectacular example of transportation gave him an exalted status in Jason's eyes.

She'd already been treated—at Jason's insistence—to a demonstration of the Gullwing's wonders. The figures the boy rattled off regarding engine size, torque and assorted other mysteries had gone in one ear and out the other. But even she had to admit that the car itself was unusual enough to be interesting. Perhaps the most striking feature was the way the doors opened from the bottom, lifting up to arch outward from the sides in a winglike effect that gave the car its name.

John had good-naturedly demonstrated this feature for her and she hadn't had to pretend to being impressed. The exotic car suited its owner, all sleek curves and mysteries.

Several times Abby thought about gently cutting off the seemingly inexhaustible flow of words spilling from her nephew. But John didn't show any signs of impatience. He didn't talk down to the boy, never looked bored. Of course, she also had the feeling that John was accustomed to concealing what he felt.

Something told her that, even without Jason's chatter, John wouldn't have said much. For whatever reason, he seemed a man accustomed to concealing more of himself than he'd ever willingly reveal. She filed the thought away as something to keep in mind. A woman who got involved with a man like that would have to accept the shadows in his life.

Not that *she* had anything to worry about because she certainly wasn't thinking about getting involved with him. Or anyone else, for that matter.

Jason managed to more or less monopolize John's attention until long after dinner, showing him his collection of model cars, telling him how he planned to be a race-car driver or maybe a great pitcher.

It was nearly eight o'clock when Abby finally interrupted an intense discussion of engines and transmissions to tell Jason it was time to take a bath and get ready for bed.

"Oh, Aunt Abby. We was just getting to the good stuff."

"*Were* getting," she corrected. "And I suspect 'the good stuff' will be there next time you see John."

"Sure. We can talk next time, Jason."

Abby hoped her relief at hearing there was going to be a next time wasn't obvious. She stood up, gesturing to John to stay where he was.

"You're welcome to stay while I get Mara settled in bed. It won't take more than a few minutes. I could make some coffee."

"Sounds good," he said, relaxing back into the chair.

As promised, it didn't take Abby long to get Mara settled in bed, the night-light left burning, the door open a crack so Mara wouldn't feel as if she'd been left alone. She could hear the water running for Jason's bath as she walked past the bathroom.

It also didn't take long to get the coffee ready. Abby poured two cups and carried them into the living room, handing one to John. Enjoying the peace, neither of them spoke for a few moments.

"I wonder who first said that silence is golden," Abby finally said. "Do you think they knew Jason?"

John smiled. "He is a bit of a talker."

"I hope he didn't drive you crazy. I guess I hadn't realized how much he missed having someone to talk engines and baseball with."

"I don't mind."

"He and Steve were very close. It's been hard on Jason having mostly females around. I think I'll ask Dillon to come around more often."

"Jason's lucky he had that time with his father. He'll always have the memories."

Abby tilted her head, studying him. "Are you close with your dad?"

"My father's dead. And no, we weren't close. I hadn't seen him in nearly twenty years." John turned the coffee cup in his hands, his eyes fixed on the idle movement. For a moment, Abby thought he might say something more, something that would give her some insight into him. But he didn't add anything.

"Where are you from?" she asked finally.

"A little bit of everywhere, really. I've done a lot of traveling over the years. Originally I'm from Los Angeles. You don't like L.A.?" he asked, catching the shiver that passed over her.

"Bad memories. The only time I've been to L.A. was to pick up the children after Steve and Diane were killed."

"What happened?"

"They'd taken the children there for a vacation. Disneyland and all that, you know. They'd been there a week and were due to leave for home the next day. Jason had stayed overnight with a school friend of his whose parents had moved there a few months before. Steve and Diane were on their way to pick him up when someone in a truck drove by and opened up on their car with an automatic weapon."

Her voice failed her for a moment. She stopped, swallowing hard. She'd rarely talked about her brother's death, preferring to put it behind her. But there was something about John, a quiet strength, that made it easier to talk about that terrible time.

"I heard there were quite a few incidents like that on the freeways. Random shootings for no apparent reason," John said. "It's hard to lose someone you care about to something so completely senseless."

Abby nodded. He'd put his finger on what had made it so difficult to accept the deaths. There'd been no rhyme or reason to them, just a tragic case of being in the wrong place—"victims of random violence," the police had told her. She wondered if John had spoken from personal experience.

"Diane was killed instantly," she continued. "Steve managed to pull the car to the side of the freeway but he died before the paramedics got there. Mara was in the back seat. She wasn't hurt. Not physically, anyway."

"Is that why she doesn't talk?" John asked.

Abby nodded. "I took her to a child psychiatrist. She said Mara would start talking when she learned how to deal with the trauma of her parents' death. I took her back a few times, and the woman played games with her, trying to get her to act out her fears, but Mara would just sit there and look at her. She wouldn't respond. So I brought her home. I keep hoping that with enough love and attention she'll work through this."

"Kids seem to do things in their own time. She'll be okay."

"I hope so." Abby sighed, leaning her head back against the chair. It felt good to talk about it.

"So you inherited the kids and the house from your brother?"

She nodded. "Steve was a contractor so he planned to fix up the place... but he only had a couple of months. I'm afraid I'm not much good with a hammer and screwdriver. A degree in botany doesn't do much to prepare you for fixing up an old house."

"Botany? And you're working in a supermarket?"

"There isn't much call for botanists in Beaumont. In fact, there isn't much call for botanists anywhere," she admitted ruefully. "I had big plans for working on great estates all over the world, maybe traveling up the Amazon and discovering some new and valuable plant."

"Nothing wrong with that." John finished the last of his coffee and set the cup down.

"Not if you don't have kids depending on you for a home and a little security. The last thing Mara and Jason needed was more upheaval in their lives. So I moved back here and got a job."

"It's a lot of responsibility to take on. Someone else's kids, a house in need of repair. You must have been pretty close to your brother."

"We were extremely close." She glanced at a photo John had noticed earlier, occupying a prominent spot on the wall. It showed a smiling couple with two children—Jason and Mara a couple of years ago. As she looked at those bright faces, smiling into a future they couldn't possibly know they wouldn't live to see, the tragedy of their deaths was suddenly very vivid.

"Steve and I were very close," Abby murmured, looking away from the picture, her eyes a little too bright. "When our parents died, he did his best to be father and big brother to me. He and Diane helped me through school. Even if I hadn't loved Jason and Mara for their own sakes, I owed it to Steve to do my best for them."

"Any family besides this Dillon?"

"Sure. I've got an aunt and uncle with a place west of town. They've got four kids who all live within a hundred miles or so. Dillon's family is north of here about fifty miles. They've offered to help, if that's what you're wondering."

"The thought did cross my mind," he said dryly.

"I refused most of their offers."

"A glutton for punishment or an excess of pride?"

"A little of both, I guess," Abby admitted with a rueful smile. "My friend Kate says I'm an idiot not to let them do more."

"I certainly wouldn't presume to make that judgment on such short acquaintance," John said diplomatically.

"Very well said." She watched that fascinating dimple come and go in his cheek. Maybe it was the quiet surroundings or the fact that she was coming to the end of a long day, another in an endless series of long days, but she found herself wanting to put her fingers against his cheek, to feel the roughness of his beard beneath her hand.

She shook the thought away, pulling herself further up in her chair and gulping down the last of the coffee. A little caffeine would chase such foolishness away.

"Maybe I am a little silly but I know Steve wouldn't have asked for help. I want his children to feel secure, to know we're a family. I want them to know that we can make it on our own."

"Steve knew how to do the work on the house," John pointed out in a neutral tone.

"You sound just like Kate. Maybe you're both right," she admitted. "But like Molly Brown said, I ain't down yet."

"What about your sister-in-law's family?"

"No. I'd starve before I'd ask them for a penny. Not that they couldn't afford it. They're wealthy. Old money. And they wrote Diane off when she married Steve, said he wasn't good enough for her. She never saw them again. It was like something out of a bad Victorian novel, the kind of thing that doesn't happen anymore.

"After not speaking to Diane for over ten years, her mother came to the funeral. She had the nerve to offer to take the children off my hands, in the same tone she might have used to offer to help me get rid of some unwanted puppies. I told her to take a hike," she said with great satisfaction.

"Obviously your brother and his wife knew what they were doing when they gave you custody of their children."

"Thank you." Abby felt a warm glow that had nothing to do with the coffee.

John glanced at his watch. "It's getting late." Abby bit her lip against the urge to protest. It struck her suddenly that since Jason had gone in to take his bath, it seemed as if she'd talked nonstop. Maybe her nephew wasn't the only one who'd been starved for someone to talk to.

"Thank you again for the door and the lock." She followed him to the door.

"Thanks for the meal." John turned in the doorway to look at her. "And the company."

"I'm sure fish sticks and a talkative ten-year-old are two of your favorite things."

"You might be surprised." He smiled, but there was something in his eyes she couldn't quite place. Loneliness, maybe? Probably only the shadows cast by the porch light, she chided her imagination.

"I meant it when I said you were welcome anytime," she told him.

"I'll take you up on that." He hesitated a moment.

Did he lean toward her as if thinking of kissing her? Abby's lips parted softly, an invitation she wasn't even aware of until John's eyes dropped to her mouth. The moment dragged on while she waited for his head to lower. Later, she'd be shocked by her willingness to let a man she hardly knew kiss her. At the moment, all she felt was a delicious tingle of anticipation.

But it was anticipation doomed to disappointment. For the space of several slow heartbeats, they hovered on the edge of a kiss. Then John seemed to shake himself, his eyes shuttering as he drew back.

"Good night, Abby." He lifted his hand and strode off the porch.

Abby resisted the urge to watch him out of sight—mooning over the man like a teenager, she thought—and shut the door.

She hoped he'd meant it when he'd said he'd be back.

SHE NEEDN'T HAVE WORRIED. On Monday, he fixed the front door. When she got home Wednesday, he'd replaced the back door. Thursday afternoon, he repaired a length of sagging fence in the backyard that her neighbor, Mr. Frickle, had been complaining about for a year.

Sunday, he arrived before noon and began the laborious task of removing the dining-room window and repairing or replacing all the rotten wood.

By then, Abby had given up protesting. He was enjoying himself, he told her simply. Most of the materials were already in the garage, touching evidence of the dreams her brother had had for the little house.

He had the time and the skills, she had the house in need of repair. When he said it, he made it sound like some sort of even trade they were making. It was far from even and Abby knew it but she couldn't ever seem to find the right words to point out the faults in his reasoning.

Besides, if she did manage to convince him of the inequity of the arrangement, he might stop coming around. And she definitely didn't want that.

She wasn't sure what it was about John Lonigan that had made it possible for him to fit so smoothly into their lives that, before long, it was almost possible to forget how short a time they'd known him.

It certainly wasn't because he was forthcoming about himself. In fact, Abby had never known anyone *less* forthcoming than he was. It was so subtly done that it took her a while to realize how easily he evaded any talk of himself.

After a week of seeing him almost daily, she still knew little more than that he'd been raised in Los Angeles and that his parents were dead. He'd traveled a great deal, he admitted easily, but redirected her attention with a question about Jason before she could pursue either the why or where of his travels.

He spoke Spanish, maybe not all that unusual considering Southern California's large Hispanic population. So why did she find herself wondering if he'd had other uses for the language than ordering dinner in a Mexican restaurant?

Most of the time, he seemed nothing more than what he appeared—a chronic drifter who'd had an unusually large assortment of jobs. But once in a while she got a glimpse of someone else—someone dangerous.

Absorbed in cutting a paint-encrusted window loose from the frame, he apparently didn't hear her approaching with a glass of iced tea.

"I thought you—" The words caught in her throat as he spun, the razor blade held low, poised for an upward thrust that could have killed. For an instant, she was staring into the eyes of a man more than capable of delivering that thrust.

It was only a split-second glimpse into something very dark and very dangerous. John relaxed instantly, the tension going out of his wide shoulders, his fingers easing on the blade.

"Sorry. You startled me."

"So I gathered," she said, hearing the shakiness in her voice.

"I guess I've spent too much time in cities," he said easily. "That tea looks wonderful."

Abby handed him the glass, aware that her hand was not quite steady. The incident had been so quick that she might almost chalk it up to an overactive imagination. But she knew she'd never forget the look in his eyes, the icy determination to survive whatever came next. In that moment, John Lonigan had been capable of killing.

He could dismiss it as too much time spent in big cities if he wanted, and maybe that was part of it. But she couldn't help but wonder just what he'd done while he was in the city that it should have left him so quick to defend himself.

JOHN COULDN'T have said just what it was that kept drawing him back to the Taylor household. He liked to think it was just what he'd told Abby: he enjoyed working with his hands, enjoyed the feeling that he was building something lasting. He hadn't had much opportunity to build in his life.

The kids were a new experience and he found he enjoyed them as much as he enjoyed the simple physical labor. Jason never seemed to run out of words, almost compensating for his little sister's silence.

And their aunt... Abby was something else again. He admired her guts, the way she never complained. He understood her pride, even though she carried it to foolish lengths. Wasn't it stubborn pride that had cut him off from his own father for twenty years? He'd swallowed that pride too late to make up for those years, coming home only after Mike Lonigan was dead and buried.

Yes, if anyone understood pride, it was he.

Of course, he also liked Abby's sense of humor—the fact that she could almost always laugh, especially at herself. And the way her smile lit up her eyes. And the way she never ran out of patience with the children.

There were a lot of things he liked about Abby Taylor. Not that he wanted any sort of personal involvement. He wasn't geared for that sort of thing. After forty years of going his own way, he was a little too old for change.

He'd known for a long time now that he wasn't capable of the sort of deep commitment a woman like Abby would need. There'd been a woman once, a long time ago. He'd thought maybe, with her... But he'd been younger then, more flexible. That time was long past. He had too many years of drifting—running, some might have said. But if he was running from something, it was something he carried in himself and he'd been doing it too long to stop now.

Still, Beaumont, Washington, wasn't looking as stifling as it had a few days ago. The restlessness that had haunted him most of his adult life had abated, at least temporarily.

He'd told Abby nothing more than the truth when he'd said he enjoyed working on the house. For now, that was reason enough to stay in town. Reason enough to be spending time with Abby Taylor and her little family.

"HE'S DOING WHAT?" Kate stared at Abby over an untouched cheeseburger.

"I said he's doing a lot of the repairs on the house." Abby shrugged as she dipped a thick french fry in catsup. "He says he enjoys the work and Steve had already bought most of the materials. They're just sitting in the garage going to waste."

"You're letting him do all the repairs that you refuse to let your family help you with?" Kate ignored the part about the materials, recognizing it for the thin excuse it was.

"He's enjoying it," Abby said defensively.

"Oh, so now you're letting this gorgeous man work on your house solely out of the goodness of your heart, because you actually pity him?"

"I didn't say he was gorgeous," Abby protested weakly. Damn Kate for getting right to the heart of a matter, anyway.

"You don't have to say it. It's written all over your face." Kate opened her cheeseburger and layered on tomato, onion, lettuce and pickle before reaching for the catsup bottle. "If you ask me—"

"I didn't."

"—you're attracted to this man and he's obviously attracted to you."

"And how did you come to that brilliant conclusion?"

Kate ignored her sarcasm. Setting the top of the bun back on the burger, she proceeded to squash it down until the sandwich approached a size she could get into her mouth.

"It's obvious. No man spends all that time working on a woman's house just because he likes to work with his hands. It's been my experience that men can always find something to do with their hands in their spare time—like cast a fishing line or open a beer can.

"And no woman would allow a man to spend so much time working on her house unless she was hoping it might lead to something a little more interesting, like maybe playing house together."

Kate ended her sermon by taking a healthy bite. Abby wished in vain to see catsup ooze out and drip onto the collar of her friend's immaculate white silk blouse.

"Your imagination is running away with you, just like it always does. If you want the truth, I think John is a little lonely."

"Sure." Kate dabbed at her mouth with her napkin, raising one dark brow in skeptical comment. "We're talking about a tall, good-looking man in his late thirties—the absolute prime of life—who drives a car worth more money than most of the houses in this town. And he's lonely."

"You know, Kate, being handsome doesn't mean he can't have problems." Exasperated, Abby threw down a french fry. Her mild temper tantrum was rewarded when the fry landed in the mound of catsup on her plate, sending a droplet flying upward to land on the white collar of her uniform.

"I didn't say he couldn't have problems. I just think you're blinding yourself to the truth if you think he's only hanging around for a chance to use his hands on an inanimate object.''

''Really, Kate!'' Abby shot her an annoyed glance before trying to dab the catsup off her collar. She only succeeded in smearing it into a wider area.

''Don't 'really, Kate' me, Abby. I just want you to admit that you're attracted to this guy. What's so awful about that?''

''All right!'' Abby tossed her napkin down, and glared at her friend across the table. ''I'm attracted to him. Are you happy now?''

''Perfectly.'' Kate gave her a smug smile and popped a french fry into her mouth.

Abby glanced around, noticing that her raised voice had drawn a few curious glances toward their table. Flushing with embarrassment, she fixed her best friend with a positively violent look.

''You are a horrid person.''

''I know.'' Kate did not seem unduly disturbed by this pronouncement. ''People often resent those who make them face the truth,'' she said, sighing over the injustice of it.

''People also resent nosy, bullying, know-it-alls,'' Abby suggested ominously.

''True. Luckily I don't have any of those qualities.''

A snort of laughter ruined any hopes Abby might have had of making Kate see the error of her ways. She didn't know why she bothered trying. Kate Bixby couldn't stop poking her nose in her friends' business any more than she could stop breathing.

''Being attracted to John doesn't change anything. I don't have time to get involved with anyone right now.''

"Abby, that is the dumbest comment I've ever heard you make. Since when did falling in love wait until someone had time to do it?"

"It's a rather large leap from being attracted to falling in love," Abby protested. "Falling in love takes energy, and I don't have any left over these days."

"You just keep telling yourself that," Kate told her, giving her a pitying look.

"I am *not* falling in love with John Lonigan."

It was foolish even to think such a thing. Very foolish. Extremely foolish. It just went to show how much Kate knew.

"DILLON. What a nice surprise." Abby pulled the door open, inviting her cousin into the house.

"How's everything?" Dillon threw one arm around Abby's shoulders, drawing her close for a quick hug.

"Fine." Abby returned the hug. Dillon had always been her favorite cousin, the one she was closest to.

"You'd say that if the world was collapsing."

"Maybe. But as it happens, it isn't."

"Yet." Dillon ruffled her hair as if she were five years old. Abby sometimes thought it was her lack of inches that led him to occasionally revert to the way he'd treated her when she was a child and he was a moderately indulgent teenager.

But she usually came to the conclusion that, even if she were taller than his own five-eleven, Dillon would still perceive her as the child who'd tagged along behind him and her brother, making a nuisance of herself more often than not. There was a certain comfort in the thought.

"To what do I owe the honor of this visit?" she asked, leaving her arm around his waist as she led him toward the kitchen.

"Well, actually, Kate suggested I drop by. She said there was someone I ought to meet."

"Oh, honestly." Abby pulled away, frowning. "Have you ever considered beating that woman?"

"Frequently." Dillon grinned down at her. "I don't think it would do any good."

"Probably not. You'd think I was a child the way she's sending you over to check up on me."

"Not check up, exactly. She just said I ought to meet this guy. And I agreed with her." Dillon held up his hand to forestall her protests. "I'm family, Abby. You won't let me do anything around this place, and now Kate tells me this guy is here rebuilding the house. I can't help but be a little curious."

"He's not rebuilding the place." Abby suddenly remembered that John was working on the kitchen sink and lowered her voice. "He's a friend of mine and he enjoys doing odd jobs. It's no big deal."

"Is he here?"

"Yes."

Dillon waited, but she didn't make any effort to enlarge on the flat statement. "Well, do I get to meet the guy or not?"

"If you must," she said ungraciously. "But if you act like you're inspecting him, so help me, Dillon Taylor, I'll punch you out myself."

"Better get a ladder first," he said, grinning.

JOHN GLANCED UP as Abby came into the kitchen, followed by a muscular blond man with a face that could have graced the cover of a fashion magazine. The hostility he felt was instantaneous and unexpected.

He'd been working on a stubborn leak in the kitchen faucet when he heard the doorbell ring. Jason was in the backyard with George, ever hopeful that the dog would prove able to master at least one trick.

In one corner of the kitchen Mara had been playing some game known only to her. She looked up as Abby and the man entered the room, her face lighting up in one of her rare smiles. It didn't make John feel any more charitable toward the man.

"Hi, half-pint. You still my best girl?" Mara slid off her chair and trotted over to the stranger, who picked her up, settling her small weight against his hip as if it was something he'd done many times before.

John noticed that the man's eyes were really too close together. He'd never trusted people with eyes like that.

The stranger turned his attention to John, his look weighing. John returned it in kind. There was something vaguely familiar about the newcomer.

"John, I'd like you to meet my cousin, Dillon Taylor. Dillon, this is John Lonigan, a friend of mine."

Her cousin. No wonder he'd looked familiar. The familial resemblance was strong, from the color of their hair to the shape of the face. John felt a wave of relief much stronger than he had any business feeling. What difference did it make to him whether this was Abby's cousin or her lover?

But it did make a difference. Her lover he'd have been tempted to ram down the newly repaired garbage disposal. Her cousin he offered his hand.

A temporary aberration, he assured himself as he and Dillon Taylor shook hands. Some primitive male reaction that had little to do with anything real. A territorial thing.

That was all it was.

Certainly nothing deeper than that.

Chapter Five

"So, what did you think of him?" Kate pounced on Dillon the minute he came through the door of her apartment.

"Whatever happened to 'Hello'? Or maybe a kiss?"

"Hello." She reached up to give him a quick peck on the lips, drawing back before he had a chance to deepen it into something more.

"There'll be plenty of time for that later," she told him, grabbing his hand and dragging him into the living room. "First things first. Did you meet Abby's handyman?"

"You know, I'm not sure I'm crazy about the idea that you shortchange a kiss with me in order to talk about another man," Dillon complained.

There was no real force behind the complaint. He let Kate pull him down onto the thick cushioned sofa, leaning back with a sigh. The sofa was upholstered in ivory raw silk. In fact, most of the living room was ivory, with occasional splashes of brilliant color to alleviate the monotony.

He sometimes tried to imagine anyone in his family doing a room in such a completely impractical color but he couldn't picture it. The big old farmhouse where he'd grown up had had no particular decor that he could recall. Unless "kid proof" was a style.

It was one of the many things that had amazed him when he and Kate had gotten involved. The idea that he was dating a woman with a white living room. That he and that woman were lovers in a bedroom decorated in shades of palest apricot.

He and Kate had been involved for almost five years now, and he still wasn't sure what she saw in him. She was the daughter of one of the wealthiest families in town. She'd spent summers in Europe, winters skiing in Aspen. She could have gone anywhere, dated anyone, but she'd stayed in Beaumont, working in her family's department store and she'd chosen him.

Him. Dillon Taylor, farm boy. A man who grubbed in the soil for a living. A man who'd rarely traveled more than a hundred miles from the town where he'd been born. What could she possibly see in him? It was a question to which he still hadn't found an answer.

"Hey. Earth to Dillon." Kate's voice dragged him out of his sudden reverie.

"Sorry. I didn't mean to go off in a blue funk. Did you miss me?" He slid one arm around her shoulders, pulling her closer.

"Miss *you?*" She snuggled closer against his side. "Why should I miss you? It's only been two days, fourteen hours and twenty-two minutes since I saw you last."

"You forgot the forty-three seconds." He nuzzled her ear.

"I just didn't want you to think I'd missed you too much," she murmured, turning her face up to give him the proper welcome he'd been denied at the door.

"But that doesn't mean I've forgotten about Abby's handyman," she said several minutes later. She put her hand against his chest, holding him off. "If you don't tell me about this guy, I'm not going to let you eat any of the lasagna I made.''

Recognizing a serious threat when he heard it, Dillon reluctantly loosened his hold, letting her put all of six inches between them.

''Abby said I should beat you, you know.''

''You *told* her I'd sent you?''

''Sure. Why not?''

Kate rolled her eyes in silent comment. ''I'll worry about that later. Did you meet the guy or not?''

''I met him.''

''Well?''

''Well, what?''

''Well, what's he like?'' she cried, exasperated.

''He's a guy.'' Dillon shrugged, enjoying the way her eyes flashed at him.

''If you don't tell me about him, I'm going to think of something hideous to do to you and I'm going to spring it on you weeks from now when you're least expecting it.''

''Okay, okay.'' Dillon tugged on a lock of soft brown hair, smiling into her dark eyes. ''But there isn't all that much to tell.''

''I should have gone myself,'' Kate muttered.

''I don't know why you didn't. Unless Abby has forbidden you to set foot on the place.''

''I wanted a man's opinion of him. A man sees different things in another man than a woman might see in that same other man.''

''It's frightening to realize that I actually understood that sentence,'' Dillon said after a moment.

''So what's he like? What does he look like?''

''He seems like a nice enough guy. He's tall, and his hair is sort of...well, it's kind of hair-colored—brown, I guess,'' he added hastily, seeing the threat in her eyes.

"Is he handsome?"

"I guess. He's got all the usual number of features and they're in all the right places. Well, I'm not an expert on male good looks," he said defensively when she threatened to hit him with a pillow.

"How about his eyes? And if you tell me they're eye-colored, I'm going to slug you, Dillon Taylor."

"They're gray, I think. Sort of distant." He wiped a hand over his brow in mock relief when this answer seemed to satisfy her.

"What's he like? Is Abby going to get hurt?"

"I don't know." He frowned, considering the question. "It depends on what she wants out of him."

"Could you tell how he felt about her?"

"Possessive," he said promptly. "When he saw me with Abby, he wasn't at all pleased. But I don't think he likes feeling that way."

"No man likes feeling that way," she said smugly.

"No, this was more than that." His frown deepened as he sought the right words to make her understand. "We had a dog once, when I was a kid."

"A dog?" Kate looked as if she thought he'd gone off the deep end.

"A dog. He showed up at the farmhouse one day. Big mangy thing. Mama was going to shoo him off but Abby was there visiting. She couldn't have been more than five at the time. Before Mama could stop her, she'd run over to the dog and thrown her arms around his neck. We all figured she was about to get her head removed but that dog just stood there and let her hold him.

"Steve was in Florida with friends and her parents were taking a vacation—a second honeymoon, really. So Abby was staying with us for a couple of weeks. That dog continued to hang around. We all fed him and he never tried to bite anybody, but he never let anybody pet him except Abby."

"And all of this leads back to Abby's handyman somewhere?" Kate questioned skeptically.

"Well, he kind of reminds me of that dog. That dog wasn't ever really tame. Some animals are wanderers, just like some people. The dog stayed with us for about ten days. Mostly he ignored us but he'd watch Abby with a sort of confused look in his eyes. She named him something stupid, like Spot, and made big plans for taking him home with her."

"What happened?"

"About two days before her parents came to get her, the dog left. Will saw him leave just before dawn. He trotted off toward the road just as if he had somewhere he was going. He looked back once, from the end of the lane, and then he turned and walked out of sight.

"Abby cried all day. She kept asking how come Will hadn't stopped him. We couldn't make her understand that some things aren't happy staying in one place, no matter how much you love them."

Kate stared at him uneasily. "You're saying you think this John Lonigan is like that dog?"

"Could be."

"That's ridiculous. I mean, even if he has done a lot of traveling, maybe hasn't ever really settled down, that doesn't mean he can't change. He's not a dog. He's a man. If he fell in love with Abby, really fell in love, he'd change."

"Maybe."

"What do you mean 'maybe'?" She drew away, frowning at him. "Of course he'd change."

"I don't think falling in love changes a man quite as much as women like to believe it does."

"So you're saying that even if he loved Abby he'd still leave?"

"Maybe." He lifted his hands defensively when she glared at him. "Hey, I never claimed to be the Swami of love. Abby's a big girl. Contrary to your fervent belief, you can't protect her. John seemed like a nice guy. I'm sure he has no intention of hurting her."

"Well, I think they're going to fall in love," Kate said with a touch of belligerence.

"I think that would be great. I hope they live happily ever after. Now, can we discuss something a little closer to home, like how long it's been since I last kissed you?"

He knew she was still concerned about Abby but she allowed herself to be distracted.

"Ms. TAYLOR. What a pleasure to see you." Abby looked up from the register, smiling when she recognized Jason's teacher.

"Ms. Brown. How are you?"

"I'm fine. I thought I would take advantage of lunch break to run out and pick up a few groceries."

Abby began running the packages across the scanner, listening for the electronic ping that told her that the computer had registered the item.

"Actually I wanted to talk to you," Ms. Brown said as she dug in her purse for her checkbook.

"You did?" Abby threw her an uneasy look. "Anything wrong with Jason?"

"No. No, as a matter of fact, quite the contrary." The teacher gave her a reassuring smile. "These past few weeks I've noticed a marked improvement in Jason's schoolwork. I think he's finally beginning to work up to his potential. You and I had spoken at the beginning of the year and, considering the tragedy of losing his parents, I really think he's done remarkably well.

"But until recently I knew he wasn't giving all he was capable of. But his grades are improving, he's starting to participate in oral activities. In general, I'm very pleased with Jason."

Abby felt her chest swell with pride. *She* already knew Jason was a wonderful boy. But it never hurt to hear it confirmed.

"Thank you for telling me that, Ms. Brown. It means a lot to me to know that he's getting back to normal at school."

"Well, you've done a wonderful job with him. It's been a difficult time for all of you. Raising children alone is never easy."

"That's true." Abby waited while the teacher wrote out her check. She felt buoyed up by the woman's words.

"Of course, from what Jason tells me, you won't be trying to handle it alone much longer." Ms. Brown gave her an indulgent smile as she handed her the check.

"Excuse me?" Abby had been wondering if she should get Jason some small treat, something to celebrate the progress he'd made. Even if she couldn't tell him what it was for, it seemed as if she shouldn't let this occasion go unmarked.

"Jason mentioned in class that you'll be getting married soon."

"He did?" Abby hit the ground with a thump.

"Yes. It wasn't a secret, was it?"

"Secret? No, not exactly."

"Well, Jason seems very happy about the idea. You're fortunate there, Ms. Taylor. So many boys have a difficult time dealing with a new man in their mother's life. Perhaps the fact that you're his aunt makes it a little easier for him.''

''Perhaps.'' Abby gave the woman a vague smile. Ms. Brown picked up her bag of groceries and said something about being so glad to have had a chance to talk to Abby.

Abby hoped she gave an appropriate answer. She reached down to flip off the light on her aisle. Her hands were not quite steady as she picked up her purse and made her way to the rather dingy employees' lounge at the back of the store. Thankfully it was empty. One thing she wasn't in the mood for now was idle chitchat. Pouring herself a cup of water from the cooler, she sat on the cracked sofa and faced the fact that she'd been letting her own needs take precedence over what was best for the children.

Ms. Brown hadn't mentioned the name of her ''fiancé.'' But she didn't have to. Jason could have been thinking of no one but John.

Abby gulped down the water, wishing she could throw it over her face instead. She should have seen this coming. A blind woman could have seen this coming. But not her. No, she'd been going blithely along, glad there was a man for Jason to talk to. Glad there was someone around she could talk to. God, the only one of them who hadn't spilled their guts to John Michael Lonigan was poor little Mara. Meanwhile, they still knew almost nothing about him.

But that wasn't the point now. Abby scowled at a tiny crack in the plaster wall. The point now was how to deal with the situation she'd created or at least perpetrated.

John had been spending more and more time working on the house this past month. It was amazing what a few evenings and weekends had managed to accomplish. The place was actually beginning to look as though it belonged in the neighborhood.

He'd become a part of their lives. The children liked him. Mrs. O'Leary across the street had been his devoted fan ever since he'd rescued her cat from a tree.

Kate had finally met him and had pronounced him satisfactory. Dillon had driven in from the farm to help with the repairs to the garage door, and the two men had rubbed along together without a hitch. The only person who didn't like John was Mr. Frickle next door, and she discounted his opinion because he hated everyone and everything.

Her own feelings Abby flatly refused to examine too closely. As she'd told Kate, she didn't have time to get emotionally involved right now. Of course she liked John, even if she sometimes felt that he kept most of himself hidden away.

But that wasn't the point, either. Damn! Why was she having so much trouble sticking to the point here?

Because she didn't want to face the fact that there was no easy solution to the problem.

She'd let Jason—let them all, really—take John into their lives. Let hopes and dreams get built up around a man who could walk out tomorrow. There were no ties, no commitments on his part. There was no reason in the world for him to stay.

She should never have let it happen. She should have foreseen this problem with Jason and put a stop to it before it got to this point.

The problem was, what did she do about it now?

ABBY STILL DIDN'T have an answer when she got home that afternoon and found John scraping cracked paint off the house trim, preparatory to putting on a new coat.

She'd grown accustomed to seeing the exotic Mercedes parked in front of her house; grown even more accustomed to seeing John's tall figure around the place. It was hard to remember what it had been like before he'd been there; harder still to imagine what it would be like if he weren't there again.

But she had to face facts. And the fact was that they were only a temporary diversion in his life. He probably hadn't even realized what was happening; hadn't even considered the fantasies Jason might be building around him.

Abby set her jaw. Jason had baseball practice this afternoon, which meant it was a perfect time to talk to John. She didn't know quite what she was going to say but she'd think of something. Jason was too fragile, too easily hurt. She wasn't going to see his heart broken if she could help it.

"WE NEED TO TALK."

John set the scraper down on the windowsill and dusted his hands on the seat of his jeans before turning to face Abby. He'd watched her reflection in the window as she approached. The set of her shoulders had told him that she had something on her mind.

Mara was settled in the kitchen with a glass of milk and some cookies. Jason was at baseball practice. It had surprised him to find he missed the boy. He'd become accustomed to him being underfoot, his enthusiasm more hindrance than help.

In fact, there were a lot of things about his life these days that surprised him. Like the pleasure he was taking in seeing the old house start to sparkle again.

He'd worked his share of construction jobs. Right after he'd left home, he'd worked construction to survive. He'd also driven big rigs, dug ditches and done a stint as a short-order cook.

After he went to work for the government and put his flair for languages to use, he'd held quite an assortment of jobs over the years, all of them covers for the real reason he was in a particular place. He'd found his various covers more or less enjoyable but they'd never been anything more than a job, something to be done as well as possible because his survival depended on being convincing.

This was different. He was taking a personal pride in this place. Almost as if it were his own home.

The thought made him uncomfortable and he pushed it away. Years ago, he'd accepted the fact that he wasn't the hearth-and-home type. Some people were born to wander, the same way others were meant to sink roots. He was definitely the wandering type.

"John?" The sound of his name made him realize he'd been standing there staring at Abby, lost in thought. He shook himself, seeing the questioning look in her eyes.

"Sorry. I didn't mean to drift off on you. You said we needed to talk."

"That's right." She drew a deep breath and squared her shoulders.

"Something wrong?"

"Yes. No. In a way."

John raised his brows, watching the delicate wave of color flood her cheeks. He couldn't remember the last time he'd known a woman who blushed. It was one of many things he found appealing about Abby Taylor. Sometimes he wondered if there weren't a few too many things about her that appealed to him.

Abby wished he didn't have to stand there looking so darned attractive. Couldn't he at least button his shirt? And if he had to leave it unbuttoned, did his chest have to be quite so nicely muscular? Where was a nice, flabby looking chest when you needed one?

"What did you want to talk about?"

She dragged her gaze from his chest and met his eyes, her cheeks flushing again. She was acting like an idiot. She drew in a slow breath, forcing herself to focus on why it was so important that they talk.

"I saw Jason's teacher today. She came into the store."

"Is Jason in trouble?" John frowned in concern. To her relief, he began buttoning his shirt.

"No. Actually she told me that his grades have been picking up. He's participating more in class discussions. Overall, she's very pleased."

"That's great." He smiled, and for a moment she forgot everything but her pride in her nephew and smiled back at him. It felt wonderful to share the moment with someone who cared about Jason the same way she did.

She drew herself up short, her smile fading. She couldn't assume that. There was no reason to think that John felt the same kind of ties to Jason that she did. He was her nephew. Her flesh and blood. But what was he to John?

"So what is it we need to talk about?" he asked, sensing her quick change of mood.

"Ms. Brown also congratulated me on my upcoming marriage," Abby said baldly, watching to see his reaction.

His eyes widened in surprise before he shuttered them with the guarded look that was so familiar.

"I see. What did you tell her?"

"Nothing. I didn't know what to say." Abby paced a few feet away, her feet crunching on the gravel driveway. She turned to face him again, her chin set. "It made me think. I won't have the children hurt again."

"You can't protect them forever," he said quietly.

"I know that. But they're still coping with losing their parents. I don't know if they could deal with any more hurt right now."

"Maybe not."

"They've lost so much already."

"True."

"They're so young. So vulnerable right now. I don't think they could bear it if they lost another person they cared about."

"It would be very hard."

"And there's nothing tying you here. Nothing to stop you from leaving."

"I'm not going anywhere anytime soon."

"But there's no reason you can't," she said, feeling as if she wasn't getting her point across. "And I don't want them hurt. I *won't* have them hurt."

"Abby." John covered the distance between them in one long stride, catching her hands in his, stilling their restless motion. "What is it you want me to do?"

Abby stared at their linked hands. Hadn't she been asking herself the same question all afternoon? And she still didn't have an answer. His hands felt strong around hers. She could feel the slight roughness of calluses.

"I don't know," she said at last without lifting her gaze from their hands.

In the silence that fell between them, she heard the soft trill of a bird perched somewhere in the oak above them and the sound of someone starting a car farther down the street.

"Do you want me to leave?" John asked quietly. "I can go now and not come back, if that's what you think is best."

"No." The answer was out before she had a chance to think. She lifted her head to meet his eyes. Was it her imagination or was there a deep sadness there? A loneliness, maybe even a vulnerability? "No, I don't want you to go," she said slowly. "Unless you want to."

"It's been a long time since I've felt as if I almost belonged somewhere," he said slowly, not answering her question directly.

"I just don't want to see the children hurt." She tightened her fingers over his, trying to get across the strength of her feelings.

"I don't want that, either. I promise you that I'll do my damnedest not to hurt either of them."

And what about me? Will you try not to hurt me?

The thought was so vivid that, for a moment, Abby almost thought she'd said it out loud.

"It's just that they're so little," she whispered.

"I know." He cupped one hand over her cheek.

She saw herself reflected in his eyes and wondered if he could see the yearning in hers. His head lowered and she let her lashes drift down. Her breathing was suspended as she waited for his mouth to touch hers.

It was a soft kiss, making no demands, offering reassurance and comfort. Was it her imagination or was there a deeper promise underneath?

Her lips softened under his, her hands coming up to rest against his chest, feeling the sun-warmed muscles beneath the thin shirt. His hand slipped into her hair as she leaned into him, letting the kiss deepen. He smelled of hot sun and sawdust, warm, earthy scents that filled her senses.

She nearly murmured a protest when he began to break the kiss. She didn't want the kiss to end. She wanted it to go on and on. She wanted one kiss to lead to another. She wanted to feel the strength of him against her without the irritating barriers of their clothing between them. She wanted him like she'd never wanted anyone or anything in her life.

The strength of the thought stilled any protest she might have made. Opening her eyes, she stared up at him, knowing, with a shivery certainty, that it wasn't only the children who'd opened their hearts to this man.

He'd said he wouldn't hurt the children. But what about her?

Chapter Six

When he was a small boy, John had watched the happy families on television and wondered why his family wasn't like them. Ozzie and Harriet, Lucy and Desi—life was always full of laughter in their households. There hadn't been a whole lot of laughter in the Lonigan family.

His mother had been a dark-haired beauty who threw herself into everything in life. Whether it was laughter or rage, she felt the emotion to the depths of her soul and generally spread what she was feeling to anyone near her.

Some days, she'd loved her son passionately, smothering him with affection, telling him he was her perfect child. Other days, she'd had neither the time nor the patience for a growing boy, pushing him away for some childish misdemeanor or weeping bitterly because he didn't love her enough.

In reality, he'd loved her too much. He'd spent his youth seeking her approval, wanting her to love him all the time, not just when he was perfect. It was only as an adult that he'd been able to see her instability.

His father had loved his mother deeply. And she'd loved him with the same passion she gave to everything in her life. But it wasn't a love that could survive the daily grind of life.

Nothing Alicia Lonigan felt survived the day-to-day pressures of living for very long.

By the time Mike Lonigan realized that, they had a son to think about. They'd stayed together for the sake of the child. Some of John's earliest memories were of hearing his parents fight—his mother's voice shrill and ugly as she accused his father of trying to destroy her. His father had rarely raised his voice but there'd been a bitter edge to the low rumble of his words that had sent a shudder through the young John.

Always, after one of their fights, his father would leave the house. He never slammed the door but there'd always been something very final sounding in the way he'd closed it. No matter how many times he came back, every time he left, John wondered if this time he was going to stay away.

Alicia would either shut herself in the bedroom she still shared with her husband, filling the small house with the sound of her weeping or she'd come find John. Drawing him into her embrace, she'd cry slow, painful tears that never reddened her eyes and tell him that he wasn't to worry. No matter what his father did to her, she was never going to leave her precious little boy. She stayed in this hateful house where she was so unhappy because she loved him so much.

As he got older, John had had the occasional, cynical moment when he'd wondered if the real reason wasn't that she needed him as a stick to beat his father with. But such thoughts had been fleeting and quickly pushed aside, the guilt he felt translated into another strike against his father.

He and his father never managed to get along for more than a short period. Mike Lonigan had been a police officer, devoted to his job. He'd had firm ideas of right and wrong. He'd also had high expectations for his only son.

As an adult, John could look back and see that his father had been doing his best. He hadn't been a demonstrative man. Being married to Alicia had made him even less so. The more tempestuous she became, the more taciturn he grew, as if to balance out her excesses.

Mike had wanted his son to be strongly focused on something. Sports, music, academics—he would have settled for anything. In the way of children since time immemorial, John had been equally determined to drift through his youth, accomplishing as little as possible.

Naturally, Alicia had sided with her son in any conflict with her husband. At the time, it had seemed as if his mother was the only one who understood him, who cared about him.

From his father, John had inherited a stubborn determination to go his own way. His father was just as determined to make sure he got off to what Mike considered a good start in life. The clashes between the two had been inevitable.

His mother died when he was sixteen. John had grieved, but there'd been a niggling feeling of relief that she was gone. No more hysterical fits followed by passionate apologies and avowals of love.

The guilt had translated, in human if unjust fashion, into an even more bitter resentment of his father. For two years, the small house had rocked with their arguments. Two weeks before his eighteenth birthday, John had packed a duffel bag with his clothes and a few favorite books and left home, vowing it would be a cold day in hell before he returned.

And he hadn't returned. With time and distance, he'd come to see his childhood with a clearer vision than had been possible when he was in the midst of its emotional turmoil. He'd forgiven his father for his sins, both real and imagined. He'd thought about writing, maybe even going home to mend fences. But he didn't make it home until after his father's death.

He'd never grown any roots and told himself that was exactly the way he liked it. No strings. No commitments except the ones he chose to make and they were always of a short duration. He'd been lucky enough to find a job with the government that called for someone of just his qualifications. It didn't hurt that there was no one to grieve if he failed to return from one of the trips he was sent on.

After his father's death, he'd quit his job, taken his portion of the money from the sale of his father's liquor store and bought the Gullwing. He'd spent the past two years drifting around his own country instead of someone else's.

He had his life arranged just the way it should be. If he was sometimes lonely, that was the price he paid for having incurable wanderlust.

There'd been a woman once that he might have settled down for. She'd told him that he wasn't so much wandering as he was running. Running from commitments he thought himself incapable of making. For her, he'd have tried to make those commitments. But she'd died and he'd taken it as just one more sign that he wasn't meant to be one of the lucky ones who could settle in one place and set down roots.

But he'd never quite forgotten that youthful craving for a home and the stability that went with it.

At age forty, for the first time in his life, he was getting a taste of what a family could be. Abby, Jason and Mara were a family in the real sense of the word. For a few short weeks, they'd opened the doors to a world he'd only seen from the outside.

Of course it wouldn't last. Nothing ever did.

"Now, this is going to last a lot longer than any of us will." The man at the lumberyard clapped a grizzled hand on the pile of cedar boards. "You build it right and a cedar fence'll last a long time. Ain't the cheapest but it's one of the best."

"Sounds good. You can deliver it this afternoon?" John was writing a check as he spoke.

"Heck, we're slow enough today, I can just about follow you home."

"Good." Perfect, in fact. He'd call Bill and let him know that his lunch hour was going to be a little longer than usual. Bill wouldn't care. If the truth were told, he'd hired John as much for company as for help in the store.

He wanted the wood delivered and stacked in the back-yard before Abby got home. If she saw the delivery truck, she'd know it was new wood and she'd argue that she couldn't afford a new fence. Well, he could afford it and she didn't have to know he'd bought it. She could think it was just another batch of the seemingly inexhaustible supply of materials her brother had bought for the house.

John paid for the wood and gave directions to Abby's house. They were already loading the fencing on the truck when he pulled the Gullwing out of the parking lot. He supposed there were those who'd say he was crazy to spend his money on a house that didn't belong to him, a place he didn't even live in.

Some might even suggest that he was getting more involved with the Taylors than he had any real business doing. Bill had mentioned it once or twice, commenting on the amount of time he was spending on the little house, not to mention the time he was spending with Abby Taylor.

He and Bill had developed something of a friendship in the months John had been working for him. The older man's concern grew out of that friendship, so John refrained from suggesting that he mind his own business.

The answer was a straightforward one. He was enjoying himself. These past few weeks were one of the rare times in the last twenty-odd years that he hadn't felt a restless need to move on, to see what was over the next horizon.

Besides, he didn't have anything else to spend his money on. The small apartment over the liquor store came with the job. He had no one to support but himself. And other than his car, his tastes were pretty simple.

So, there was no reason in the world he shouldn't buy fencing to put in Abby's backyard. For some reason, it gave him pleasure to think of the fence sitting there long after he was gone and no doubt forgotten.

If it occurred to him that he was spending a lot of time justifying his actions, he pushed the thought away.

The delivery truck arrived at Abby's, as promised, only a short while after John did. The wood was unloaded and stacked in the backyard. After the men were gone, John stood in the grass for a few minutes, soaking in the sunshine and the scent of the wood.

"I certainly hope you're not planning on putting a fence up on *my* property line." The sound of Elmer Frickle's whiny voice slithered into the peaceful moment.

John turned to look across the low, sagging fence. It was a struggle to keep his upper lip from quivering in a sneer. Elmer Frickle had been born and raised in the house he now lived in. He'd cared for his aging parents, inheriting the house on their deaths. There were those who might have considered that a charitable deed. As far as John was concerned, the man was such an almighty pain in the butt, he wouldn't have been surprised to find Elmer's parents had been glad to go just to get away from him.

"I'm going to put it up on Abby's property line," he said, keeping his tone neutral.

"Well, you certainly can't do that. No, no. I can't have that at all." Elmer tugged fussily at the pseudosafari hat that protected his pasty white complexion from the sun.

"What's the problem, Mr. Prickle? You told Abby the fence had to be replaced."

"It's *Frickle*. And certainly I told her that. Certainly, certainly. Of course I did. It's a disgrace. Just look at it. A disgrace." He swept his short-fingered hands in a gesture that encompassed the aging picket fence.

"Then what's the problem?" John asked, hanging on to his patience with a conscious effort. After all, Abby was the one who had to live next door to this guy. It wasn't his place to antagonize the man.

"She can't just have *anyone* put up the fence. Certainly not. Not at all. I have just the man in mind. Fine work. I can't have anything but the best," Elmer finished smugly, tugging on the hat again.

"Is that the guy that gave her the outrageous estimate two weeks ago?"

"You get what you pay for," Elmer said, drawing himself up to his full five foot five inches, indignation in every line of his pudgy body.

"Do you plan on paying for this guy, Mr. Pickle?"

"No, no. Certainly not. And my name is Frickle. *Frickle.* I'm on a fixed income, you know. Besides, Ms. Taylor is the one with the noisy children and that dreadful dog."

George had been examining the pile of fencing but he turned to give Elmer a thoughtful look as if fixing the man in his mind. John knew George was just as likely to be contemplating the thought of taking his twentieth nap of the day as he was thinking about going for Elmer Frickle's throat. But Elmer gave the huge dog an uneasy look and edged an inch or two away.

"It's her responsibility. Hers," he added hastily.

"Then you'll just have to put up with her choice of labor, Mr. Trickle," John said calmly.

"*Frickle*," he spit out, glaring at John. "You think I don't know what's going on." John's calm refusal to give in touched off the malice that was never far from Elmer Frickle's surface. "You think you're fooling me with all your pretending to work on the house."

"I'm not interested in your opinion one way or another, Fickle." John arched one dark brow in a lazy comment, as if he couldn't imagine how Elmer could have thought otherwise.

"Frickle! My name is Frickle!"

"Odd name." John studied him. "Frickle Tickle? Named for a rich uncle, were you?"

"No, no. Stop calling me that! My name is Frickle! Frickle!"

"Frickle Frickle? That's even worse."

It was rather like shooting fish in a barrel, John decided, watching the old man's face flush an alarming shade of red. It should have been beneath him but he didn't feel any guilt. The guy had been hassling Abby for months now. It wouldn't hurt him to get a little of his own medicine.

"It's not Frickle Frickle!" Little flecks of saliva had appeared at the corners of his mouth.

"I wish you'd make up your mind," John murmured, allowing a trace of annoyance to show.

"Elmer," he got out stutteringly. "My name is Elmer."

"Then why did you say it was Frickle?"

"Because it is."

John's brows climbed in shock. Frickle's face was turning the shade of a ripe plum. His fingers were clenching and unclenching in spasms of frustrated rage. John didn't have any doubt that if the other man had been holding the means to do the deed, he would have been lying dead at Frickle's feet.

"My name is Elmer Frickle. Elmer Frickle. Elmer Frickle." Each repetition was louder than the last until the final words were just under a scream.

John let a second go by before shrugging as if the subject had long ceased to interest him. "Why didn't you say so in the first place?"

"I... You... I..."

"You really should have that stutter looked into, Mr. Trickle. They can do wonders these days with therapy."

He turned away, snapping his fingers at George. For once in his life, George actually obeyed a signal, though it was possible he'd decided to head for the shady porch on his own. Whatever his reason, his timing was perfect. He and John strolled casually across the lawn, leaving Elmer Frickle gasping and sputtering on his side of the soon-to-be-replaced fence.

"I should be ashamed of myself, shouldn't I?" John paused by the porch to scratch George's floppy ear. George grunted a denial, leaning heavily against John's leg. "It was childish, unworthy of me."

He pondered the scene for a moment, seeking some feeling of guilt. But there was none to be found. In fact, he felt rather pleased with himself.

THE WEEKEND John started work on the fence, the weather made an unseasonable leap from spring to summer. The sun seemed twice as hot as it had been during the week, blazing down out of a clear blue sky, pouring heat over the town.

By Sunday afternoon, John had cleared away the first section of the old fence and had the new fencing in its place. Elmer Frickle had watched the operation from the safety of his kitchen window, peering through the curtains under the mistaken impression that he couldn't be seen. Halfway through the morning, John had looked directly at him, given him a wide smile and waved. The round face had disappeared in a frantic flutter of curtains.

Abby had choked back laughter and told John he was *not* a nice person. From the twinkle in her eyes, he was fairly sure she meant it as a compliment.

After that, Elmer continued to keep an eye on the fencing operation but he was a bit more discreet in his spying. As far as John was concerned, one of the best things about the new fence was that it was going to be too high for the nosy old man to see over.

Lunch was leftover fried chicken and cold potato salad, washed down with gallons of iced tea. After lunch, Abby put Mara down for a nap and Jason retreated to the garage where he was building some unidentifiable object with scraps of wood. John stretched out on the grass, finding a shady spot under a tree and closing his eyes.

Abby felt strangely restless. She had a few things of Jason's that needed mending—it never ceased to amaze her that he could leave in the morning in a new shirt and come home in the afternoon with a button missing—but she wasn't in the mood for sewing.

She wandered around the yard, nipping a spent flower here or a withered leaf there. She'd spent more time on her plants since John had been coming around. In some odd way, his presence had lifted some of the weight from her shoulders and it wasn't just because of the work he was doing.

For lack of something better to do, Abby got out the hose and began sprinkling one of the flower beds. John was apparently asleep, his head propped on his hands. She let the water run, her attention more for his prone form than for the plants.

She'd had a long talk with her nephew after that surprising conversation with his teacher. She'd explained to him that John was a visitor in their lives, that it wouldn't do to build up too many expectations around him. Not to mention the fact that he'd lied to his teacher when he told her that Abby was engaged.

She wasn't sure just how much of what she'd said had gotten through to him. Life didn't work out the way it did on television, she'd told him. She and John weren't getting married. With a ten-year-old's logic, Jason didn't see why not. Everything would be great if the two of them got married and they were a real family.

The problem was that she more than half agreed with him. She was beginning to think everything might be great if they were a real family.

Slanting another glance at John's relaxed form, she felt a spurt of annoyance that he should look so completely relaxed while she was drifting around watering plants that didn't need watering.

He'd taken off his shirt after lunch. His bare chest was lightly dusted with dark hair tapering to a tantalizing line that arrowed across his stomach to disappear into his jeans. They were well worn and now the faded blue denim rode low on his hips and clung lovingly to his thighs.

He looked completely relaxed. Supremely male. Totally attractive.

Abby's annoyance increased.

Men. They had the sensitivity of water buffalo. She could just about bet that *he* didn't spend time lying awake at night wondering where this odd arrangement was taking all of them. Of course he didn't. Why should he? He could simply pack up and drive off into the sunset in that stupid, macho car of his.

It was hard to say which of them was more surprised when Abby turned the hose on John's relaxed body. Since she'd only planned on sprinkling the flower bed, she hadn't turned the pressure on very high so it wasn't a hard spray of water that landed on his bare chest. More of a light shower. But it was more than enough to bring him jack-knifing into a sitting position, a rather vivid oath exploding from his lips.

Abby stared, too startled by her own actions to even think to turn the hose nozzle another direction. Her fingers tightened on the trigger grip, turning the light shower to a hard spray that caught him full in the face. John lunged upright, the move taking him out of range of the hose.

Time seemed to stand still.

He stared down at himself as if he couldn't believe that he'd gone to sleep bone-dry and awakened nearly soaked from head to foot. Water dripped from his dark hair to join that already beaded on his shoulders. His jeans were soaked from waist to knee.

Abby stared at him, her mind a total blank. A smile tugged at the corners of her mouth. He couldn't have looked more shocked if George had suddenly begun spouting Shakespeare.

She wiped the smile off when he looked at her. His expression was unreadable, his eyes in shadow. Since she still held the hose, there was no sense in trying to pretend she wasn't the guilty party. And the best defense was always a good offense.

"You were sleeping too heavily. I thought you might have a nightmare."

John blinked, absorbing this absurdity. "So you turned the hose on me to prevent me from having a nightmare?"

"That's right." Abby watched a drop of water drip off the end of his nose, and bit her lower lip. "Wasn't that nice of me?"

"Nice?" John pondered the idea. "You know, in New Guinea, a woman who wakes a man suddenly pays a terrible price." He took a step forward.

"She does?" Abby eased back a step, feeling her pulse increase in response to the gleam in his eyes.

"A terrible price," he rumbled ominously.

"It's a good thing this isn't New Guinea," she said, trying to sound a little braver than she felt. "Besides, I'm armed." She lifted the hose nozzle, wishing it looked a little more threatening.

"You need a better arms dealer, honey." He took a long stride toward her. With a squeak, Abby abandoned the extremely dubious protection of the hose and sprinted for the safety of the house.

He caught her before she'd gone more than a couple of yards, one long arm catching her around the waist and lifting her completely off her feet. Abby shrieked, wiggling wildly. It was only later that she realized that she'd never for a moment feared that he might drop her.

"Hold still for your punishment," he ordered her, his stern tone ruined by an undercurrent of laughter.

"Never! I'll never surrender my person to your dastardly plans, you fiend."

"What?" John dropped her into the cool grass, following her down before she could roll away. "My dastardly plans?"

"That's right. I'll fight till the last breath leaves my body," she promised nobly.

"With dialogue like that, someone may shoot you to put you out of your misery," he said dryly. "And don't think I've forgotten your punishment."

Abby shrieked again as his fingers found the sensitive skin of her sides and tickled mercilessly. Her hand came up to press against his chest. Crisp, curling hair flattened under her palms. Hard, damp muscles lay just under her fingers. Her T-shirt had twisted upward during their mock struggle and John's hands were on bare skin.

Their eyes met, gray colliding with brown, awareness meeting awareness.

In the space of a heartbeat, the laughter faded, replaced by something much more potent.

Abby was suddenly aware of the rough brush of denim against her shorts-clad legs. Her fingers flexed against his chest, an unconscious testing motion that made his eyes widen and then narrow.

His hands softened on her sides, spreading out to test the softness of her skin. Abby's legs shifted restlessly, her hands sliding upward to rest on his shoulders.

It was hard to say who moved first. Did she lift her head or did he lower his? The kiss seemed so inevitable that it hardly mattered.

His mouth was just the way she'd remembered it, warm and firm. But this kiss was nothing like the first they'd shared. That had been a gentle kiss, reassuring, comforting, only hinting at deeper possibilities. This kiss wasn't about comfort.

This kiss was fire from the moment their lips met. John's mouth slanted over hers, demanding everything she could give, promising even more in return.

Her mouth opened to him. His tongue slid across her lower lip, dragging a shivering response from her. Her fingers slid into the thick, damp darkness of his hair, pulling him closer. The hard width of his chest pressed against her breasts, teasing her nipples to tightness.

The sun beat down on them, but Abby didn't feel its heat. She didn't feel the cool scratchiness of the grass against her bare legs. All she felt was the sensual weight of John's long body, the rough brush of his cheek against hers, the contrasting softness of his hair sifting through her fingers.

With her eyes closed, her senses were filled with him. His scent—a mixture of sweat and soap. The brush of denim, the feel of his hands on her skin, cupping her rib cage, his thumb riding dangerously near her aching breasts.

A brass band could have marched through the yard and Abby wouldn't have known it—wouldn't have cared. This was what she'd been waiting for, what she'd been missing. From the moment they met, everything had been leading up to this.

Later, she wondered what would have happened if George hadn't decided to take a hand in the proceedings. Actually it was more of a nose in the proceedings. Seeing the two of them lying in the grass, clearly enjoying themselves, George conceived an immediate urge to join in this fun new game. Accordingly he loped across the lawn and thrust his cold, damp nose in John's ear.

"Dammit all to hell!" John jerked upward, breaking the kiss. The abrupt interruption left Abby feeling bereft, disoriented, as if she'd been awakened too quickly.

George snuffled happily at her face, blowing away the lingering cobwebs. Abby stared up at John, who still leaned above her, his lower body pressed to hers with startling intimacy.

His eyes were, as usual, unreadable. From his expression, she might have imagined the torrid kiss. But there was no mistaking the heavy pressure of him against her hips.

His eyes met hers for a long moment. Without a word, he rolled away from her, shoving George out of the way.

Abby lay where she was, still breathless. She'd expected him to walk off, but he held his hand down to her. She hesitated a moment before taking it, not sure she wanted even that small contact right now.

He drew her to her feet as if she weighed no more than a child, releasing her as soon as possible.

"I'll get back to the fence," he said, his eyes slanting across her face without meeting hers.

"Yes. Yes, that's a good idea." Abby doubted if he even heard her murmured agreement since he was already moving away.

She stood where he'd left her, watching as he bent to pick up a board and set it in place. To look at him, you'd never guess that he'd just turned her world inside out.

Chapter Seven

For two days, the fence remained half-done. John stayed away and Abby told herself she was glad. With one kiss, the polite facade they'd been keeping had been proven just that—a facade. She no more thought of John as a casual friend than she thought the moon was made of green cheese.

And since the last thing she needed was any sort of involvement, it was just as well that he'd had the tact to stay away. She was glad he hadn't come over. Very glad.

The fact that the house felt empty had nothing to do with his absence.

The third afternoon after that shattering kiss, Abby picked Mara up at preschool. She hadn't slept well the night before, lying awake instead to wonder if something might have happened to John. What if she'd assumed he was staying away because of the kiss when, in reality, he'd been injured?

What if he'd had an accident? The Gullwing was lovely but it wasn't very substantial. What if a pickup ran a stop sign and hit John? He could be hurt. Maybe that was why he hadn't come back to finish the fence.

And if he *had* been hurt, was unconscious, how would anyone know to contact her? He could die and she'd never even know.

At one o'clock, she'd actually had her hand on the phone to call the hospital when she'd realized the absurd lengths to which her imagination was taking her. In a town the size of Beaumont, a serious accident would be front-page news.

John hadn't been in an accident. He was simply doing the intelligent thing and staying away, giving them both a chance to put what had happened into perspective.

Really, she was making a big deal out of nothing. Basically, they'd exchanged nothing more than a simple little kiss. Well, maybe not "little," and come to think of it, it wasn't all that simple.

So her thoughts had spun most of the night and for a good part of the day. Driving Mara home from preschool, she had to fight off the urge to drive by Bill's liquor store just to see if she could see any sign of John.

It took a concerted effort to keep up a smiling face for Mara. From the look in Mara's eyes, Abby wasn't sure she was successful.

She turned onto their street, her eyes scanning ahead, automatically seeking the sleek black car parked in front of her house.

And there it was.

Abby hadn't known she was holding her breath until she released it on a sigh of relief.

"John's here."

She pulled into the driveway, aware that her fingers weren't quite steady as she shut off the engine. She drew a deep, calming breath before getting out of the car.

It was only because she'd been concerned about him that she was feeling a little breathless now. Relief. That's all it was. Relief. She opened Mara's door and unlatched her seat belt.

She certainly wasn't nervous about seeing him again. Not a bit.

Mara scrambled out of the car and scampered down the driveway, headed for the backyard.

The sound of a hammer hitting wood rang clear in the air. Abby smoothed her hands down the sides of her tunic top. Should she change out of her work uniform? She squelched the thought. She and John were just friends, no matter what that silly kiss had made it seem like. She wasn't going to go changing her clothes to impress him like a teenager.

It wasn't as if she were in love with him, she reminded herself fiercely. She followed Mara, her pace slower.

What on earth was she going to say to him?

JOHN HAD HEARD the car pull in. Even over the sound of the hammer on the fence and Jason's chatter, the uneven chug of the engine was audible. He ought to give the car a tune-up, he thought. He set a nail in place and tapped it with the hammer to get it started.

His thoughts weren't on the car or the nail he was driving. He'd lost track of what Jason was saying the minute he'd heard Abby's car.

What the hell was he supposed to say to her?

It was a question he'd asked himself time and again these past two days and he still didn't have an answer. Maybe he was making too big a deal out of it. After all, what had really happened? They'd shared a kiss. Nothing earth-shattering. Just a kiss.

And if that's all it was, why had he stayed away for two days?

Because he was annoyed with himself for letting the kiss get out of hand, he told himself. He'd been enjoying these past few weeks. Enjoying the work on the little house, the time spent with Abby and the two children.

He'd been aware of being attracted to Abby. Hell, what red-blooded man wouldn't be? But he didn't want that attraction to get in the way of the relationship they'd established—a relationship that had more to do with companionship than sex. He wanted to think of Abby as . . . well, in sort of a sisterly light.

With that one kiss, he'd seen just how impossible it was to think of Abby Taylor as his sister. The minute he'd felt her sun-warmed skin under his hands, that little fantasy had been shattered.

He'd spent two days wondering where they went from here. He'd even considered packing his duffel into the Gullwing and leaving Beaumont, Bill's Liquor and Abby Taylor behind.

But he'd promised her he'd do his best not to hurt the children and leaving without a word was hardly the way to keep that promise. Besides, he couldn't leave her with the fence half-done. And the roof still needed repairs. And the kitchen cabinets needed an overhaul.

And he missed them. He missed Jason, who never seemed to run out of questions. Little Mara, with those solemn blue eyes that seemed to see so much more than they should. The house, which had begun to look as if it held hope for the future. Hell, he even missed the damned dog.

And Abby. Most of all he missed Abby.

He told himself it was because he hadn't had many friends in his life—even fewer women friends. The problem was, it wasn't just a sexual attraction he felt. He liked Abby. He liked the way her nose wrinkled when she laughed; the way she stuck her tongue out when she was concentrating on something. He liked the fact that she never whined about the hand life had dealt her.

Anyway, whether he liked her or not, he had to at least finish putting up the fence.

So he'd come back, ignoring the small voice inside that hinted that maybe he'd come back because he simply couldn't stay away.

"Hey, Aunt Abby and Mara are home." Jason's shout made John miss the nail he'd been aiming for. The hammer missed his thumb by an uncomfortably close margin and hit the fence post with enough force to jar his arm.

Wincing, he set the hammer down on top of the post and turned away from the fence, flexing his hand. Mara was running across the grass, her fair braids bouncing on her shoulders, a sheaf of papers clutched in one small hand.

"Hi, squirt." John crouched down to her level, giving her a smile that would have surprised many people who thought they knew him.

She skidded to a stop in front of him, a rare smile revealing her tiny white teeth. Thrusting out her hand, she invited him to look at the papers she held. John took them from her, shuffling carefully through the stack of crayon drawings, pausing to admire each one.

It had taken Mara longer to warm up to him than it had Jason. But once she'd decided to let him into her affections, she'd done so wholeheartedly. Looking at a drawing of a house with a dog sitting next to it, John found himself wondering what he'd missed by not being here the past two days.

The thought shook him. God, how had he let himself be drawn so deeply into this situation?

SEEING JOHN kneeling in front of Mara, admiring her drawings, Abby felt her heart give a funny little bump. It was mainly for the children's sake that she'd been hoping he'd come back, she told herself. They'd have been devastated if he'd gone out of their lives without a word.

John didn't look up as she approached, though she didn't doubt that he was aware of her presence. If he hadn't noticed on his own, Jason's greeting must have told him she was there.

"Hi, Aunt Abby. John's got another section of the fence done. I've been helping him. Neat, huh? Old man Frickle has been glaring at us the whole time but he hasn't said anything. I think he's scared of John, don't you?"

"Keep your voice down, Jason," Abby told him, glancing at her neighbor's window. Mr. Frickle was visible as a squat shadow hovering to one side. Abby had to restrain the urge to stick her tongue out at him, just to see what he'd do.

"Okay. But I still think he's scared of John." Jason clearly approved of this idea. Elmer Frickle had few qualities that endeared him to ten-year-olds, what with his constant complaining about any noise Jason might make, not to mention George's mere presence on the other side of the fence.

Actually, Abby couldn't think of any qualities Elmer Frickle had that would endear him to anyone, ten years old or not.

"Whether he is or isn't, it's none of your business," she told Jason in halfhearted reproach.

"Yeah. But it would be neat if he was, wouldn't it?"

John's gaze met hers as he rose to his feet, his eyes gleaming with amusement at Jason's unrepentant attitude. Abby lifted her shoulders as if to say she'd tried.

The small incident helped smooth over any awkwardness. After that, it was simple enough to fall into familiar patterns, as if that explosive kiss had never occurred.

If there was a tendency to avoid touching each other, a certain awareness that hadn't been there before, it was easy to ignore that.

Things were back to normal. She'd been foolish to make such a production out of one little kiss. It hadn't meant a thing.

"So, have you admitted that you've got the hots for tall, dark and handsome out there?" Kate nodded out the window to where John was working on Abby's car.

"Kate!" Abby flushed, giving the window an uneasy look.

It was raining and John had pulled the car under the section of extended roof that served as a halfhearted carport. He was stooped over the engine compartment, doing whatever it was that people did when they stooped over engine compartments. Jason hung on the front bumper, watching John's every move, thrilled to hand him tools and even lend an occasional hand.

"What?" Kate asked innocently. "He can't hear me."

"Would you care if he could?" Abby asked in exasperation.

"Of course. Because then I couldn't trust you to tell me the truth. So, have you admitted you lust after his body?"

"Of course not. Because I don't," Abby added hastily and untruthfully.

"Liar." Kate got up and opened the refrigerator with the familiarity of an old friend. Pulling out the pitcher of lemonade, she sat down at the table again. "It's obvious that you're very attracted to him."

"It is not! Is it?" Abby had the sudden, awful thought that maybe it was obvious to John.

"Only to someone who's known you as long as I have," Kate reassured her. "So, when are you going to do something about it? I'll keep the kids for you, if you'd like."

"What for?" Abby was still worried about the possibility that John might think she was mooning over him.

"So you can do something about it," Kate said, looking as if she suspected her friend's intelligence.

"So I can— You mean so John and I can— Really, Kate, you have the most awful mind."

"What's awful about it?" Kate protested, raising her brows. "You're attracted to him. He's obviously attracted to you."

"He is?" Abby didn't like the way her heart gave an eager jump. "Don't be an idiot."

"You're the idiot if you haven't noticed the way he watches you. Good heavens, Abby, the man looks positively starved."

"Does he?" Abby smiled, pleased despite herself.

"Yes, he does. And my offer to take the kids still stands, even if you do think I'm awful."

"I appreciate it, Kate, but I won't need to take you up on it." She ruthlessly suppressed any hint of regret in the refusal.

"Why not?" Kate pursued the issue with the lack of tact that was one of her more exasperating attributes.

"Because I'm not going to get involved with him."

"Not get involved?" Kate's eyes widened. "You think you're not involved now? My God, Abby, the man practically lives here. He's all but rebuilding this house. The children adore him. If that's not involved, then what is?"

"I'm not going to get any more involved," Abby clarified, wondering uneasily if you could draw lines for that sort of thing.

Kate frowned, unusually serious. "You know I'm fond of Jason and Mara. And you know how much I admire the way you gave up a lot of your dreams to take them on and give them a home."

"It wasn't a big sacrifice," Abby said.

"I know. I know. They're your family. And even if you wanted to, how could you refuse when Steve took over raising you when your parents died. I know all that." Kate waved one hand dismissively. "I'm not arguing with any of that."

"Then why do I have the feeling you're about to lecture me about sacrificing my life?"

"You know I'm right, Abby." Kate was not in the least deterred by Abby's exaggerated sigh. "You're twenty-six, not ninety-six. What about your needs?"

"What do you want me to do? Have a torrid affair with the next man that comes along?"

"Why wait for the next man?" Kate nodded significantly to the scene outside the window. John was explaining something to Jason, the boy hanging on his every word.

"No. I'm not going to have an affair with John." Just the thought sent an unnerving tingle up her spine.

"Why not?" Kate asked as if they were discussing whether or not to have a manicure. "He's perfect. He's attracted to you. You're attracted to him. You get along. What more can you ask for?"

"I can't."

"Why not?"

"Because it might turn into something more," Abby burst out finally, surprising herself almost as much as Kate.

But now that the words had been said, she realized the truth of them.

"Oh, honey, you're not falling in love with him, are you?" Kate's dark eyes were all concern.

"No, of course not. But I'm afraid I could," she admitted with a stark honesty only possible between close friends.

"Would that be so bad?"

"I've told you before, I don't have the time or the energy to get involved with someone. Everything I have has to go to the children." Abby's eyes pleaded with her to understand.

"I know you love them, Abby, but you can't sacrifice your whole life to them. Steve and Diane wouldn't have wanted that. You know it as well as I do."

"It's not my whole life. It's just for now. It's only been a year since the shooting. They still need me so much."

"It's not fair that you should have to shoulder this all on your own." Kate sat back in her chair, a frown creasing her forehead. "What about Diane's snooty family? Couldn't they help?"

"Absolutely not. You know how they were about her marrying Steve. And then suggesting I could hand the children over to them like unwanted packages. I'll starve before I'll ask them for help."

"Okay, okay." Kate lifted her hand in apology. "I know how you feel about them. I just worry about you."

"Well, don't." Abby forced a smile. "I'm doing just fine."

Kate's eyes drifted out the window to John. "What if he's the one, Abby? The one we used to dream we'd always meet? What if he's yours?"

"Then his timing stinks," Abby said lightly. "Enough talk about my nonexistent love life. How are you and Dillon these days?"

It was an effective diversion. Kate drew her eyes from John to look at her glass of lemonade, her expression moody.

"We're okay, I guess."

"You guess? What's wrong?"

"Nothing. Nothing really. I mean, really, there's nothing wrong."

"Then why do you look so glum?" Abby had only asked about Dillon to distract Kate from the subject of John, but hearing the unusual uncertainty in her friend's voice, her interest sharpened. It wasn't often that Kate Bixby was ambivalent about anything.

"I'm not glum. Not really. Do I look like the mistress type?" she asked abruptly.

"Mistress type? Where on earth did you get that idea? Not from Dillon," she asked, incredulous.

"Not in words of one syllable," Kate muttered.

"Then why are you asking?"

Kate hesitated, looking as if she wished she hadn't brought the subject up, but her need to talk to someone overcame her reluctance.

"I've been in love with Dillon since I was twelve years old."

"Since you fell in the stock tank and he pulled you out. You had the most awful crush on him."

"Well, it's a crush that didn't go away," Kate said moodily. "I could have gone to college anywhere in the country. I could have traveled all over the world, if I'd wanted to. But I didn't. I stayed right here in Beaumont."

"Because you were in love with Dillon." Abby remembered all the arguments they'd had about Kate's stubborn belief that if she stayed in Beaumont, sooner or later Dillon would notice her as something more than his cousin's best friend.

"I watched him date other women. It seemed like he dated everyone else in the whole damn county. Half the women in town were in love with him at one time."

"Not quite half," Abby demurred but her comment was ignored.

"Then five years ago, he finally realized I was alive. We started dating and one thing led to another and...well, you know where it all ended up."

"You and Dillon fell in love and he spends every moment he can spare from the farm with you."

"Aha! You see?"

Abby blinked, wondering what it was she was supposed to see. "You knew Dillon had to spend a lot of time at the farm when you got involved with him."

"I don't mind the time he spends at the farm," Kate cried. "Why doesn't he take me with him?"

"To the farm?" Abby asked in amazement. "There are animals at the farm, Kate. And manure and all sorts of untidy things."

"You do think I'm the mistress type." Abby was stunned to see tears fill Kate's eyes.

"No, of course I don't. It's just that you never really liked getting dirty. Even when we were kids you— Why on earth would you want Dillon to take you to the farm?" she asked bluntly.

"Because it's customary when two people get married." Kate dug into her purse for something to blow her nose on, finally coming up with an Irish linen handkerchief with her initial embroidered in one corner.

"You and Dillon are getting married?"

"No." Kate's eyes filled with fresh tears. "That's just it."

Abby groped her way through the tangled conversation, sure that it made sense, if only she could figure out just what they were talking about.

"The problem is that you're not getting married?"

"Yes."

"And you want to get married?"

"Yes."

"Does Dillon know you want to get married?"

"Of course not!" Kate's eyes flashed through the tears. "Do you think I'm going to beg him to marry me like...like the heroine in some cheap novel? I want *him* to want to marry me."

"I see." And she did see. Kate's pride wouldn't let her make the first move. "Maybe if you just hinted a little? No, I suppose not." She caught the look in Kate's eyes and decided not to pursue that line of thinking.

Before she could think of anything more concrete to offer Kate, Jason came bursting into the room, full of chatter about how great it was to change spark plugs. John followed more slowly, moving to the sink to wash the grease off his hands.

Kate left soon after that. Abby watched her leave, wishing there was something she could say to make her friend feel better. There were times when she could have cheerfully strangled Kate, but she was still her best friend and she didn't like seeing her unhappy.

Maybe *she* could gently hint Dillon in the right direction.

But the next day, something happened that put Kate and Dillon completely out of her mind.

"ABBY, you've got a call." Sherry Daniels held up the phone. Abby glanced at the clock on the wall of the employees' lounge. She only had five minutes left on her break and she'd wanted a chance to repin her hair and freshen her makeup.

Reaching for the phone, she murmured her thanks to Sherry before putting the receiver to her ear.

"This is Abby Taylor."

"Abigail. I'm glad I caught you. When I called earlier, your employer said you'd be taking your break about now."

"Mrs. Delevan?" Abby hadn't talked to her sister-in-law's mother since the funeral nearly a year ago but, there was no mistaking those cultured tones.

"Yes. There's something I wish to discuss with you."

"I'm afraid I'm due back at my register in just a few minutes." Abby didn't bother to put any warmth in her tone. She didn't like Patricia Delevan and she saw no reason to conceal that fact.

"This won't take long. Actually I could have had my attorney contact you but I thought, as a courtesy, that it might be better if I spoke to you first."

"Your attorney?" Abby's fingers tightened around the receiver. "I can't imagine what either you or your attorney would need to speak to me about."

"It's about the children, naturally. You remember we spoke at Diane's funeral."

"Diane and *Steve*'s funeral," Abby said tightly. Even now that he was dead, the woman was trying to cut him out of her daughter's life.

"Yes, of course." The tone was cordial. Too cordial. The only time Patricia Delevan sounded like that was when she'd just managed to pull off a coup, particularly one that was going to blight someone's else's life. "When we spoke at the funeral, I told you that I wanted custody of my grandchildren."

"And I told you that wouldn't be possible. *I* was given custody of the children in their parents' will. You know that as well as I do. Now, if that's all you have to say, Mrs. Delevan, I really do have to be going."

"But it isn't all I have to say." The plummy courtesy left the other woman's voice, revealing the iron will beneath.

"I've decided to fight for custody of my grandchildren, Abigail."

"You'll lose."

"I don't think so. I have information that could prove you an unfit guardian for impressionable young children."

"What information?" Abby tried to inject scorn into the question, but fear had all but closed her throat.

"You're carrying on a cheap affair with some common laborer, flaunting it in front of the children. You've been seen in a torrid embrace in broad daylight. The man is there at all hours of the day and night. Heaven knows what the children have been allowed to see."

The room was suddenly much too small. There wasn't enough air for her straining lungs. Abby sank onto the cracked sofa, her fingers knotted around the phone.

"The children haven't seen anything," she offered at last.

"Perhaps we should let the courts decide." The other woman let the implicit threat hang in the air.

Abby closed her eyes. A court battle. The children caught in the middle, confused and frightened. God, what would that do to them so soon after losing both their parents?

"Don't do this," she whispered, beyond caring that she was begging.

"Naturally I'd rather avoid any scandal," Mrs. Delevan said, the false warmth reappearing now that she sensed a possible victory. "Perhaps if the two of us could talk?"

"When?"

"I see no reason to put it off. How about tomorrow? One o'clock. We could meet at the Hauf Brau," she suggested, naming the nicest restaurant in Beaumont.

"No. We'll talk but we'll meet at my house." Abby knew she was at enough of a disadvantage without letting the other woman stage this meeting on her own ground.

"Very well. I'll see you then."

Abby sat clutching the receiver long after the only sound coming out of it was the dial tone. In the space of a few minutes, she'd been brought face-to-face with her worst nightmare. She couldn't lose the children. No matter what, she couldn't lose the children.

Chapter Eight

John was straightening the bottles on the shelves behind the cash register. Bill was seated on a stool at the end of the counter, perusing the newspaper, reading an occasional item to John who listened with half an ear.

When the bell over the door jangled, both men turned toward the interruption. The last person John expected to see was Abby. She pushed the door open with one hand, brushing back a loose strand of hair with the other. She glanced around until her eyes fell on him.

"John." Just his name, but it was enough to tell him that she was upset.

"What is it?" He moved to the end of the counter, brushing past Bill, who abandoned the paper to watch this encounter with unashamed interest.

"It's the children," she muttered, her eyes distracted.

John felt his heart stop, a hundred images flashing through his mind, each more horrific than the last.

"What's happened?" He caught her hands in his, squeezing them, not sure if he was offering comfort or seeking it. "Has there been an accident?"

"No. Oh, no. I'm sorry. I didn't mean to make you think that. They're all right." She closed her eyes, drawing a deep breath. "I'm not thinking clearly at the moment," she said, opening her eyes again and giving him a shaky smile.

"That's okay." John felt his heartbeat slow to something approaching normal. He hadn't realized just how much Jason and Mara had come to mean to him until he'd thought something might have happened to one of them. The realization shook him.

"I'm sorry to bother you at work. I just needed someone to talk to. Could you take a break, do you think?"

"You take as long as you need," Bill offered. He heaved his considerable bulk off the stool and moved around behind the counter. "I don't suppose we're going to get a deluge of customers this time of day."

"Thanks, Bill." John glanced around, seeking someplace they could talk comfortably. "I have a room upstairs," he told Abby.

The room was almost sterile in its neatness. John had spent so many years living out of a suitcase that he'd never had a chance to collect the sort of things that most people use to clutter up their living spaces. He'd also lived in cramped quarters enough to appreciate the value of putting things away.

There was only one chair. He gestured Abby to it while he sat on the side of the bed. Abby seemed to be gathering her thoughts. It occurred to him suddenly that this was the first time he'd seen her anywhere other than at her house.

"Tell me what happened," he said at last, when she didn't show any signs of speaking.

"Mrs. Delevan called me at work today. Diane's mother," she clarified in answer to his questioning look.

"The children's grandmother," he said, getting an inkling of what might have happened.

"Only in the strictest sense of the word," she said fiercely, glaring at her hands where they lay linked in her lap. "She's only seen them once at the funeral. She was never there for birthdays or Christmas or to patch up a skinned knee."

"Okay." In a room as small as his, it was a short distance from the bed to the chair. John reached out, catching one of her hands in his. Abby clutched his fingers, grateful for the support. "Tell me what she said."

"She wants the children," she whispered.

"But you have custody of the children. Your brother and sister-in-law left them in your care. Right?"

"Yes."

"Then what can this woman do? You are their legal guardian. Unless she can prove you're an unfit parent, I don't see what she can do."

"She says she's going to prove I'm unfit."

"Ridiculous. Anyone who knows you knows you're a terrific parent."

"Someone saw us kissing." She lifted her eyes to his face, her own swimming with tears. "She says I'm flaunting my affair in front of the children. That who knows what they've been exposed to."

"That's absurd." John released her hand, sitting back on the bed. "We're not having an affair."

"I know. But we *did* kiss and the children might have seen that."

"So what? Seeing us kiss isn't going to ruin their psyches."

"But think how it could look in court. I can't lose them, John. I just can't."

"Abby, no court is going to take the children away from you just because you kissed me." Her fear seemed unreasonable to him. Sure, she could be facing an ugly court battle. That was reason enough for her to be upset. But she wasn't going to lose the children.

"You don't understand. They could make it seem so ugly. *She* could make it seem that way." Abby got up, turning to stare out the small window at the street below. "They're wealthy. The Delevans have connections. Her husband was a judge for almost twenty years. Her brother is a judge. They know senators and congressmen. They lunch with the governor."

"Abby, you're jumping ahead of yourself. You're assuming that the system isn't going to work."

"What if it doesn't work?" She turned to look at him, her eyes fierce. "What if they pull the right strings, grease the right palms? I could lose the children."

"That's not going to happen." But his words lacked conviction. The problem was, she could be right. He'd seen it happen. Given enough money and enough influence, the Delevans stood a pretty fair chance of getting custody of their grandchildren.

Jason and Mara could be yanked out of the home Abby had spent nearly a year building for them. All the security she'd tried so hard to wrap them in could be snatched away in the blink of an eye.

Over his dead body.

The strength of his own reaction threw him off balance. This wasn't his fight, he reminded himself, scrambling to keep his accustomed distance from the situation. Sure he liked Abby and he was fond of Jason and Mara. He'd hate to see the little family broken up.

But it wasn't really his problem. It wasn't as if they were *his* family. He didn't have a family.

But it was her supposed affair with him that was being used as a weapon in this fight. Didn't that make it his fight, too?

"Where did you leave things with her?" he asked, his tone neutral.

"She's coming to the house tomorrow at one. I took a day of vacation," she added irrelevantly.

"Maybe when you talk to her, you'll be able to make her see reason. If she cares about her grandchildren at all, maybe you can make her see that they should be left with you."

She looked at him as if he'd lost his mind. John wondered if she was right. This wasn't his fight. He didn't get involved in things like this. So why was it that the thought of Jason and Mara being taken from Abby filled him with a deep dark rage?

"Patricia Delevan doesn't give a damn about anything but her precious family name," Abby said, biting each word off. "Aside from pure spite, the only possible reason she could have for wanting Jason and Mara is so that everyone knows how wonderful she is to take in her grandchildren."

Her words were followed by a lengthy silence while John struggled with his inner demons. Part of him wanted to take her in his arms and tell her that they'd fight this together, that he'd do anything he had to to make sure she kept the children. But that urge was fighting against a lifetime of noninvolvement. A lifetime of avoiding emotional situations.

The result of the inner battle was that he couldn't think of a thing to say.

Abby waited and he saw the hope fade from her eyes, to be replaced by a sort of blank acceptance. That look hurt. It hurt more than it had any right to. What difference did it make to him what she thought? He'd never made her any promises.

"I probably shouldn't have bothered you," she said at last.

NO RISK, NO OBLIGATION TO BUY... NOW OR EVER!

CASINO JUBILEE
"Match'n Scratch" Game

Here's how to play:

1. Peel off label from front cover. Place it in space provided at right. With a coin, carefully scratch off the silver box. This makes you eligible to receive one or more free books, and possibly other gifts, depending upon what is revealed beneath the scratch-off area.

2. You'll receive brand-new Harlequin American Romance® novels. When you return this card, we'll rush you the books and gifts you qualify for ABSOLUTELY FREE!

3. If we don't hear from you, every month we'll send you 4 additional novels to read and enjoy. You can return them and owe nothing but if you decide to keep them, you'll pay only $2.96* per book, a saving of 33¢ each off the cover price. There is *no* extra charge for postage and handling. There are *no* hidden extras.

4. When you join the Harlequin Reader Service®, you'll get our subscribers-only newsletter, as well as additional free gifts from time to time just for being a subscriber!

5. You must be completely satisfied. You may cancel at any time simply by sending us a note or a shipping statement marked "cancel" or returning any shipment to us at our cost.

> **YOURS FREE!**
>
> *This lovely Victorian pewter-finish miniature is perfect for displaying a treasured photograph and it's yours absolutely free — when you accept our no-risk offer!*

*Terms and prices subject to change without notice. Sales tax applicable in NY.

CASINO JUBILEE
"Match'n Scratch" Game

CHECK CLAIM CHART BELOW FOR YOUR FREE GIFTS!

YES! I have placed my label from the front cover in the space provided above and scratched off the silver box. Please send me all the gifts for which I qualify. I understand I am under no obligation to purchase any books, as explained on the opposite page.

(U-H-AR-10/91) 154 CIH ADE3

Name

Address   Apt.

City   State   Zip

CASINO JUBILEE CLAIM CHART

🍒🍒🍒	WORTH 4 FREE BOOKS, FREE VICTORIAN PICTURE FRAME PLUS MYSTERY BONUS GIFT
🍒🔔🍒	WORTH 3 FREE BOOKS PLUS MYSTERY GIFT
🔔🔔🍒	WORTH 2 FREE BOOKS

CLAIM N° 1528

▼ DETACH AND MAIL CARD TODAY! ▼

HARLEQUIN "NO RISK" GUARANTEE

- You're not required to buy a single book — ever!
- You must be completely satisfied or you may cancel at any time simply by sending us a note or a shipping statement marked "cancel" or by returning any shipment to us at our cost. Either way, you will receive no more books; you'll have no obligation to buy.
- The free book(s) and gift(s) you claimed on the "Casino Jubilee" offer remains yours to keep no matter what you decide.

If offer card is missing, please write to: **Harlequin Reader Service** P.O. Box 1867, Buffalo, N.Y. 14269-1867

▼ DETACH AND MAIL CARD TODAY! ▼

BUSINESS REPLY MAIL

FIRST CLASS MAIL   PERMIT NO. 717   BUFFALO, NY

POSTAGE WILL BE PAID BY ADDRESSEE

HARLEQUIN READER SERVICE
3010 WALDEN AVE
PO BOX 1867
BUFFALO NY 14240-9952

NO POSTAGE
NECESSARY
IF MAILED
IN THE
UNITED STATES

"No. That's all right." He felt awkward as he stood up, as if his body suddenly didn't fit him anymore. He stared at his hands for a moment as if uncertain how they'd come to be on the ends of his arms and then he stuffed them into his pockets. "I wish there was something I could say to help."

"So do I."

He slanted her a quick glance but could read no sarcasm in her expression. She glanced at her watch.

"I'd better be going if I'm not going to be late picking Mara up."

"Sure. Sure." He opened the door for her, standing back to let her start down the stairs first. She paused after a couple of steps, looking back over her shoulder at him.

"Will you be over this afternoon?"

"No." He cleared his throat. "Actually, Bill asked me if I could work this evening. He's got something he wants to do," he added vaguely.

"Oh." Abby turned and continued down the stairs. John followed, feeling as if he'd somehow grown shorter in the past few minutes.

Bill turned to look at them, his eyes bright with unconcealed interest. Abby returned his nod with a half smile, heading directly for the door. John followed her, wanting to say something, not knowing what to say.

She hesitated at the door, looking back at him as if giving him one last chance.

"Good luck with your meeting tomorrow." He could have bitten his tongue off the minute the words were said. The disappointment that flooded her face was like acid in his throat.

"Thank you." She said it as politely as if he were a stranger who'd just performed some small courtesy for her.

Before he could say another word, she'd pulled open the door and was gone.

Probably just as well, he told himself, trying to believe it. He'd never given her any reason to think he could solve all her problems. He was no knight in shining armor ready to slay dragons in the form of nasty in-laws. He'd never pretended to be anything but what he was—a wanderer.

"Pretty girl," Bill commented.

"Yeah." John turned away from the door, wandering back to the counter, his hands still in his pockets, his shoulders slumped.

"Kind of woman that makes a man think about settling down, having a home."

"If a man is suited to that sort of thing." John leaned one hip against the counter and stared at a display of breath mints.

"Every man is suited to that sort of thing, given the right circumstances."

John blinked, focusing his gaze on Bill's round face. "As a matchmaker, you're about as subtle as a Howitzer," he said dryly.

"Some people don't respond to subtlety," Bill said, his eyes twinkling. "That's one fine woman just walked out of here. From what little you've said, she's got grit. Taking on two kids like she did, raising them, trying to make it on her own. A woman like that doesn't come along that often."

"I didn't say they did. But some people just aren't meant to settle down."

Bill's response was short and to the point. Despite himself, John grinned.

"Better watch your language. Your wife catches you talking like that, she's liable to wash your mouth out with soap."

"She'll have to catch me first. You listen to me. A man doesn't get all that many chances to settle down with a damn fine woman. And a man who passes a chance like that up doesn't deserve another one."

"I'm just not a settling man, Bill. This is the longest I've lived in one place in over twenty years." It was important that Bill understand.

"Doesn't that tell you something?"

"It tells me I probably should have left weeks ago."

"Buffalo chips. Don't be a damn fool, boy."

The novelty of being called "boy" wiped out any annoyance John might have felt at the abrupt tone.

"You think I haven't been watching you? A couple of months ago, you were starting to get that restless look about you. I figured you'd be giving me notice any day. Not that I blamed you. Any fool can see you've done a bit of traveling and that you planned to do a good bit more.

"About the time you started going over to the Taylor place, all that restlessness just seemed to drain right out of you. I'd wager my bowling trophy that you haven't had the urge to leave since you met Abby Taylor."

John stared at him, his silence acknowledging the truth of the words. Oh, he'd thought about leaving, but it hadn't been the familiar restless urge to find out what lay over the horizon that had made him think about leaving.

"So what are you suggesting?" he asked, lacing his tone with sarcasm. "That I marry her?"

Bill shrugged. "Just don't do something you'll spend the rest of your life regretting."

No matter how much John wanted to dismiss the older man's words, they lingered in his thoughts. Lying in bed, staring up at the ceiling, he found sleep elusive. He thought about what Bill had said, that every man was the settling type given the right circumstances. It didn't seem likely that

a small farming town in the back of beyond should provide him with the right set of circumstances, yet he'd lingered here.

He'd let Abby down. It wasn't a comfortable thought but
it was one that had to be faced. She'd come to him not for
help, but for support, and he hadn't provided it. The intensity of his emotional involvement had caused him to
back off, just as he'd done all his life.

Only with Eileen had he ever come close to making a
commitment to something besides his job. An English-
woman with pale brown hair and a complexion that held all
the dewiness for which the British Isles were famed, she'd
worked with him in a squalid little town in North Africa.

It had been a long-term assignment, and at some point
their relationship had gone from professional to deeply
personal. They'd talked about quitting when this job was
finished, getting out and building a life together in what
they'd referred to as the "real world."

Looking back, John wondered if Eileen had ever believed he'd really take that step, make a commitment to her,
to building a future. He wondered himself. Eileen had been
killed in a bomb blast, set off to catch a local dissident.

John frowned at the ceiling. He'd loved Eileen as much
as he'd ever loved anyone. He'd actually believed he was
willing to give up the job, step into the much more dangerous waters of building a life with another person.

Now he wondered if she hadn't been right when she'd
looked at him with faintly sad eyes and called it a lovely
dream that wasn't likely to come true. If she'd lived, would
he have quit?

What difference did it make? Irritated, he sat up, swinging his legs off the bed. The wood floor was cool under his
bare feet as he moved over to the window. Standing to the
side out of long habit, he looked out at the silent street. It

was long after midnight. The little town slept, just like he ought to be doing. But every time he closed his eyes, he saw Abby's face, her eyes showing her hurt.

And what the hell business did she have being hurt by anything he did? He hadn't made her any promises, hadn't told her she could rely on him.

So you're just going to stand by and watch her lose the children? John's hand clenched into a fist at his side. The thought of Jason and Mara being taken from Abby was like a hot knife in his gut.

Dammit! He didn't want to care. He hadn't planned on caring.

But care he did. Whether he wanted it or not, he did care, more than he'd cared about anything in a very long time. And he couldn't just do nothing.

Straightening away from the window, he reached for his clothes. Maybe he never would have made the commitment Eileen had wanted from him. But he was older now. He'd seen a lot more of the world. Maybe Bill was right. Maybe any man was a settling kind of man, given the right circumstances. And whether he stayed or not, he wasn't going to see Abby lose those children. Not without a fight.

ABBY HAD BEEN UP since before dawn. Since she hadn't been sleeping anyway, getting out of bed wasn't much of a change. She'd started cleaning in the kitchen, and by the time the children were up she'd finished both the kitchen and the living room. It wasn't so much that she cared what Patricia Delevan thought of her home. She simply had to have something to do or she was going to go completely crazy.

She took the children to school and drove the long way home, trying to kill time. But even after she finished scrubbing the bathroom, there was still nearly two hours to go.

She showered and washed her hair, blowing it dry and piling it on top of her head in a soft twist that made her look older, more businesslike. She took time to get her makeup just right.

She knew just the image she wanted to present. Cool and collected. In control. That wouldn't be easy when facing Patricia Delevan. On the few occasions they'd met, the older woman had always managed to put her on the defensive.

But this time would be different, she told herself. This time *had* to be different. She wore a suit of palest peach with a rich ivory silk blouse. It felt strange to be wearing something so dressy. She spent most of her time either in her work uniform or the jeans she wore around the house.

When the doorbell rang, she was as prepared as she was ever likely to be. Taking a deep breath she went to the door, feeling as if she were opening it to the devil in a thin disguise.

"Abigail. How nice you look." The arch of Patricia's brow carried all manner of genteel contempt. Abby felt her temper stir.

"Patricia," she said coolly, taking pleasure in seeing the other woman's eyes widen at the use of her given name. She was damned if she'd call her Mrs. Delevan like some poor peon in an old novel. "Won't you come in."

First round to me, she thought, feeling a small surge of confidence.

But it wasn't a feeling that lasted long. As soon as they'd settled in the living room, Abby in a chair, Patricia Delevan on the sofa, the gloves came off.

"I hope you're going to see reason about this, Abigail. You must know there's no sense in trying to fight me."

"I don't know that at all. I do have legal custody of the children, given to me by their parents. Steve and Diane wanted me to raise their children and they made their wishes quite clear in their will. I think that would weigh heavily in court."

"Oh, I won't deny that you have some claim." Patricia waved one perfectly manicured hand, somehow managing to both acknowledge and dismiss that claim. "But I am the children's grandmother, a relationship many people regard as a bit closer than that of an aunt. And obviously I can offer the children so much more when it comes to the material things in life."

Pale blue eyes surveyed the neat but small living room, dismissing it as beneath consideration. Abby struggled against the urge to leap up and violently disarrange the neatly coiffed gray hair.

"I certainly wouldn't dispute that the Delevans can offer more in a material sense than I can hope to give Jason and Mara. But I think there are other things that are more important."

"Oh, please. Is this where you're going to give me a nauseating little speech about love being more important than mere wealth?"

"Your daughter apparently thought so." Abby slid the knife in without a trace of remorse, seeing it strike home in the way the older woman's mouth tightened, her eyes flaring with old emotions.

"Diane was a little fool," Patricia spat. She stopped, drawing a deep breath, letting the mask slip back into place. "My daughter made her choices and you can see where it got her."

"Steve was a wonderful husband. Diane was very happy. Something you might have seen if you hadn't written her out of your life. I don't think that will look good in court—

you refusing to speak to your only child because you didn't approve of her marriage.''

"That's something I have certainly had ample time to regret." Abby was stunned to see tears shimmering in the other woman's eyes. "I made a terrible mistake and then I let pride keep me away from my daughter and my grandchildren. But now I want a chance to atone for my mistakes. To give my grandchildren all the advantages I can provide them. Is that too much to ask?''

She fumbled in her purse, drawing out a lace handkerchief to dab her eyes. Abby stared at her, thrown completely off balance. She'd been prepared for almost anything, but not this sudden vulnerability.

"I...I don't—" She broke off as Patricia lifted her head. The tears were gone, the artfully applied makeup was undisturbed. There was nothing to show that a moment ago the woman had been nearly overcome with emotion.

"I think a judge might forgive me, don't you?" Patricia suggested, her eyes glinting with cool amusement.

Abby stared at her, feeling her stomach twist. The woman was evil. There was nothing behind those pale eyes but a frightening determination to get what she wanted. And she didn't care who she had to destroy to get it.

She groped for something to say, some defense she could offer, but this woman didn't care that the children were happy where they were. She didn't care that she'd be tearing them away from everything that was familiar. All she cared about was getting her way.

And she'd succeed.

Abby saw it as clearly as if she could read the future. She was going to lose Jason and Mara. Oh, she didn't doubt that the court would allow her visitation rights. But how long would that last? How long before the Delevans moved their grandchildren to another state? Put them in boarding school? All in their best interests, of course.

She could take them and run, but how long could she hope to keep ahead of the kind of power the Delevans held? And when she was caught, chances were she would lose the children anyway.

She was their legal guardian. There was no one to stop her from moving to another state. Never mind how she'd get hold of the money. She'd swallow her pride and ask Kate. But there was nothing to stop them from suing her for custody in another state.

"The children are happy with me," she offered, hearing the pleading note in her voice and hating it. But she'd get down on her knees and beg if she thought it would do any good.

"Children are adaptable." Patricia flicked a minute piece of lint from the hem of her linen dress.

"Mara. Mara hasn't spoken since the accident. You can't throw her life into turmoil again."

"The child needs psychiatric care. I'm sure the courts will agree with me that you've been most remiss in not providing it."

"You can't do this." Abby's protest was hardly more than a whisper.

"On the contrary. I can and I will. Of course, we can avoid a great deal of unpleasantness if you'll simply agree to sign custody of the children over to my husband and myself."

"No. I'll fight you every step of the way." Abby wanted to sound strong and sure but she heard the fear in her voice and knew the other woman could hear it as well.

"Well, that's your choice, of course."

Abby searched desperately for some argument she could offer, something that might sway Patricia Delevan from a path that was going to mean misery for the children.

"I can't lose the children," she said, as much to herself as to the older woman.

"You should have thought of that before you began your sordid little affair."

"But we're not having an affair."

"I doubt the courts will believe that."

"Oh, I think they might."

Both women started, turning toward the door. They'd been so intent on their conversation, neither of them had heard it open.

"John." Abby felt her heart leap. Logically she knew there was nothing he could do to reverse the disastrous situation but she no longer felt quite so alone.

"Sorry I'm late. It took me a little longer to make those calls I'd told you about." He stepped farther into the room and pushed the door shut behind him.

"Calls?" Abby groped for a memory of him mentioning any calls. When she'd seen him yesterday, she'd had the distinct impression that he had distanced himself from her problems completely.

"Has it been rough?" He came forward, dropping a kiss on her forehead before sitting on the arm of her chair.

"Yes." Had she actually passed out from stress and was now in the midst of some bizarre hallucination?

"Well, I think I've got everything straightened out. Don't worry." His eyes seemed to be sending her some message, but she was too dazed to guess what it might be. He'd set his arm around her shoulders and she could only lean into his support and pray that he knew what he was doing.

"You must be Mrs. Delevan." John's eyes were a cold gray as he looked at her.

"And you must be Abigail's handyman. I suppose I can understand the attraction, my dear," she said to Abby. "If you like the brawny, brooding type."

Abby felt the tension in John's arm, but there was nothing but amusement in his smile. "You might as well pull your claws in. You've lost the battle and the war."

"Oh, really?" Patricia arched one brow. "I don't think so. It's noble of you to ride to her rescue, of course, but it won't do any good. Abby's tacky little affair with you was just the final nail in the coffin. I've been planning to get my grandchildren for some time now. This simply made it a little easier."

"Actually, Abby and I are going to be married." Feeling Abby jerk in surprise, his arm tightened warningly around her shoulders. "I don't think that's going to help your case any."

"It's true that a fiancé won't be as useful to me as a lover, but we can work around that." She smiled, showing perfect white teeth.

Abby had the feeling that she'd dropped into the Mad Hatter's tea party. Nothing made any sense. Why was John telling this woman they were engaged? It could only put off the inevitable. She was bound to find out the truth before long.

"I really think you should drop this," John said quietly.

"I'm sure you do. But then the losing side always hopes the other side will decide to drop the battle. Now, I really don't see that we have anything more to say to each other so I'll just—"

"Sit down." The icy command made Abby jump even though it wasn't directed at her. Patricia Delevan, on the point of rising, sank back into her seat, reacting automatically. The moment she realized what had happened, angry color swept into her face.

"How dare you speak to me in that tone of voice."

"I'll speak to you any way you like," John said coolly.

"I can have you destroyed along with your mistress," she said furiously.

"You're not going to destroy anyone. You're not even going to make trouble for anyone."

"We'll see about that." She stood up, her slender body rigid.

"Yes, we will." John rose to his feet, using his size to intimidate.

"If you attempt to offer me any physical harm, I'll not only take the children, I'll see the two of you in prison." Her voice was steady, even though her eyes were showing a touch of fear.

"I have no intention of touching you," John said contemptuously. "I don't have to."

"Then get out of my way."

"Not quite yet. I have a few things you should hear."

"I don't have any interest in anything you might say."

"Shut up." The succinct command made Patricia's jaw snap shut. Abby swallowed the urge to giggle at the woman's stunned expression.

"How dare—"

"I made a few calls this morning. To some friends in Washington, D.C."

"I don't care if you called Timbuktu."

"And they made a few calls to friends of theirs in the state capitol. I see I've caught your attention." His smile made Abby shiver. Patricia's fingers knotted on the soft leather of her purse.

"I don't see what relevance this has."

"Let me explain." John dropped the false courtesy, his voice becoming crisp and hard. "My friends asked a few questions about why your husband retired so abruptly, just when his name was being mentioned as a possibility for the governorship.''

''Lawrence was simply exhausted by the demands of his profession.'' Her voice shook.

''Lawrence was about to come under investigation for taking bribes.''

''That's not true.'' But there was no conviction in her voice.

''He retired rather than be faced with the scandal and the possibility of indictment.''

''No, he was exhausted.'' She broke off, changing her tack. ''You couldn't prove anything after all these years.''

''I don't have to. All I have to do is pull a few strings, poke into it a little, let the papers get hold of it. Your husband is still a prominent figure in this state, but he won't be for long if a scandal erupts around his name. No more cozy dinners with the governor. No more mention in the society columns.''

''It would never work. No one would care after all these years.'' But there was no conviction in her voice.

''Do you really want to take that chance? You have a great deal to lose. If you take us to court over the children, I'll make certain that every investigative reporter in the state has reason to look into your family's past. And what they don't find, I will.''

''You can't do that. You'd have to know people, have connections.''

''I know enough people, Mrs. Delevan. And I can always meet the ones I don't know. Think about it. Is it really worth dragging our family through the mud to get custody of two children you don't even really want?''

''Of course I want my grandchildren.'' But the strength had gone from her voice. She was beaten and she knew it. ''Naturally, I only want what's best for them. Perhaps I've been a bit hasty in this matter." The words were pulled from her.

"Very hasty," John said, watching her without mercy.

She looked at him with hatred in her eyes. Defeat was not something she experienced often. She'd started this war, confident that she would win, just as she'd won at everything else in her life.

But she was not a stupid woman and she recognized a superior force when she saw it. What John was threatening would destroy her cozy little world. Of course, he might be bluffing. But the look in those eyes was confident. He didn't look like a man who bluffed.

Abby hadn't moved from her chair. She watched the confrontation between the other two, feeling as if she was seeing a struggle between two titans. Patricia Delevan glared at John, seeking some hole in the wall he'd built around her. John simply waited, knowing she had no choice but to give in.

"As I said, I may have been hasty." She struggled to make her retreat seem a matter of choice. "Perhaps the children will be better off with you, after all, Abigail."

"Yes." Abby couldn't have said more than that if her life had depended on it. She could feel herself crumbling inside. She wasn't going to lose the children.

"Yes, well. I guess I'll be on my way." John stepped back, clearing the path to the door. She hesitated a moment, hatred in her eyes. "I won't forget you."

"I'm flattered," he said, smiling at her.

Abby watched her leave, hardly able to believe that the nightmare was over. The door shut behind her with a distinct click.

"I thought she was going to take the children away from me," Abby murmured. "You stopped her."

"It was a good thing her husband was something less than perfect." John pushed his hands into his back pockets, rocking back on his heels.

"How did you find that out?"

"I know a few people." He shrugged. "You just have to know who to ask."

"Who on earth do you know who could find out that kind of information so quickly?"

John shrugged again. "I've met all sorts of people over the years. I did a bit of work for the government here and there."

And from the closed look in his eyes, that was all the information she was going to get out of him. Abby was too relieved to care. He could keep all the secrets he wanted as long as she got to keep Jason and Mara.

"You actually stopped her." She clasped her hands together in her lap to stop their trembling. "Thank you."

"You don't have to thank me. I don't want to see Jason and Mara taken away from you any more than you do."

"You told her we were getting married," she said slowly, sorting through her tangled thoughts. "What happens when she finds out that was a lie? What happens when you . . . when you leave?"

"There's a simple solution." John crouched down in front of her, prying her hands apart, holding them in his.

"Marry me."

Chapter Nine

Obviously the stress of the past twenty-four hours had done something to her hearing. Or she really *was* hallucinating. It wasn't possible that he'd just asked her to marry him. Well, not asked precisely.

"Excuse me?"

One side of his mouth kicked up in a half smile. "You heard me. Marry me."

Abby closed her eyes. He'd repeated it. Could you hallucinate the same thing twice? There had simply been too many shocks piled one on top of another. She couldn't even really feel the impact of this one.

When she opened her eyes, he was still crouched in front of her, his hands holding hers, watching her expectantly. She opened her mouth. Closed it again. And then said the only thing she could think of.

"Why?"

"Because it's a good idea."

"It is?" She drew her hands away. It was too difficult to think with him touching her. Not that she felt capable of much intelligent thought one way or another.

"Sure. Think about it."

She stared at him for a moment and then brought her fingers up to rub at her temple. "Look, it's been a rough twenty-four hours. I'm not really thinking too straight. Why is it such a good idea?''

If she'd been secretly hoping he was going to say he was madly in love with her, she was doomed to disappointment.

"Okay." John stood up, apparently not in the least disturbed by her rather confused reception of his proposal. "If we were married, you wouldn't have to worry about the battle-ax who just left. I may have scared her off permanently but, like you mentioned, if I weren't around, she might try again."

"It's very nice of you to be concerned about that but we can't get married just to foil Patricia Delevan."

"There's also the kids to think about." John paced back and forth across the room, more animated than she could ever remember seeing him. "You've said yourself that Jason, in particular, really misses having a man's influence in his life. He likes me. I like him. If I worked at it, I suspect I could be a fairly good influence. And Mara seems to like me."

"Of course she does. Both of them care about you a great deal. But—" She broke off as he held up his hand, indicating he wasn't through.

"You could use some help, with the children and with the house. Two incomes will go quite a bit farther than one. I've got some money in the bank, a few thousand. It would give you a pad."

"No." Abby stood up. She circled her chair and stood gripping the back of it, her eyes fierce. "I'm certainly not marrying you or anybody else for their money. What kind of a woman do you think I am? Do you think I'm a . . . a gold digger or something?"

"Of course not." John stopped his pacing to face her across the chair. "If you were a gold digger, I'd be a poor bet. I'm far from wealthy. Most of what I have is tied up in that car out there. But wouldn't it be nice not to have to worry about every penny?"

"Of course it would. But that's not reason enough to get married." She couldn't believe they were actually discussing marriage. Yesterday, when she'd gone to him, upset over Patricia Delevan's call, it had seemed almost as if he didn't care. She'd left him feeling as if she were all alone. No one but herself to depend on. Not that he'd owed her anything else. But she'd had to admit to a feeling of hurt.

Then he'd shown up like St. George to fight the dragon, slaying it quite thoroughly. And before she'd had a chance to adjust to that, he was suggesting that they get married. Not because they loved each other but because she needed him.

"There's one thing you haven't mentioned," she said, lifting her head to meet his eyes directly. "Just what would you be getting from this marriage? You've told me what it could mean to me and to the children but you haven't said a word about what you'll be getting out of it."

"A home." The simple answer was unexpected and disarming.

"A home? That's all?"

"That's quite a lot."

"I don't understand." Abby moved around the chair, sinking back into its support. At the moment, she needed all the support she could get. "You want to marry me just to get a home?"

She glanced around the living room, noting the cracks in the plaster and the scuffed wooden floor she hadn't managed to get refinished.

"I don't think you'd be making a very good bargain. You could buy a place of your own."

"I didn't say I wanted a house. I said I wanted a home."
He sat on the edge of the sofa, leaning forward, elbows on
his knees. "All my life, I've drifted from one place to another, never settling in one spot long enough to put down
roots, never really wanting to. I've spent more time here
than I've spent in any one place since leaving home."

Abby, who'd spent most of her life in one place, tried to
imagine what it would be like to always be on the move. She
thought maybe she was beginning to understand what he
meant when he said he wanted a home.

"You don't marry someone just to put down roots," she
said gently.

"Why not?"

"Well, because you don't have to, for one thing. You
don't have to marry me to stay in Beaumont. You can stay
and make a home for yourself without that."

"I don't know how," he said simply.

"Sure you do. I mean, there's nothing to know. You
just . . . Well, you can—" She broke off, staring at him.

How did you go about explaining how you made a
home? Especially to a man who'd never had one? There
wasn't a recipe for it. You didn't take a house and then go
out and buy a package of Genuine Home Atmosphere for
it.

"You can't marry for that," she said finally, knowing the
answer wasn't as strong as she'd have liked.

"Why not? Abby, I've never in my life wanted to settle
in one place. I always figured I'd spend my entire life
drifting around the world until I got too old to catch a bus.

"But I'm forty years old and it's beginning to occur to
me that I don't have a whole hell of a lot to show for forty
years of living. I've never stayed anywhere long enough to
build friendships. I've nothing to speak of by way of family.

"Maybe it's turning forty or a midlife crisis." His smile was self-deprecating. "But I'm beginning to think I'd like something more to show for my life than a car and a passport with a lot of stamps in it."

"But marriage..." Abby shook her head, trying to grasp the enormity of what he was suggesting. She rubbed her fingertips over her skirt, keeping her eyes on the aimless movement. "You've talked about how good this would be for the children and how it would help me. You've told me what you'd be getting out of it.

"But marriage is a big commitment, John. It isn't like we love each other." She held her breath, not sure what she hoped to hear from him. Did she want him to drop to one knee and vow undying devotion? What would she say then?

"We like each other," he said slowly. "Isn't that enough? Passionate love isn't always the best foundation for a marriage."

There was something in his voice that made her think he had a particular marriage in mind. A look in his eyes that spoke of bitter memories. Who was he thinking of?

"Are you planning on this being a real marriage?" she asked, her voice hardly above a whisper.

"Yes."

The flat answer made her shiver, but she couldn't have said whether it was with anticipation or uncertainty. She jumped when John's hand cupped her chin, turning her face to his. Her eyes met his reluctantly.

"Would it be such a hardship to have a real marriage with me, Abby?" There was tenderness and a certain humor in the gentle question.

She remembered the kisses they'd shared. Those kisses had haunted her dreams. No, it wouldn't be a hardship.

She shook her head, a delicate flush coming up in her cheeks. "No, it wouldn't be a hardship," she whispered.

"I wouldn't rush you. We could get married right away, but you can take all the time in the world getting used to the idea." His fingers stroked her cheek, the movement both soothing and evocative.

Abby closed her eyes. The idea of having someone to share her burdens with had a strong appeal. So much of what he'd said made sense. He was wonderful with the children. She didn't doubt that they'd welcome him into the family without a hitch.

And she couldn't say it would be a hardship to think of him as a husband instead of a friend. The attraction between them was strong. He was offering her a solution to nearly all of her problems.

But she'd never thought of getting married to solve problems. She'd always assumed she'd fall in love with someone, they'd date, they'd get married—all in the proper order.

"I can't make a decision like this right now," she said abruptly. She stood up, moving away from him. Cupping her hands around her elbows, she shook her head. "I need time to think, John. I ... So much of what you've said is true."

She turned to look at him. He'd risen when she did and now he stood there watching her, looking so solid, so strong. Abby wanted to go to him, feel him put his arms around her and know that she wasn't ever going to be alone again.

But she'd always prided herself on her strength. And she needed to be strong now. She had to make the right decision now, for her sake, as well as for the children. Their futures depended on her making the right decision.

"I've got to think," she said again.

"Okay. I understand I've sort of sprung this on you out of the blue." He moved forward, stopping in front of her.

Abby tilted back her head to look at him. His gray eyes were so full of understanding that she felt tears sting at the back of hers. "I'd do my best to take care of you, Abby."

"I know," she whispered.

"Let me know when you decide."

"I won't take long. I promise."

"See that you don't." But a smile took the sternness out of the words. He lifted his hand, stroking his fingers across her cheek. "We make a good team. Don't forget that." He bent and dropped a soft kiss on her mouth.

He was gone without waiting for a response, to either the kiss or the words. Abby stood where he'd left her, her eyes focused on nothing in particular.

"HE DID WHAT?" Kate's voice rose to something perilously close to a shriek.

"Sshh." Abby looked around uneasily.

They were standing in the lingerie section of Bixby's Department Store, which was where she'd tracked Kate down, after having searched half the store for her.

"He did what?" Kate repeated in a whisper that rose to a squeak at the end.

"He asked me to marry him." Even saying the words out loud didn't make it feel real.

"And what did you say to him?"

"I said I didn't know," Abby admitted. "Can we go somewhere a little more private?" Several women were beginning to eye them strangely.

"Come on." Kate wove her way between the tables of camisoles and petticoats. Abby trailed behind, wondering if it had been such a good idea to come here. Sometimes talking to Kate could make an issue even more confusing than it had been to start.

Kate led the way to an upper floor, where the administrative offices were. Kate's office was small but comfortably furnished. As she admitted, it paid to be the boss's daughter.

"Now, tell me everything, from the beginning."

Abby sank into the chair across the desk from Kate. She'd already decided not to tell her friend about the incident with Patricia Delevan. Even though it seemed to have sparked John's extraordinary proposal, it wasn't really relevant to her problem.

"There isn't all that much to tell. He asked me to marry him and I said I had to think about it."

"Are you in love with him? Is he in love with you?"

Trust Kate to get right to the point. Abby fiddled with the strap on her purse.

"Marriages can be built on things other than love," she said, avoiding a direct answer.

"So you're not in love."

"No." *Are you sure?* her heart whispered. She pushed the thought away.

"So why get married?"

"Well, the children—"

"If you tell me you're thinking about getting married for the sake of the children, I swear I'm going to smack you over the head, Abby Taylor." Kate's dark eyes flashed a warning as fierce as her words.

"I have to consider them."

"No one said you didn't. But you can't get married *because* of them. Tell me why *you* want to marry John. And don't tell me you don't want to because I know you do. If you didn't want to, you would have just told him so. You've only come to talk to me because you want me to talk you out of it."

Abby opened her mouth to deny it and then closed it again without saying anything. One of the most annoying things about being best friends with someone all your life was that they had a tendency to get to know you frighteningly well.

She'd convinced herself that she just wanted to get Kate's opinion before she made her decision. Then she'd weigh the pros and cons and make up her mind in a rational fashion.

Kate had seen right through to the truth. She wanted to say yes to John, had wanted to from the moment he asked her.

"I hate it when you're right."

"It's one of my best qualities," Kate said smugly. "Do you want a cup of coffee or something?"

"No. I just want to know what to do."

"Well, you *want* to marry him. What's wrong with that?"

"I don't know. It's not the way I'd dreamed. What happened to falling in love and dating and all that stuff?"

"That doesn't necessarily turn out the way you dream, either," Kate said. "Look at Dillon and me. We dated. We fell in love. Or at least we seemed to. Five years later, you don't see me wearing a wedding ring." There was a trace of bitterness in her tone but she went on before Abby could say anything.

"John's willing to offer you a pretty big commitment after knowing you just a couple of months. He must feel pretty strongly about you."

"Maybe." Abby sighed. "He says he wants a home and a family, a chance to build something."

"Sounds like a pretty firm commitment to me. Do you care about him?"

"Of course."

"And he cares about you?"

"I think so."

"You already know Jason and Mara like him and that he's good with them. You may not have known him very long but you're not exactly talking about an unknown quantity here, Abby."

"You sound like you think I should do it," Abby said, half wishing Kate would try to talk her out of it.

"I think you've already made up your mind that you're going to do it," Kate said, leaning back in her desk chair and rocking it from side to side. Abby avoided her eyes.

"It's foolish."

"Maybe."

"It could be a disaster."

"It could be wonderful."

"Whose side are you on, anyway?" Abby cried, exasperated. "I came to you for a calm, rational opinion."

"My calm, rational opinion is that you should go with your gut feeling."

Abby stared at her, feeling something dangerously akin to relief bubbling up inside. She'd come here to have Kate talk her out of doing something that her head told her was risky. Instead, Kate was telling her to follow her instincts.

And her instincts were urging her to say yes to John, not to let this opportunity slip by.

Or was it her heart that was speaking so clearly?

"You been to see that girl of yours?"

John glanced over his shoulder at Bill who was in his customary position at the end of the counter. The paper was spread in front of him but his eyes were fixed on John.

"Anyone ever tell you that you're nosy?" John asked conversationally.

"My wife does all the time. Says I'm worse than an old woman the way I poke my nose into other people's business." Bill didn't seem particularly remorseful.

"Your wife is obviously an intelligent woman."

John finished counting a stack of fives and clipped them together. Later, he'd make a trip to the bank to deposit the money.

"So, have you seen her?"

John grinned, shaking his head. It was impossible not to like Bill. Sometimes he wondered if he and his own father might not have had a relationship like his with Bill if he'd made it home before Mike Lonigan's death. Bill reminded him of his father or of what his father might have been years after he'd left home. Older, wiser, less driven.

"Yes, I've seen her." There was no sense in not answering. Bill would just keep asking.

"She looked upset when she left yesterday," Bill commented. John let several seconds slide by without saying anything. He glanced at Bill, shaking his head when he found the older man watching him expectantly.

"Don't you ever give up?"

"Nope. Persistence is my strong suit. She feeling better today?"

"I think so." John finished counting the money and slipped it into the bag to go to the bank. The bag went into a drawer beneath the register. He locked the drawer and then turned to lean one hip against the counter.

"Actually I took some of your advice," he said.

"Well, I'd guess you're about the first. What did you do?"

"I asked her to marry me."

"Hot damn." Bill's eyes widened in shock.

John knew just how he felt. He still wasn't quite adjusted to the idea himself. Not that he hadn't given it plenty of thought. He'd been up most of the night before thinking about it. He'd thought about it in between making phone calls, starting at 6:00 a.m. It had been in the back of his mind while he was coaxing people into digging up dirt on Judge Delevan.

He'd thought about it, all right. But it still didn't seem quite real. He, who'd never thought he was much on commitment, had just proposed to a woman. With two kids, no less.

Talk about plunging in feetfirst.

"You won't regret it," Bill said, rattling the paper in his enthusiasm. "She's got grit. Anybody can see that."

"She hasn't said yes, yet," John cautioned him.

"She will."

"I'm glad one of us is sure." John half laughed, covering up his uncertainty. It had surprised him to realize how badly he wanted Abby to say yes. It shouldn't matter so much. After all, it wasn't as if he were in love with her.

"Well, now that you'll be staying here in town, I've got a proposition for you." Bill's confident assumption that Abby was going to accept made John smile.

"What kind of a proposition?"

"Well, I've been doing some thinking lately."

"A dangerous occupation," John murmured, his smile widening when Bill shot him a stern look.

"As I was saying, I've been doing some thinking and it occurred to me that I'm getting on in years. Not quite ready to put out to pasture, mind you, but I certainly ain't no spring chicken."

Bill leaned back on the stool, fixing John with a serious look. "I was thinking it might be a good idea if I was to take on a partner. Somebody who had a vested interest in the place, so to speak."

"Bill, I—"

"Don't say no till you've thought about it. You're taking on a family now. This place ain't much but it draws a pretty decent income. Got a good location. I wouldn't pitch a fit if you wanted to make a few changes."

He looked around the rather plain building. "Matter of fact, a few changes might be a good idea. But I don't have the energy to make them.

"The wife's been after me to take some time off. She wants to go visit the grandkids and they're scattered all over the country. You'd think out of six kids one of them could have settled within driving range," he grumbled.

"I'd have to think about it, Bill. To tell the truth, I've never thought of myself as a businessman," he said honestly.

"Never thought of yourself as a family man, either, I'll bet," Bill shot back. "But you're about to be. Maybe you don't know yourself quite as well as you thought you did."

He heaved his bulk off the stool, folding up the paper with a snap. "You think about it as long as you like. I'm not out beatin' the bushes for partners. You let me know if you think you're interested, and we'll work out the details."

"Thanks, Bill." John watched the older man leave. Every afternoon about now, Bill went to a bar a few blocks away and played pool with a couple of cronies. He said it was as close to aerobic exercise as he planned to get. After he was gone, John looked around the store, seeing it with new eyes.

Half owner of a liquor store. He'd sold his interest in his father's liquor store and bought the Gullwing. Now here he was considering a partnership in another one. His father had run that store for close to twenty years. It seemed ironic that his son might end up in the same business.

It was too soon to be worrying about things like that. He couldn't make any decisions until Abby gave him her answer. And who knew how long that might be.

He didn't have long to wait. Bill had been gone only a few minutes when the bell over the door rang. John was kneeling behind the counter, counting the liquor bottles on the bottom shelf, making notes of things they needed to reorder. He stood up and turned toward the door, feeling a quick tightness in his chest when he saw Abby.

She paled and then flushed when she saw him, hesitating before moving toward the counter. She'd discarded her jacket but still wore the skirt and blouse she'd put on for her confrontation with Patricia Delevan. She looked cool and elegant and trembling with nerves all at the same time.

"I didn't expect to see you so soon," he said by way of greeting, keeping his tone casual, as if what she had to say might not have an enormous impact on both their futures.

"I didn't expect to be here," she admitted. She stopped just across the counter, her eyes on the scuffed surface rather than on his face. "I thought about...what we talked about."

"Marriage." He supplied the word she couldn't quite seem to get out.

"I thought about it."

"Good." John waited.

The silence lengthened painfully. Just when he thought she was never going to speak again, she drew a quick breath.

"Yes, I'll marry you." She rushed the words out as if afraid to keep them inside a moment longer.

"You're sure?"

"I'm sure." She lifted her eyes to his face at last. "I want to marry you."

John wanted to kiss the shaky smile from her mouth but he contented himself with brushing his fingers over her cheek.

"Thank you."

He felt an elation out of all proportion to the moment. After all, this was more in the nature of a merger than a love match. That would have required them to love each other. And they didn't. Not a bit.

Chapter Ten

They were married three weeks later in a simple ceremony held in the little house they'd be sharing. The groom wore a suit purchased for the occasion. The bride wore a calf-length ivory silk dress with a sweetheart neckline and full skirt that swirled around her legs. The dress was a gift from the maid of honor who'd threatened violence if she argued about accepting it.

Looking at her reflection in the mirror, Abby was glad she'd let Kate give her the dress. When she'd agreed to marry John, she'd thought vaguely that she'd wear something already in her closet. Kate had been scandalized by the idea. A bride simply had to wear something special.

She felt special in this dress. Too special? she wondered uneasily. After all, this was a marriage of practicality, not passion. She wasn't exactly a traditional trembling bride. As if to prove her wrong, her hand shook too badly for her to risk using the lip brush she'd picked up.

Abby set the brush down, meeting her wide eyes in the mirror, seeing the doubts reflected there. She'd been so busy these past three weeks, planning the wedding, making sure the children understood what was happening and working full-time, there'd been little time for reflection.

From the moment she'd said yes to John, her life had been a whirlwind of activity. She'd had few doubts about her decision. But then, there'd been no time to think. Now, with the ceremony due to begin in less than thirty minutes, she was suddenly swept by a tidal wave of uncertainty.

Had she been crazy to think this would work? Could two people build a marriage on little more than mutual respect and determination?

"You look gorgeous." Kate swept into the bedroom in a swirl of pale green skirt.

"You don't think I look too...bridal?" Abby questioned uneasily.

"Abby, you *are* a bride. You're supposed to look bridal."

"I just don't want to look like I'm expecting this marriage to be something it's not," Abby said.

"Just what isn't it going to be?" Kate clicked her tongue in exasperation. "The two of you are going to have a real marriage, in every sense of the word. Or so you've told me. You *are* a bride. There's no reason you shouldn't look like one."

"I guess." Abby let Kate fuss over her hair, telling herself that it was a little late for doubts now.

Her stomach was churning with nerves. Her palms were damp. She wanted nothing so much as to climb out a window and run away. And even more, she wanted to see John, to have him tell her that this was the right thing to do. Somehow, when he said it, she believed him. It was only when she was alone that she began to doubt her own sanity.

She watched Kate carefully coax a stray lock of hair into place. The French braid that pulled Abby's hair back from her face was Kate's handiwork and she'd fussed with it off and on most of the morning.

"Maybe we should have just gone to city hall." Abby pressed her hand over her churning stomach.

"Over my dead body would you have gone to city hall. You promised me that I could be in your wedding."

"That was when we were eight years old."

"A promise is a promise," Kate said firmly.

"Oh, Kate, what if I'm making a mistake?" Abby put her hands over her cheeks, suddenly sure that she couldn't go through with the wedding.

"Abby, there are no guarantees in life. Even if you and John were madly in love, that doesn't mean you'd have a happy marriage."

"That's what he said."

"See, great minds think alike. Besides, you look too beautiful *not* to get married."

A soft tapping on the door interrupted them. What if it was John coming to tell her that he couldn't go through with the ceremony? As sure as she'd been a moment before that it was a terrible mistake, she was suddenly just as sure that she couldn't bear for him to call the wedding off.

Abby had to try twice before she could find enough voice to call out permission to enter.

"I hope I'm not intruding." Lily Dushane stepped into the room, her smile hesitant.

"Of course not. I'm just sitting here trying not to panic."

Abby glanced up at Kate, unsurprised to find her staring at the other woman with her mouth slightly ajar. Lily was, without doubt, the most beautiful woman Abby had set eyes on. With her blue-black hair and emerald-green eyes and a face like a perfect cameo, she was inclined to knock the breath out of people when they first saw her.

"Kate, I don't think you've met Lily Dushane. Lily, this is my friend, Kate Bixby."

"Pleased to meet you." Kate stuck out her hand, blinking the dazed look from her eyes.

"Abby told me that you helped her pick out her dress. It's really quite beautiful." Lily's smile was as exquisite as the rest of her.

"Lily's husband, Trace, is John's best man," Abby told Kate. "She and Trace came up from California to be in the wedding."

"Are you related to John?" Kate asked, regaining her voice.

"In a way. His father helped Trace and me when we first came to Los Angeles. He practically adopted us. I guess that makes us almost-relations." Turning to Abby, she said, "I wondered if you already had your 'something borrowed.'"

"Actually I don't. I have my mother's earrings for the something old and my garter is blue. My dress is the something new. I was going to borrow something from Kate."

"Well, if you'd like, you could borrow my cameo." She held out her hand to show a delicate gold cameo on a fine gold chain. "Trace gave it to me for a wedding gift and it's very dear to me. I know we only just met yesterday but I'd like to think we're going to be friends. It would mean a great deal to me if you'd wear it for your something borrowed."

"Oh, Lily, how sweet." Abby touched her finger to the lovely necklace, blinking back the tears that had been all too close to the surface today. "I'd be honored. Would you put it on for me?"

She turned her back, watching in the mirror as Lily slipped the necklace around her neck and bent to work the tiny clasp. The cameo lay in the hollow at the base of her throat, adding a final, delicate touch to her gown.

"Thank you," Abby said, her voice husky with emotion.

"Thank you for making John happy." Lily's eyes met hers in the mirror. "He's been alone too long."

Abby touched her fingers to the cameo, lowering her eyes. Obviously, Lily thought this was a love match and Abby didn't have the courage to tell her otherwise.

"YOU LOOK AWFULLY CALM for a bridegroom." Trace's comment brought John's head around to look at the other man. He'd been staring out the window at the new fence that lined the west side of the property.

In a way, that fence had been instrumental in getting him where he was today. If he and Frickle hadn't had that confrontation over it, the old man might not have taken his revenge by calling Mrs. Delevan to give her the ammunition she'd tried to use to browbeat Abby into giving up the children.

He'd wanted to have a serious talk with the old man but Abby had talked him out of it. Elmer Frickle was the sort who'd turn around and sue for harassment. From the nervous way the old man scuttled off anytime he happened to see John, maybe the talk wasn't necessary anyway.

"Anybody home?" Trace asked when John didn't say anything.

John shook himself out of his thoughts. "I don't recall you being all that nervous before you married Lily."

"True, but then I'd been in love with Lily most of my life. And I wasn't taking on a ready-made family."

"Trying to talk me out of it?"

"Hell, no. I think Abby's great. I think the kids are great. I just want to see you sweat a little." He grinned with friendly malice.

"I'm so glad I have you here to offer me support in my hour of need," John said dryly.

"Anytime."

John glanced at his watch and reached for his suit coat. He shrugged into it and tightened his tie, slanting Trace a glance out the corners of his eyes.

"To tell the truth, I didn't expect you to come."

"So I gathered." Trace was perched on the arm of a chair, one leg swinging idly. "I had the feeling it was Abby's idea to let us know you were getting married."

"I didn't think it would hold all that much interest for you," John said honestly.

"You're family, John. As close to it as Lily and I have. If your father hadn't taken us in when we were kids, I'd have ended up in prison and God knows what would have happened to Lily."

"I suspect you gave Mike as much as he gave you."

"Maybe. But this isn't about repaying debts. It's about being part of a family."

"Well, I'm glad you came." The words were awkward. He wasn't accustomed to showing his emotions. To tell the truth, it meant more to him than he'd ever have believed that Trace and Lily had dropped everything to fly to Washington for his wedding.

Family. That was what he'd told Abby he hoped to get from this marriage. Maybe he'd been a little hasty in assuming that he didn't already have some.

THE WEDDING went off without a hitch. All present agreed that the bride was beautiful but pale. The groom was handsome, if a little reserved.

The ceremony was performed outside under a clear blue sky. Mara charmed everyone in her baby-blue dress, tossing rose petals on the grass pathway, her small face solemn with the importance of the occasion.

Jason had been pressed into service to give his aunt away and he was puffed up with pride and self-consciously aware of his new suit. Kate had found someone to play the flute, adding an almost medieval air to the gathering.

Hearing the music start, Abby nearly bolted back into the house, sure that she couldn't go through with the marriage. But everyone was out there waiting, already standing for the arrival of the bride. Jason was holding out his arm, his young face so serious it made her want to burst into tears.

She forced a shaky smile and set her hand on his arm. Drawing a deep breath, she let Jason lead out the back door and down the steps.

The pathway between the rows of folding chairs seemed as long as a football field. Abby kept her head down, afraid to meet anyone's eyes for fear the uncertainty she felt would be obvious.

What on earth had she been thinking of when she agreed to this marriage?

It was a good practical decision.

It was madness. Marriage was a serious commitment. She hardly knew this man.

She knew she trusted him. Knew he would do his best to take care of her and the children.

But what about love? Could she go through her life married to a man she didn't love?

Who says you don't love him, her heart whispered.

Abby almost stumbled, the question hitting her with the force of a blow. It was absurd. Ridiculous. She wasn't in love with John.

But she could be.

She lifted her head, looking forward to where he stood in front of the minister, waiting for her. He looked so tall and strong. Solid. It wouldn't be hard to love a man like that.

The sound of the flute soared in the air, and Abby felt her heart lift as if in response to the music. John stepped forward as Jason stopped. He took her hand from the boy with the proper solemnity. Feeling her fingers tremble, his eyes met hers.

Abby felt her nervousness drain away. She might not see love in his eyes but she saw tenderness and concern, a reassurance that she was doing the right thing. He cared about her. It was enough for now.

"ALONE AT LAST." John shut the door behind the last of the guests and reached up to loosen his tie. "I was beginning to think your cousin Charlie was going to spend the night."

"He and Sally don't get out that often. I guess they wanted to make the most of it." Abby sank into a chair, slipping one foot out of its shoe and flexing her toes.

"Feet hurt?" John asked sympathetically. He settled on the sofa, stretching his long legs out in front of him.

"A little," she admitted. She wished she felt as comfortable as he looked.

Kate had taken the children for the night, which meant that she and John were now alone. Completely alone. Always before, the children had been there, if not in sight then just in the next room.

It felt strange to be totally alone with him. Stranger still when she looked at the plain gold band on her finger.

"I think everyone had a nice time," she said, wanting to break the silence.

"They seemed to." John tugged off his tie and opened the top button on his shirt. "When you said you were just going to invite your family and one or two friends, I had no idea it would be so many people."

"I have a big family."

"And a protective one. Your uncle Arnold grilled me pretty thoroughly as to my future job plans. And your cousin Nick was concerned that I might have bought my car with drug money."

"Oh, dear."

"Your aunt Mary had a similar thought. She seemed to think I might be hiding from something, either the government or gangsters. She finally settled on gangsters, I think."

"I'm sorry." Abby felt her cheeks warm.

"Don't be. At least she placed me with the good guys."

"It never occurred to me that they'd do that. How embarrassing."

"Don't worry about it." John leaned back on the sofa, his smile easy. "It's nice that they're concerned about you. I don't mind fielding a few questions."

No, he probably didn't mind, she thought. If there was one thing she'd learned about him since she'd met him, it was that he was awfully good at fielding questions without ever really answering them.

The silence that fell between them might have been comfortable if she hadn't been vividly aware of their isolation. Absurd, she scolded herself. There were neighbors all around. Besides, it wasn't as if she were afraid of him.

Was she?

"I'm glad Trace and Lily could come," she said.

"I am, too. It was nice to see them again."

"You wouldn't even have told them about the wedding if I hadn't insisted."

"True. You can say I told you so, if it will make you feel better."

"I'll restrain the urge."

"Thank you."

Silence fell again. Abby stared at her hands, wishing Kate and her aunts hadn't been so nice about doing all the cleanup before they left. A pile of dirty dishes would have been a welcome distraction about now.

She jumped when John shifted position on the sofa, her eyes flying to his face. He was watching her, his gaze unreadable, as usual. Abby was suddenly vividly aware that she'd just married a man she'd known only a few months. What did she really know of him, after all.

"I'm not going to bite, Abby."

"I know." She twisted her wedding ring around on her finger.

"I told you I wouldn't push you. I want this to be a real marriage but I'm not going to rush you into anything."

"I want a real marriage, too," she whispered, staring at the shiny gold band.

"It doesn't have to happen tonight."

"No, it's better to get it over with."

John's snort of laughter made her realize what she'd said.

"Oh, dear. I didn't mean it that way." She felt her cheeks warm and pressed her fingers to them. "I just meant that there was no sense in putting it off. Oh, that's not much better."

"You make it sound like taking nasty medicine," John said. An undercurrent of amusement deepened his voice.

"I don't mean it that way," she said miserably. "It's just that I guess I've just realized that I don't really know you very well. I mean, I don't know that much about you."

"There's not much to know."

"Isn't there? Why do I have the feeling that's not quite true?"

"Because you have a suspicious nature?" he suggested, apparently not at all disturbed by her doubts.

"Maybe. But you never talk about yourself."

"There's not much to say."

"You told me you worked for the government," she said, persisting in the face of his indifference. "For how long?"

He hesitated, and she wondered if he was going to lie to her, but his answer came with a reluctance that made her think it was the truth.

"Sixteen years."

"What did you do for them?"

"This and that."

"Were you a spy?" she asked boldly.

"I don't think they like the term spy. Operative maybe, or agent. I think 'spy' is passé."

"Well, were you one?"

"What difference does it make?" He arched one eyebrow to emphasize the question. "Would it matter if I had been?"

"It's just that I don't know anything about you," she muttered fretfully.

"Come here."

"Why?" She eyed him uneasily.

"Just come here." He leaned forward and caught one of her hands, pulling her toward him. Abby left her chair reluctantly, settling on the sofa a good foot away from him. But John wasn't having that. She stiffened as he slid her over so that her thigh was pressed to his.

"You said you weren't going to pounce," she muttered uneasily.

"This isn't pouncing. This is sitting together." His arm settled over her shoulders. "You know, I don't think I told you how beautiful you looked today."

"Thank you." When he made no move to kiss her, Abby relaxed slightly.

"I think Jason and Mara are happy that we got married."

"Yes. Sometimes it's hard to tell what Mara is thinking but I know she likes you." Talking about the children seemed so safe that Abby shifted into a more comfortable position against him.

"They're great kids. I've never thought of myself as father material. I'll have a lot to learn."

"I think you have to go pretty much on instinct." She felt his fingers in her hair but she didn't protest. It felt so nice to be sitting close to him, talking in quiet tones. It was easy to put aside the questions he still hadn't answered and think only of the comforting strength of him.

"You've done a great job with them." His fingers were gentle as he loosened the elaborate braid Kate had spent so much time on.

"Mmm." Abby closed her eyes as her hair tumbled loose over his hand.

"You have the most beautiful hair," he whispered.

Hardly aware of her actions, Abby tilted her head in unconscious invitation. John's lips brushed over the top of her ear before finding the sensitive skin behind it. A delicious shiver worked its way up her spine.

His mouth touched the delicate line of her jaw, tracing his way with kisses until he'd found the corner of her mouth. Her lips parted in anticipation of his kiss, but he moved instead to her chin and then the tip of her nose and then the other corner of her mouth.

The light kisses teased at her senses, awakening a hunger but not satisfying it. Abby's hand came up to touch his chest, her fingers flexing in an unspoken plea.

John feathered kisses over her cheeks and across her eyelids. He found the pulse that beat at her temples and tasted the sensitive lobes of her ears. Abby murmured a protest when his mouth slid the length of her throat. Her lips ached for the touch of his. Why didn't he kiss her?

When he returned to her jaw and began to repeat the tormenting sequence all over again, her fingers slid upward, burying themselves in dark hair at the back of his neck. She turned her head blindly, finding his mouth. She could taste the smile of masculine triumph but she didn't care.

Control of the kiss was hers for only a moment. John's hands cupped the back of her head, holding her as his mouth slanted across hers with avid hunger. Abby's mouth opened to accept the thrust of his tongue.

Her fingers tightened in his hair as he lifted her without breaking the kiss and set her on his lap. She was surrounded by him. Her world filled with the scent and feel of him. Her breast was pressed against his chest, her thighs lay across his.

But in the midst of the passion, there was tenderness. He demanded nothing she didn't already want to give. His hands were gentle as he found the zipper at the back of her dress and slid it down. Abby found her own fingers on the buttons of his shirt, trembling but eager.

He eased her back, lowering the dress to her waist. Abby was suddenly self-conscious, aware that the low-cut silk camisole concealed very little. John slipped the delicate straps from her shoulders, first one and then the other. The silk slid downward until it barely concealed the dusky shadow of her nipples.

Abby shivered as his hand came to cup one breast, his thumb brushing gently over the peak. Her palms lay flat against his chest, bare between the edges of his shirt.

"Abby." Her eyes lifted reluctantly to meet his, half-afraid of what hers might reveal. "I'm getting an overpowering urge to pounce," he told her huskily. "If this isn't what you want, tell me now."

He was offering her a chance to draw back, to end this now before it went any further. She stared at him, her eyes dazed as she struggled to bring order to her thoughts.

She could feel his heart beat beneath her hands, strong and steady, faster now. And his eyes. How could she ever have thought his eyes were cool? They were molten silver now, all fiery warmth and promise.

And there was no real choice to make, after all. It had been made from the moment he started kissing her. Perhaps even earlier, when he'd slipped the fine gold band on her finger or maybe when she'd agreed to marry him.

She wanted him, not because it would make their marriage stronger, not because she wanted to provide the children with security. She wanted him because of who and what he was. Because it wasn't possible *not* to want him.

She let her hands slide up to his shoulders, leaning forward, giving him her answer in the yielding pressure of her breast against his hand, in the slumberous plea in her eyes.

John groaned, his fingers sliding under the thin protection of the camisole to cup her bare flesh. His touch was gentle but hungry, erotic yet tender.

Abby lost herself in his kiss. All her fears melted away, revealed for what they were. She hadn't been afraid of John. She'd been afraid of what he could make her feel.

When he stood up, still cradling her in his arms, she linked her arms around his neck, leaning her head against his shoulder as he carried her toward the bedroom.

The bedroom was dark, but John carried her unerringly to the bed, setting her on her feet next to it. Abby watched as he shrugged out of his shirt, discarding it in a white pool on the floor. Her dress and his pants soon joined it.

When he reached for her, she came into his arms willingly. All her doubts had vanished like mist before a warm summer sun. She'd never in her life been as sure of anything as she was that this was the right choice.

Chapter Eleven

Happy the bride the sun shines on. Abby wondered if there were any old rhymes to cover the day after the wedding. If so, she hoped rain was a good omen. The blue skies of her wedding day had disappeared behind thick gray clouds the next morning.

She woke slowly, aware of a feeling that something important had changed. She didn't have to open her eyes to know that the morning was well advanced. She'd slept better than she had in years and she felt at once rested and luxuriously lazy.

Rolling over on her back, she stretched out her hand, seeking the solid form of her brand-new husband. But she was alone in the bed. She opened her eyes, half relieved, half disappointed. Now that she knew he was gone, she realized she could hear the shower running.

Abby hitched herself up against the pillows, pulling the sheet up to cover her breasts as she contemplated her wedding night. It had been everything she'd ever dreamed of.

John was a tender, passionate lover and he'd wrung a response from her that she'd never thought herself capable of giving. He'd made her feel as if she were the most important thing in the world to him, as if nothing mattered but her pleasure.

The memory of it brought a flush to her cheeks. At least on a sexual level, her marriage was off to a smashing start. The only thing missing had been a pledge of undying love.

She frowned and plucked at the sheet where it was tented over her knees. There hadn't been much time for deep introspection lately. It seemed as if, from the moment she'd agreed to marry John, there'd been something that needed to be done every minute of every day. If she wasn't making arrangements for the wedding or taking care of the children, she was at work.

This was the first chance she'd had to draw a deep breath in three weeks. She'd thought that once she said yes to John's proposal, the doubts would be gone. When that hadn't happened, she'd thought maybe after the wedding she'd be a little more sure of the choice she'd made. And surely, after spending a wonderful night in her husband's arms, it wasn't possible that she'd have as many questions as she had three weeks ago.

But the questions were still there. The nature of them had changed slightly but they were still there. She wasn't quite so concerned with whether or not she should have married him as she was with *why* she'd agreed to marry him. All her arguments about doing it for practical reasons were beginning to sound a little hollow.

When they'd made love the night before, she **hadn'**t been thinking of what a practical decision she'd made. She hadn't thought of anything beyond how right it felt to be in John's arms, as if she'd finally come home after a long, long journey.

She'd felt fulfilled, not just physically but emotionally. Complete in a way she'd never known before. As if she'd been waiting for this moment, this man all her life. Thinking about it, it was almost frightening.

Was it possible that her feelings for John were deeper than she'd allowed herself to believe? Had she been lying to herself all this time, pretending she was marrying him because it was the smart thing to do? Talking about building a marriage based on friendship, not passion, when the truth was that she was already more than half in love with him?

When she thought about it, she still had so many unanswered questions about him. Even last night, he'd managed to sidestep her question about his job with the government. Just what had he done with his life before she met him? He hadn't said he hadn't been a spy or operative or whatever he wanted to call it. He'd dodged the question without really answering.

Who had he been? Did it really matter?

Before she could answer her own questions, she heard the shower shut off. The sound galvanized her into action. She shot out of bed and raced to the closet. The last thing she wanted was for him to come out of the shower and find her lying in bed as if she were waiting for him. As if she were expecting—well, never mind what he might think she was expecting. Because she wasn't.

Abby was just belting the gold silk robe around her waist when she heard the bathroom door open. She spun around, feeling all nervous and quivery inside, as if they hadn't just spent the night in the same bed.

Seeing her, John paused in the bathroom doorway. His skin was still moist from the shower, his hair falling in thick damp waves onto his forehead. He wore nothing but a navy-blue towel knotted around his hips.

Abby felt her stomach clench and her mouth go dry. She had never in her entire life experienced quite such a wave of pure, unadulterated lust.

"Good morning."

She had to swallow before she could return the greeting. "Good morning."

"I hope the shower didn't wake you." He took a step into the room and Abby reached unobtrusively for the edge of the closet door.

"No. No, it didn't wake me. I don't know what happened. I don't usually sleep this late. I mean, I guess I must have been tired after the wedding and all."

She was stammering like an idiot. And from the way he cocked one dark brow, it was obvious that he'd noticed. She stopped, drawing a deep breath. This was ridiculous. She was a grown woman, not a giddy teenager.

"Don't mind me. I'm not quite rational until I get my first cup of coffee."

John's slow smile made her heart skip a beat.

"For a minute there, I thought I'd grown horns and a tail."

"No. This is just a little new to me." Abby pushed the heavy fall of hair back from her face. "It's a little disconcerting to have a half-naked man in my bedroom, even if we are—well, even if it is perfectly respectable."

"Married," John said, his smile taking on a rueful edge. "You seem to have a hard time with that word."

"I guess I'm not used to that, either," she admitted.

"Well, it has been less than twenty-four hours." He walked over to the chair where his duffel bag lay, apparently not in the least disturbed by the fact that he was wearing only a towel.

Abby wished she could be as casual about it. As it was, she could hardly drag her eyes from the muscled length of his back. She could remember the feel of those muscles under her hands, the only solid thing in a world that was spinning madly around her.

The rasp of the zipper on the duffel bag made her jump, startling her out of her memories and bringing a flush to her cheeks. John pulled out a pair of jeans and a black T-shirt, setting them on the arm of the chair. Shorts and a pair of sneakers soon followed, the sneakers hitting the floor with a thud.

The harsh scrape of the zipper made her realize she'd been staring at him as if turned to stone. She cleared her throat and wished she could clear her mind as easily.

"I'll empty out some drawers and make room in the closet," she said.

"I don't want to crowd you." He turned to look at her and she had to make a conscious effort to keep her eyes from dropping to his bare chest.

"You'll need someplace to put your clothes and things." She was grateful to have an excuse to look elsewhere. Moving to the dresser, she pulled out the top drawer, slamming it shut when she saw the piles of lacy undergarments. She simply could not empty a lingerie drawer in front of him. The next drawer was safer, T-shirts and shorts. She could manage those even under that disconcerting gaze.

"You can't keep your clothes in a duffel bag," she said brightly, scooping a handful of T-shirts. "I mean, now that we're m-married and you live here, you'll need— Oh, my." She turned to find herself staring at a seemingly endless expanse of masculine chest.

"Abby, I'm not going to bite." He reached out to take the T-shirts from her, tossing them back into the open drawer before taking her hands. "You can relax."

"I'm sorry." She shook her head before looking up at him, her expression rueful. "I guess I'm just not used to this yet."

"Neither am I." His eyes smiled at her. "It'll come with time."

"But you are going to need someplace to put your clothes. And the rest of your things." He smelled of soap and after-shave, a heady combination.

"There isn't anything else." His hands slid up her arms to her elbows, drawing her a step closer.

"Nothing else?" Abby's eyes widened. For the first time that morning, she forgot to be nervous. "Just the duffel bag?"

"That's it. I never stayed in one place long enough to collect things." His hands were inside the loose sleeves of her robe, his thumbs circling softly against the skin of her upper arms.

"I . . . I guess you've done a lot of traveling." She could feel her knees shaking and she had to lock the joints to keep from melting into a boneless heap at his feet.

"Quite a bit."

His hands left her arms, and Abby drew a quick breath, not sure if she was relieved or regretful. But her breath was stolen when his fingers found the sash of her robe and began tugging on it idly.

"You never wanted to settle in one place?" she asked breathlessly. Had he moved closer or was she leaning toward him?

"Never had the urge. Until now."

He was definitely closer. Much closer.

"What . . . what did you do all those years you traveled? I mean, to earn a living." His breath brushed over her mouth at the same instant she felt the belt fall to the floor.

"Oh, a little of this and that." His hands found the bare skin beneath the robe. His mouth found hers. And Abby forgot all about her questions.

"I COULD HAVE KEPT Jason and Mara another day, you know," Kate said. "Given the two of you a little more time alone."

"Thanks, but I didn't want the children to feel as if they'd been shut out. This is going to be a bit of an adjustment for them, as it is." Abby poured lemonade over ice.

"Well, Jason seems to have adjusted pretty well." Kate nodded to the scene in the backyard.

The morning's rain had given way to a rather steamy sunshine. John was tossing pitches to Jason who was wearing his catcher's mitt. Dillon sprawled in a lawn chair, calling out occasional advice. Mara sat on his lap, her doll tucked under her arm, her eyes following the motion of the ball.

"He likes John. But I'm not sure it's sunk in yet that John is more than a large playmate. I don't know how he's going to take it if John has to tell him no about something."

"How are you going to take it?" Kate asked, her eyes shrewd.

"I don't know." Abby nibbled on her lower lip. "I want him to be a father to them. I mean, if I didn't, I wouldn't have married him." She shrugged. "I guess maybe we're all going to have a bit of adjusting to do."

"Sometimes you have to make a few adjustments in your life, even if they aren't comfortable." Something in her tone made Abby look at her friend. Kate was staring out the window, her eyes fixed on Dillon's relaxed form.

"Is something wrong between you and Dillon?" Abby asked.

"No." Kate dragged her eyes away from him, her smile perhaps a shade too bright. "Same as always. Now, why don't I carry the lemonade, you bring the sandwiches."

She picked up the tray of glasses and pushed open the screen door with one hip, calling out lunch was served.

Abby frowned after her as she reached for the platter of sandwiches. She was definitely upset about something. She'd known Kate long enough to recognize the signs. But she'd also known her long enough to know that Kate wouldn't talk about it until she was good and ready.

JOHN SLATHERED shaving soap along his jaw and chin. He frowned into the mirror, wondering if he should grow a mustache again. Did Abby like mustaches? He shook his head and dabbed soap over his upper lip. He'd never in his life had to consider someone else's opinion on something personal.

But then, lately he'd been doing a lot of things he'd never done before. Things like getting married. Like sharing a house with a wife and two children. Like planning a future.

He'd never thought much farther ahead than the next assignment. In part, because there was no sense in planning any farther since there was always the possibility that each new assignment would be his last. He'd always thought it was just his nature that he lived mainly in the present and gave little thought to the more distant future.

But there was something about getting married and finding oneself with a ready-made family that tended to shift one's way of thinking. He had more than himself to consider now.

He stroked the razor along his jawline. Bill had mentioned taking him on as a partner again. He had named a figure that seemed reasonable. It would take most of the money he had in the bank. In the past, that wouldn't have concerned him, but now he had to think about what was best for Abby and the kids.

He grinned at his reflection. God, listen to him. He sounded like a typical suburban husband. He wondered what the people he'd worked with for so many years would think if they could see him now. They wouldn't believe it. *He* hardly believed it.

Really, it was amazing how quickly he'd adjusted to this abrupt change of life-style. Domesticity agreed with him more than he'd ever have imagined it would. Of course, everything wasn't perfect.

Jason had been delighted that his aunt was marrying John. He'd even, somewhat unwisely, pointed out that he'd known this was going to happen when he told his teacher Abby was engaged. But there'd been a few adjustments to be made there, too.

Jason hadn't stopped to think that John's presence meant he would no longer be the man of the family. Watching him, John could all but read his thoughts. There was a part of him that was secretly glad to be relieved of the responsibilities he'd perceived to be his. Now he was free to be just what he was—a ten-year-old boy. But he resented the changes, too.

Three weeks ago, John had been helping Abby with the dishes after dinner. Watching her elbow-deep in soap suds, it had suddenly struck him that he'd never realized how sexy a woman could look in an apron. But then, Abby seemed to look sexy in just about anything.

He brushed aside her hair and bent to kiss her nape.

"Stop that." She lifted one shoulder as his mouth moved to nibble the tender skin under her ear. Since she also leaned back into the kiss, John ignored her protest, switching his attention to her other ear. She sighed, her hands still in the water.

Cupping his hand under her chin, he tilted her head back, his mouth settling over hers, feeling her instant response.

It was not a passionate kiss, as kisses went. With two children in the house, passionate kisses did not occur in the kitchen. It was more in the nature of a promise to continue the encounter later.

Abby turned into his arms as he linked his hands at the small of her back. It still disconcerted him to realize that he enjoyed these small moments of intimacy as much as the more passionate embraces they shared in the privacy of their bedroom.

"We're never going to get the dishes done this way," Abby murmured against his throat.

"We'll get a dishwasher." He brushed a kiss over her forehead.

"That would be nice, but dishwashers are expensive."

"I've got money. And if you say a word about not wanting me to spend it on the house, I'm going to dunk your head in the sink," he promised lightly. Meeting his eyes, Abby swallowed the protest he could see forming. In two weeks of marriage, the only argument they'd had was over her continued refusal to allow him to spend money on the house.

"Well, I didn't marry you so you could fix this place up," she muttered.

"That's it. I'm going to dunk your head in the sink."

She protested laughingly when he scooped her up in his arms and dipped as if to put her in the sink.

"Do we get a dishwasher?" he questioned, pressing his advantage.

"All right. All right." Abby barely got the word out through her laughter. She threw her arms around his neck, just in case he should change his mind.

Lowering her to her feet, John savored the feeling of her against him. Her feet had just found the floor when something made him lift his gaze from Abby's flushed cheeks to the doorway, aware that they were no longer alone. His eyes met Jason's. The boy couldn't have looked more shocked if he'd just seen a murder.

His white face and accusing eyes made it clear that when he'd thought of his aunt getting married he'd never thought in terms of someone else having a claim on her.

He'd darted away before John could say anything, even if he could have thought of something to say. Since then, Jason had been waging a subtle struggle for power. John didn't think Abby had noticed the change. Maybe it was one of those strange masculine games that only men, whether they were ten or forty, understood.

Jason wasn't overtly rude. He was too smart for that. Instead he'd chosen a more subtle route. He no longer spent any time with John that he absolutely didn't have to. If John was working on something around the house, which was what he spent most of his spare time doing, Jason made it a point to avoid that part of the house.

In addition to avoidance, he was trying annoyance tactics. Tools would disappear from where John had put them, only to turn up somewhere completely different. If John had cooked dinner, which he did about half the time, Jason picked at his food and mentioned how much he liked Aunt Abby's spaghetti or her meatloaf. Sidelong glances at John made sure the point wasn't being lost.

It was irritating and pathetic at the same time. The most disconcerting aspect of it was that John found himself relating more and more to what his own father must have felt trying to deal with him.

He hadn't played the same sort of games that Jason was playing. He'd had his own bag of tricks. And, of course, his had been all the more powerful because he'd generally had his mother's backing if he was caught.

Looking back on it, he could see that he must have been a royal pain in the butt. He wondered if it was some sort of divine intervention that had put him into a situation where he couldn't help but get insight into what his father must have felt.

He and Jason would work out their problems. Given time, Jason would adjust to the changes. He'd probably even come to see the advantages.

John shook his head, realizing that he'd been staring into the mirror for several minutes without moving the razor an inch. He wasn't sure if it was marriage or turning forty that had made him so introspective.

He was stroking the razor over his upper lip when he realized that his reflection wasn't alone in the mirror. Mara had come to stand in the doorway of the bathroom, watching him with those solemn blue eyes.

John swallowed a curse as the razor slipped, removing a chunk of skin he hadn't planned on losing. Grabbing a tissue to stem the trickle of blood, he turned to face his small visitor. He was grateful that he'd wrapped a towel around his hips. He wasn't quite ready to cope with finding himself nude in front of a five-year-old.

"Hi. You want to sit up here where you can see better?"

She hesitated a moment before nodding. John felt a surprising rush of emotion when she held up her arms to him. There was something so trusting in the gesture. When he thought of what she'd gone through in her young life, it struck him as incredible that she had any trust left to give. It made him wonder if he was worthy of that trust.

He set her on the edge of the sink. She watched intently as he picked up his razor. He finished shaving his upper lip and rinsed the blade, giving her a sidelong glance as he did so. Something in the way she was watching him made him think there was more to her interest than simple curiosity.

"Did you watch your daddy shave?"

Mara's eyes jerked to his. John had noticed that no one ever mentioned her parents in front of her, as if afraid that mentioning them would bring back memories of them being killed.

Mara nodded slowly, as if uncertain of the memory.

"Did you ever help him shave?" he asked, groping his way, trying to imagine what a father and his four-year-old daughter might have done together. "Maybe you helped him put on the shaving cream," he guessed.

Mara nodded again, a little more sure this time.

"You know, I missed a spot or two," he said consideringly. "Would you like to help me?" He dipped the brush in the shaving cup and held it out to Mara. She took it from him hesitantly. He guessed her father had probably used shaving cream out of a can.

"Here, you just dab it on my face like this." He closed his fingers over her small hand and pulled it to his face, showing her how to dab the brush over his jaw. Her eyes widened in surprise and then her small face crumpled in a smile that went straight to his heart.

A few minutes later, his enthusiastic assistant had covered his face with shaving cream. From forehead to chin, there was hardly a centimeter that wasn't concealed by white lather.

John grinned at her, waggling his eyebrows up and down and she put her hand over her mouth, her eyes dancing with delight. She dabbled her fingers in the shaving cup while he picked up the razor and began the task of finding his face again.

"I bet you miss your mommy and daddy a lot, don't you?"

Some of the innocent pleasure faded from her face, making John almost regret the words. But pretending nothing had happened obviously hadn't worked. It was a year since her parents had been killed and she still wasn't speaking.

"I know it hurt me a lot when my mom and dad were killed." He kept his tone casual. Mara's head jerked up, her eyes fixed on his face with an intensity at odds with her age. She didn't have to speak for him to know what she wanted.

He stroked the last of the shaving cream from his jaw and reached for a washcloth. Dampening it in the sink, he spoke over the sound of running water.

"My parents were killed by a bad man, just like yours were."

God, what was he doing? He was no child psychologist. Maybe the worst thing in the world was to remind her of what had happened.

Mara reached out, tugging on his forearm, the demand plain, even without words. She wanted to know what had happened. He ran the washcloth over his face, wiping off the last of the shaving cream. Turning to face Mara, he leaned one hip against the sink and prayed he wasn't making an enormous mistake.

"My mother and father were both shot with a gun, kind of like what happened to your mom and dad. I was older than you were but it still hurt a lot. I wanted to crawl away somewhere and hide. I bet you feel like that sometimes, too."

Her lower lip shook. John wanted to snatch her up in his arms and tell her he'd always keep her safe, that she never had to be afraid of anything again.

"Maybe sometimes you're scared that something awful will happen to your Aunt Abby or your brother or maybe even you. I know I was real scared after my parents died."

Her eyes widened as she considered the possibility of him being scared.

"And I thought maybe it was my fault my mom and dad were gone. I thought maybe I'd done something terrible and they'd been taken away because of it."

From the way she started, he knew he'd touched a nerve. Her eyes dropped to her lap.

"Is that what you thought, Mara? That it was your fault your mom and dad weren't with you anymore?"

A quick intake of breath made him glance over his shoulder. Abby was standing in the doorway, her face pale. But he didn't spare her more than a glance. His attention was all for Mara.

She lifted her head to look at him, her eyes uncertain.

"You know, what happened to your mom and dad wasn't your fault, Mara. And what happened to my mom and dad wasn't my fault, either. I know it's hard to understand but sometimes terrible things happen and it's not really anybody's fault at all."

He watched her as she tried to absorb what he was saying. It was a pretty big concept for such a little girl. Too big, maybe. Maybe he should have just kept his mouth shut and let time heal her wounds. But then, time hadn't done such a great job so far.

"You think about it, okay?" He waited until she nodded and then caught her around the waist. He dropped a kiss on her forehead before setting her on the floor. "I bet your Aunt Abby has breakfast ready."

"It's…it's on the table," Abby said, forcing a smile for the little girl. She waited until Mara was out of hearing before turning to look at him.

John folded his arms across his chest and waited, wondering if she was going to tear a strip off of him.

"Do you think that was wise?" She seemed more concerned than angry.

"I don't know," he answered honestly. "She's got to come to terms with what happened, sooner or later."

"I wish you'd talked to me about it first."

"It was sort of a spur-of-the-moment thing. If I'd thought about it ahead of time, I would have discussed it with you first."

Would he? he wondered. *Would it have occurred to him to get her opinion?* He'd been walking his own road for so long, it was hard to think of consulting someone else before he did anything.

"Well, maybe it will be for the best," Abby said, though she clearly had her doubts. She twisted her hand in the cotton apron she'd put on to protect her clothes. "What you said to Mara? Is it true?"

"Which part?" Though he could guess what she was talking about.

"The part about your parents being shot. Is that true?"

"Yes. My mother was murdered when I was sixteen. They caught the killer and he spent twenty years in prison before being released. He killed my father a few months after getting out."

"Oh, my God." Abby pressed her fingers to her mouth, her eyes wide. "How awful."

"It was a long time ago." John shrugged.

"Why didn't you tell me this?" she whispered.

"There wasn't any reason to," he said, surprised that she thought there was.

"No reason? I'm your wife."

"It was a long time ago," he said again. "It doesn't have anything to do with us. I only told Mara about it because it seemed like it might help me get her to see that what happened to her parents wasn't her fault. I hope I did the right thing.''

''I hope so, too,'' she murmured.

AT TWO O'CLOCK in the morning, Mara woke screaming.

Chapter Twelve

It seemed to Abby that one second she was asleep, the next she was on her feet and not quite sure how she'd gotten there. Mara's second scream jolted her from the stupor and she stumbled toward the door. John was there ahead of her, looking fully alert as he yanked the door open and ran out into the hall.

"What's wrong?" Jason's voice was shrill with fright as he rushed out of his room. "What's wrong with Mara?"

"Probably just a bad dream," John told him soothingly, intercepting him when he would have run into his sister's room. "Let your aunt go in to her first."

Abby noted the interchange with one part of her mind. By the time she'd pushed open Mara's door, all her thoughts were focused on her niece.

Mara was sitting up in bed, her eyes wide in the dim glow of the night-light. When she saw Abby she gave a hiccuping sob and stretched her arms out. Abby's feet hardly touched the floor as she went to her. Sitting down on the bed, she scooped the little girl into her arms.

Mara's arms circled Abby's neck and clung as if she'd never let go. Her small body shook with the force of her weeping. Abby blinked back her own tears as she rocked

Mara back and forth, murmuring meaningless words of comfort.

Abby stayed with her, even after she'd cried herself back to sleep. She continued to hold her, rocking her gently as if her presence would ward off a return of the nightmare that had awakened her niece.

The sun was beginning to hover on the eastern horizon when the sound of the door being pushed open startled her out of a light doze. Mara still slept, one arm dangling out of Abby's hold. She slept with that abandon peculiar to children, her small body completely lax, her mouth slightly open.

"Come to bed." John crossed the room, moving with that silence that always surprised her in a man of his size.

She was too tired to protest as he lifted the child from her arms. Mara barely stirred as he settled her against the pillows and pulled the blanket up over her.

Abby rose slowly, her muscles stiff from sitting in one position for so long. She gave a startled gasp when John scooped her up in his arms, holding her as easily as she'd held Mara.

He carried her into their bedroom and laid her on the bed. Abby sighed as her head touched the pillow. It felt like heaven. But she couldn't go to sleep quite yet.

"Jason?"

"Jason's fine," John said, his voice unusually gruff. "He's been asleep for hours."

"Have you been awake all this time?" She forced her eyelids open, studying his face in the gray dawn light.

"Go to sleep," was the only answer he gave her. He pulled the covers up over her shoulders but Abby caught his hand when he would have moved away.

"Mara's nightmare wasn't your fault."

"Go to sleep," he said again, pulling his hand gently away.

She was too tired to do anything else.

ABBY WOKE feeling as if she hadn't had any sleep, which wasn't far from the truth. She staggered out of bed and into the bathroom where several splashes of cold water helped clear the sleep from her eyes.

A glance at the clock told her there was no time for the shower she was longing to have, not if she was going to get to work on time. Of course, whether she went to work at all depended on how Mara was. She tugged on her robe and left the bedroom.

She found Mara in the kitchen with Jason and John. John was leaning against the counter, a cup of coffee cradled in one hand. Other than the slight shadows under his eyes, John looked no worse for the wear. His eyes seemed to shift away from hers but it could have been her imagination since he turned almost immediately to pour her cup of coffee.

Mara seemed absolutely normal. She was munching her way through a bowl of cereal, her feet swinging back and forth under her chair.

Abby blinked tears from her eyes as she took the cup John handed her. There was no sign that Mara's nightmare had remained with her into the daylight hours.

"Do you think we should send her to school?" Abby asked John quietly.

He shrugged. "Don't ask me. It's pretty obvious I'm no child psychiatrist." There was bitter self-condemnation in his words.

"We don't know that your talking to her about Steve and Diane is what caused her nightmare," Abby argued, keeping her voice low.

"Has she ever had a nightmare like that before?"

"No." She gave the answer reluctantly, knowing it was only going to add to the guilt he felt.

The look he gave her said it all. He didn't need to bother with a verbal reply.

"Even if that is what caused it, it doesn't make any sense to blame yourself. You did what you thought was right."

"The road to hell is paved with good intentions," was his only answer. He scowled down at his coffee cup.

Obviously there was no arguing with him, especially not when she was confined to whispers. When he saw that Mara had taken no permanent harm, he'd stop feeling so guilty.

At least, she hoped he would.

BY DINNER that night, Abby had managed to put the incident in a more positive light. Maybe Mara having a nightmare was an indication that she was starting to come to terms with her parents' death.

John had provided dinner, bringing home Chinese takeout. Abby couldn't help but wonder if it was an urge for moo goo gai pan or a guilty conscience that had inspired him. It didn't matter. Tonight, after Jason and Mara were in bed, she'd talk to him and make him see that he couldn't blame himself for doing what had seemed right at the time.

He spoke little at dinner, and though there was nothing unusual about that, it did seem to Abby that he was even less communicative than usual. As if to make up for it, Jason was full of the day's events at school.

In the midst of listening to him describe, in intricate detail, the precise events that had led up to a food fight in the cafeteria, Abby forgot to keep an eye on Mara's progress with her meal.

Generally a light eater, Mara had only one culinary passion, and it was egg rolls. Given her choice, she'd probably have had egg rolls with every meal. As long as she made a show of eating the rest of the meal, Abby made it a point to keep the egg roll supply replenished.

But tonight, tired from lack of sleep, distracted with John's continued silence, and her ears full of Jason's story, she slipped up on her duty. Mara had finished her first egg roll and had fulfilled her part of the bargain by eating several bites of chow mein. She put down her fork and waited politely.

Since the box of egg rolls was on the other side of the table and she was well aware that leaning across the table was severely frowned upon, and since no one seemed to be paying any attention to what she regarded as a grave lack, she did the obvious thing.

Pointing at the important box, she made a request.

"Egg roll."

Jason was just approaching the climax of his story when Abby heard Mara's request. It was a measure of her tiredness that she had reached for the box and handed it to Mara before she realized that a miracle had occurred.

She stared at her niece, sure that she must have imagined it. But if she'd imagined it, then she wasn't alone. John was sitting as if turned to stone, his eyes intent on Mara. Even Jason had broken off his story to stare at his little sister.

Only Mara seemed unaffected, crunching contentedly into the crisp egg roll. She looked the same as she always did, certainly not like a child who'd just done something incredible.

Abby wanted to scream and shout. She wanted to grab Mara and dance wildly around the room with her. But she didn't do any of those things. She drew a slow breath and forced her voice to calm steadiness.

"Could you say that again, Mara?"

Mara looked at her, the moment extending so long that Abby thought she'd retreated into silence. For a wild moment, she wondered if those would be the only words Mara would ever speak.

"Egg roll."

"Hey, she said something." That was Jason, stating the obvious and expressing the amazement they all felt.

"You like egg rolls, don't you, Mara?" Abby was hardly conscious of stretching her hand along the table toward John as she waited to see if Mara would reply. But his fingers closed over hers, strong and hard.

Again, there was a lengthy pause while Mara seemed to consider whether to answer. She studied the egg roll clutched in her hand and gave a decisive nod.

"Yes."

Tears burned the backs of Abby's eyes. She forced them back. Mara didn't seem to see anything extraordinary in her sudden vocal expression. The best thing to do was to treat it exactly as Mara was doing—as if it were no big deal.

Her eyes met John's, needing someone who could share the miracle with her. His eyes were blazing with happiness, the gray now a glittering silver. There was nothing held back in that look, none of the barriers that were so much a part of him.

And in that look she saw not just the surface he usually revealed but the man who lay beneath that surface.

The man she'd fallen in love with.

"SORRY I'M LATE." Abby slid into the booth across from Kate, breathless from hurrying. "My last customer was a lady with about a thousand coupons, and half of them were expired."

"That's okay. I ordered you a salad. So, how's the little chatterbox?"

"Well, I wouldn't exactly call Mara a chatterbox. But in the week since she spoke the immortal words 'egg roll,' she's begun to talk more and more. I think part of the problem may be that in the year since she quit talking her mind has learned a lot of new words but her mouth isn't sure how to get around them yet."

"In a few months, you'll probably be wishing you could find a way to shut her up," Kate said.

"It'll take a while before I get tired of hearing her talk. Every word she says still seems like a miracle."

"How's Jason taking it?"

"Oh, he was impressed for a day or so and then it got to be old hat."

Abby leaned back as the waitress brought two salads and set them on the table.

"So, how's married life, now that you've had a few weeks to settle into it?" Kate gave her salad a liberal dusting of pepper.

"It's fine. It takes some getting used to."

"You're not sorry you took the jump?"

"No, I'm not sorry," Abby said softly, poking her fork into her salad without interest.

"Aha!"

Abby jumped, dropping her fork with a clatter. Glancing across the table, she saw Kate looking at her with an expression that could only be called triumphant.

"What?"

"I knew it all along." Kate waved a forkful of lettuce at her before popping it into her mouth and chewing with a smug air.

"Knew what?" Abby questioned, wondering if she'd missed out on an important piece of the conversation somehow.

"You're in love with John," Kate said.

"What makes you say that?" Abby hadn't quite adjusted to the idea herself. She wasn't sure she was ready to talk about it, even with Kate.

"You've got that dreamy look in your eyes. Just like you used to have when you looked at Jerry Ballard during recess.

"That was when I was ten years old," Abby protested. "And I wasn't in love with him. I had a terrible crush on him."

"Well, the look hasn't changed. You're in love with John."

"Well, what if I am?" Abby was aware that she sounded more like a cross ten-year-old than a mature woman.

"I think it's great. I figured it out a long time ago."

"How could you have? I only just realized it myself a few days ago."

"You always were slow." She ducked the napkin Abby threw at her. "And prone to violent fits of temper, too."

"You're impossible," Abby complained, laughing reluctantly.

"But I'm right. You wouldn't have married him if you hadn't been more than half in love with him. And I wouldn't have encouraged you to do it if I hadn't thought you were."

Abby remembered all the times she'd told herself that it wouldn't be hard to fall in love with John and knew that Kate was right. She'd been at least halfway to being in love with him for a long time. These past few weeks of marriage had just pushed her the rest of the way.

And now she was head over heels in love with a man who'd married her because he wanted a family.

She blinked against the sudden sting of tears.

"Hey, what's wrong?" Kate was all concern. "It's good to love the man you're married to, isn't it?"

"Not if he doesn't love you back," Abby whispered, grabbing for a napkin and dabbing her eyes with it.

"How do you know he doesn't?"

"I know." Abby sniffed away the threatened deluge. "It's like living with an iceberg, Kate."

"An iceberg? You mean, in bed?"

"No! No, of course not. *That* part is just fine." Abby flushed, thinking that "just fine" hardly described it. "I mean, in the sense that he doesn't let much of himself show."

"Well, men are inclined to be more reserved. They don't like to spill their guts the way women are always doing."

"No, it's more than reserve." Abby frowned, trying to find the right words. "It's like there's a part of him that he lets the world see, but it's only a small part of who he really is.

"I don't even *know* who he is," she said, frustrated. "He's told me almost nothing about himself, what he used to do, where he's lived. He just sidesteps questions.

"He keeps most of himself hidden. I don't know if it's because he's afraid of being hurt or if he doesn't trust me enough to let me see that part of him."

"Maybe he just needs a little more time."

"Maybe. But I feel like he hasn't made a real commitment to this marriage. I know. I know." She waved a hand to forestall the protest she saw hovering on Kate's lips. "Marriage is a big commitment, and I don't mean he isn't committed to the marriage."

"Then what do you mean? You've lost me completely."

"I don't know," Abby said, frustrated by her inability to find the right words to express something she could feel so clearly. "He's holding back emotionally. He's committed, but not a hundred percent. He told me what he wanted from this marriage was a family. And you can't have a family without giving a hundred percent. He's trying to stay on the surface."

Kate shook her head. "Maybe you're expecting too much. From what you've told me, the man has spent most of his life traveling all over the world. Now he finds himself in Beaumont, Washington, married and a more or less stepfather to two children. That's quite a change in lifestyle, Abby. Give him a little time."

"Maybe." But Abby didn't believe it was simply a matter of time.

"Enough about me," she said, shaking off the melancholy mood that threatened. She reached for her neglected salad. "What are you doing these days? How's Dillon? I haven't seen him in ages."

"Neither have I."

"This is a pretty busy time of year on a farm."

"Actually, Dillon and I are no longer seeing each other."

"What?" Abby lowered her fork to stare at her friend.

"I decided to break it off." Kate's casual air might have fooled someone who didn't know her. But twenty years of friendship had given Abby the ability to see past the tough front Kate liked to put up.

"What happened?"

"Nothing." Kate shrugged, as if she hadn't been in love with Dillon Taylor most of her life. "I just decided it was time to move on to other things."

"What other things?"

"I don't know," Kate wailed, grabbing for a napkin, her calm facade shattering.

"Oh, Katie, I'm so sorry." Abby reached for her friend's hand, the childhood nickname taking them both back to the days of first boyfriends and all the terrors attendant on growing up.

"Thank you." Kate blew her nose, blinking rapidly to dispel the few tears that had managed to escape and cling to her lashes.

"What did Dillon say?"

"Not much. I don't think he cared. Maybe he was relieved to get rid of me." The thought brought a new wave of tears.

"Stop it. Of course he wasn't relieved. Dillon loves you. Did you tell him how you feel? About wanting to be something more than his lover, I mean?"

"Of course not!" Kate looked at her as if she'd lost her mind. "I'm not going to beg him to marry me."

"I didn't say you should beg him to marry you. Just maybe hint him in the right direction."

"If he hasn't figured it out by now, I don't see how hinting is likely to do any good." Kate pulled a compact from her purse and inspected the damage to her face.

"So you just told him to get lost without giving him the slightest idea of why?"

"He ought to know why."

Abby leaned back in her seat. If it hadn't been for the fact that Kate was obviously hurting, she would have been hard-pressed not to laugh out loud. Calm, pragmatic Kate, who was always so full of advice for everyone around her, turned into a blithering idiot when it came to her own love life. It was almost a pleasure to see.

"Maybe if I talked to Dillon—"

"Don't you dare!" Kate's head shot up, her eyes flashing fire at the very thought. "If you say one word to him about me, our friendship is at an end, Abby. I mean it."

"Okay. I won't say anything." Beneath the table, Abby crossed her fingers in a childish gesture. First chance she had, she was going to point out to her cousin the error of his ways.

She didn't have any doubts that Dillon loved Kate to distraction. Once he knew why Kate was upset, they'd be able to work things out.

She only wished her own problems were as straightforward.

"JOHN? You've got a call." Bill's voice carried easily into the storeroom. In fact, John thought, chances were it had carried halfway down the block. He picked up the case of beer he'd come to get and left the storeroom, bumping off the light with his elbow.

"Who is it?"

"Says it's Jason's school," Bill said.

"His school?" John frowned. Dusting his hands on the seat of his jeans, he reached for the phone.

"Hope it's nothing serious," Bill said as he handed it to him.

The call was brief. John was frowning when he hung up the phone.

"Problem?" Bill asked.

"Jason got in a fight at school. Abby's at lunch so they called me." He thrust his fingers through his hair. "They want me to come pick him up. He's been suspended."

"Well, boys have been getting into fights at school for a long time," Bill said comfortably. "You'll have a talk with him."

John stared at him. It was only just now sinking in that everyone—Bill, Jason's teacher, Jason—was expecting him to deal with this situation. Just the thought made him want to break out in a cold sweat. He'd rather have faced a knife-wielding assailant in a dark alley than have to deal with one ten-year-old boy.

"You okay?" Bill's question made him realize that he'd been standing there staring at the older man, probably looking as sick as he felt.

"I've never dealt with anything quite like this," he admitted slowly.

"Oh, it's not that hard." Bill settled onto his favorite stool, leaning his elbows on the counter.

"That's easy for you to say," John commented, his smile rueful. "You've raised six kids. What am I supposed to say to him?"

"It's not that bad." Bill laughed, his round face creasing. "I'd rather deal with a boy than a girl any day. They're easier to figure out. When our kids were little, I never knew what Sally and Lisa were thinking. Left it up to my wife to try to figure that out. But the boys, they weren't so bad. Usually they told you just what they were thinking. Boys aren't as likely to hide their feelings from you."

"So what do I say?" John asked. "Jason and I haven't done too well together since the wedding," he admitted.

"Well, that's natural. It's bound to be something of an adjustment for the boy."

"I understand that. But it's not going to help our relationship out much if I play the heavy-handed parent."

"You might be surprised." Bill pulled a stick of gum out of his pocket and began unwrapping it with precise movements. "One thing I learned about being a father is that a kid's got to respect you. Loving comes easier. But respect has to be earned.

"You have yourself a serious talk with Jason, tell him that he can't go around punching other people in the nose. Maybe you ground him for a week or so. He isn't going to love you for it. But he'll respect you."

John kept Bill's words in mind as he drove to the school. He wasn't sure what to expect when he picked Jason up. Did they wrap you in chains for fighting these days?

Had they been too harsh with Jason? He was just a kid and he'd lost his parents a year ago. There'd been a lot of changes in his life. Had they made allowances for that? And what about the other boy? Were they letting him get off scot-free?

By the time he arrived at the school, John was feeling as defensive as if he were the one who'd been suspended. Jason had probably been provoked, he thought, striding up the concrete path. Had they even bothered to find out the whole story or had they just picked on Jason to punish because they knew he didn't have a father to stand up for him?

Later, it would occur to him that his reaction had been a little overboard. But in this, his first test as a parent, he was discovering how completely illogical a parent could become when faced with a possible criticism of his child.

He strode into the school prepared to slay dragons if necessary.

As it happened, Jason was not in chains. Nor did he look as if he'd been browbeaten or subjected to emotional torture. Despite a split lip and the beginnings of a black eye, he looked smugly pleased with himself. A look that disappeared when he saw John.

"What are *you* doing here?"

"They couldn't reach your aunt so they called me."

John had already talked with the principal. She had told him that both boys involved in the fight were being suspended for two days, allaying his suspicion that there was any bias toward Jason. In fact, her calm acceptance that this sort of thing happened now and again had made him see how ridiculous his thinking had been.

"I don't want you," Jason said sullenly.

"Well, you've got me. Let's go."

Jason picked up his pack, the same one he'd once told John to stuff money into. Now it held his books. His feet dragging, he followed John out of the office and down the silent halls.

John hadn't been in a school in a long time and it struck him that the place looked a great deal smaller than the schools he'd gone to. Or maybe it was just that he was a great deal bigger.

John stopped next to the car, pulling open the door and then turning to watch Jason's sullen approach. The boy looked as if he were on his way to prison, his shoulders slumped, his head drooping down, the pack dragging on the ground at his side.

John was torn between the urge to laugh, which he knew would be fatal, and the urge to shake the boy. He did neither. He simply waited without speaking while Jason slouched toward the car. The laughter nearly won out, though, when he saw Jason quickly glance around, hoping that someone might be there to see him getting into the exotic car.

Neither of them spoke on the short drive home. Unless you could count the occasional muffled sigh from the passenger. John ignored the pathetic sounds. He still wasn't sure he was the right person to handle this. Maybe he should wait until Abby got home, let her deal with this.

No. His hands tightened on the wheel. He couldn't make her be the bad guy. Besides, wasn't it supposed to be better to deal with these things immediately, get it over with? But what did he know about ten-year-old boys? Having been one once didn't make him an expert on them.

Once home, Jason's lethargy disappeared. He ran ahead of John, letting himself into the house. By the time John got inside, he'd tossed his pack on the sofa and was heading for the back door, apparently planning on making the most of his unexpected afternoon off.

"Jason."

John's voice made him slow but he didn't turn. For a moment, John thought he was simply going to ignore him.

"I'm going to go see George," Jason said, his tone less certain than John was sure he'd like it to be.

"No, you're not. You and I need to talk."

"I don't have to talk to you." Jason turned to look at him, his young face taut with emotion. "You're not my dad."

And that was the heart of the problem, John thought. If Jason accepted him as an authority figure, he felt as if he were being disloyal to his father.

"No, I'm not. And I'm not trying to be your father."

"Yes, you are. Marrying Aunt Abby and moving in here and everything."

John stifled a sigh. He felt woefully ill prepared for this. Nothing he'd done in the past twenty years had given him any idea of how to handle the boy's hurt and resentment. Now if only Jason had been pointing an AK-47 at him, then he'd know what to do.

"Sit down, Jason."

Jason hesitated, obviously deciding whether or not to push his luck by continuing out the back door. John didn't say anything. He simply raised his brows. Jason decided not to test that look.

He edged back into the living room and sat on the sofa. The way he held himself made it clear that he was only here under protest. It was also obvious that he had no intention of listening to a word John had to say.

John sank into a chair, staring at Jason broodingly. How many times had he sat in front of his own father just like that, his mind closed to anything Mike Lonigan might have to say, convinced that his father's sole purpose in life was to make him miserable?

Had his father felt the same frustration he was feeling now? Had he been torn between the urge to shake some sense into him and the need to reach out and make him see that life didn't have to be as hard as he was making it?

"What were you fighting about today at school?"

"None of your business." Jason slanted him a quick look, filled with a pathetic mix of fear and resentment.

"Okay. You don't have to tell me. I'll just tell you that you're grounded for the next week."

Jason's head jerked up, his eyes wide. "But I've got baseball practice!"

"You should have thought of that before you got in a fight. You want to tell me what happened?"

Jason jumped to his feet. "I don't have to tell you nothin'. You think just 'cause you married Aunt Abby that you're the boss around here. But you're not."

"Sit down!" John's stern tone made the boy sink back onto the sofa despite his determination to grant him no authority.

John studied the flushed young face, wishing he wasn't floundering in the dark.

"I thought you wanted me to marry your aunt," he said, opting for an oblique approach. "You told your teacher we were engaged long before we had any plans to get married."

"Yeah." Jason stared at the floor.

"And when we told you we were getting married, you seemed happy about it."

"Yeah, but that was before—" He broke off, obviously afraid he might say something that would help John understand what the problem was.

"Before what? Before you saw me kissing your aunt?" John ventured. From the way Jason's body twitched, he knew he'd struck a nerve.

"You're old enough to understand that married people kiss, aren't you?"

"Yeah, but..." Jason's hands clenched on his knees.

"But you don't like the idea of sharing your aunt?" John suggested. "You know she doesn't love you any less just because she's married to me."

Jason slanted him a quick glance from under his lashes— the only sign that he'd heard. John leaned back in his chair, studying the boy. Had he been as annoyingly uncommunicative as this when he was Jason's age? *At least as bad.* He sighed.

"Look, I'm going to be blunt. I think you're mature enough for me to just lay it on the line."

Jason's shoulders straightened in unconscious response to being called mature. The look he shot John was still wary but it held curiosity, too.

"I'd like for us to be friends, the way we were before," John told him. "But, friends or not, I'm not going anywhere. You can continue to play these little games, but I'm not going to leave.

"And you should think about whether you really want me to leave. One of the reasons your aunt and I got married was that we wanted a good home for you and Mara."

"We don't need you," Jason burst out, his hands clenching and unclenching on his knees. He glared at John, his eyes dark with resentment.

John almost grinned in relief. At least he was talking.

"Well, I guess you were doing pretty well before I came along," he agreed slowly. "But did you ever think about how hard it was on your aunt, without another adult around to help her?"

"*I* helped her," Jason said fiercely.

"I know you did." John paused, choosing his words carefully. "But it's not the same as having another adult around. You're only eleven, Jason." He shamelessly added in the birthday that was still a few weeks away. "You just can't do all the things I know you'd like to do to help your aunt."

"We were doing okay," Jason muttered sullenly.

John sighed, staring at the boy's down-bent head. Who would ever have thought the day would come when he'd identify so strongly with his own father?

"You know, when I was your age, I had a chip on my shoulder even bigger than the one you're carrying around. I thought I was as smart as any adult and I spent a lot of time trying to prove it. I got into my share of fights at school, too."

Jason's head had lifted, his eyes curious, despite his determination to show no interest in anything John had to say.

"What happened?" he asked when John showed no signs of continuing.

"I got a lot of bloody noses and black eyes. Gave my share of the same. I pushed my father away, a lot like you're trying to push me away. I told myself I didn't need him, that I was tough enough to manage just fine on my own."

"Weren't you?"

"Oh, sure." John lifted one shoulder in a shrug. "I managed. Just like you'll manage. But you know what I discovered?"

"What?"

"It's a damned lonely way to live. Don't push away the people who care about you, Jason."

"You're not my dad," Jason told him, a little less fiercely.

"No. But I'd like to be your friend. And friends aren't all that easy to find." John stood up, looking down at the boy. "You think about it."

Chapter Thirteen

Abby came awake slowly, aware that something was not quite right. Still half-asleep, she pushed fretfully at the light blanket covering her. She was too warm. The temperature in the room must have gone up twenty degrees since they went to bed. Even with the blanket off, the bed felt hot, as if she were sleeping next to a furnace.

Beside her, John stirred restlessly, muttering in his sleep. Thinking he was having a bad dream, Abby reached out, jerking her hand back when she came into contact with his shoulder. His skin felt as if he was on fire.

Her eyes flew open, the last remnants of sleep scattered from her mind. The room was light with the first pale rays of sunshine. She leaned up on one elbow, looking down at John. Even after two months, she was still half-surprised to find him in her bed. As time passed, she was realizing just how little faith she'd had in the durability of this marriage. And how big a chance she'd taken in marrying him when she hadn't really believed he'd stay.

John had pushed the covers down to his waist, obviously feeling too warm, just as she'd felt. The difference was, in his case, he couldn't escape the heat by ridding himself of a blanket—because he was the source of the heat.

Abby reached out to put her hand on his forehead, confirming what she already knew. He was running a fever, his skin flushed and hot. He frowned at her touch. His eyes opened slowly as if the small movement were an effort. For a moment, he stared at her as if he wasn't quite sure who she was.

"John? Do you feel sick?"

"Cool," he muttered. For a startled moment, she thought he was saying he was too cold, but then she realized that he was referring to her hand on his forehead. His eyes drifted shut again.

Abby stared at him, her mind blank. It didn't seem possible that he was sick. Not John. He was too strong, too vital.

"I'll call a doctor," she said, more to confirm to herself that she had an intelligent plan of action than to inform him of her intentions.

She moved to get off the bed, but his hand suddenly clamped around her wrist, stronger than she would have believed possible considering the temperature he must be running. She turned back to him, her hair swinging around her shoulders with the quick movement.

"No doctor." The words were an effort but his eyes were fierce.

"John, you're sick." She stroked his forehead and he closed his eyes, savoring the cool feel of her hand against his burning skin.

"No doctor," he repeated, enunciating each word in a way that told her how much concentration it required for him to get them out. "I'll be all right. Two, three days. No doctor. Just leave me alone."

"Okay." She stroked his forehead, smoothing the frown lines away. His hold on her wrist gradually relaxed, his fingers dropping away from her arm. Abby continued the gentle stroking until it seemed as if he'd dropped back into a light doze.

Easing away, she slid off the bed. She looked down at him for a moment before turning away. Of course she wasn't just going to leave him alone. She was going to call a doctor. John might be holding a part of himself back from this marriage but she wasn't. And she wasn't going to leave him lying there sick and feverish without trying to do something about it.

OPENING THE DOOR an hour later, Abby was surprised to find not only the doctor but Dillon on her doorstep. She'd forgotten that Dillon was coming over today to help John start the repairs to the roof. She gave him a distracted smile.

"Dr. Martin." She had to clasp her hands together to keep from reaching out to drag him over the threshold. She'd had plenty of time to convince herself that she should have called an ambulance instead of the family doctor.

"Abby." He followed her into the living room. "I can't remember the last time I made a house call." He seemed vaguely surprised to find himself making one now.

Luther Martin and his wife had been friends of her parents. He'd delivered Abby and her brother. And they'd helped the two of them when their parents were killed and Steve was left with the care of his young sister.

If she hadn't been so worried, Abby might have felt guilty about the way she'd shamelessly bullied him into stopping by on his way to the office. But John's fever seemed worse, and she was too busy worrying about him to be concerned about having used an old family friendship.

"What's wrong with John?" Dillon asked, forestalling the doctor's question.

"I don't know. He was fine last night. This morning he's burning up with fever." She addressed her answer to Dr. Martin, though the question had been Dillon's.

"Is he conscious?"

"On and off. He told me not to call a doctor. He said he'd be all right in two or three days and just to leave him alone."

"Well, now that I'm here, why don't I take a look at him? If I'm going to bill you for a house call, I might as well have a look at the patient." He gave her a comfortable smile. Abby returned it with a weak grimace.

Dr. Martin gently discouraged her from following him into the bedroom. If he needed her, he'd call her. Abby wandered back into the living room.

"Do you need me to take the kids to school or anything?" Dillon offered.

"No. Jason went in with one of his friends. And one of the teachers at Mara's school lives just two blocks away. She took Mara with her. Thanks, anyway."

Her eyes wandered to the hallway that led to the bedrooms, and she asked, "How long do you think he'll be?"

"A little more than thirty seconds, I'd think," Dillon told her dryly. "Come on. I could use a cup of coffee. A little caffeine will do wonders for you."

Abby allowed him to take her arm and lead her into the kitchen. It was difficult to concentrate on anything besides what might be going on in the bedroom. Even something as simple as making coffee was an effort.

She answered Dillon's attempts at conversation, hardly aware of what she was saying. It wasn't until he mentioned Kate that she was able to force more than a sliver of her attention on his words.

"Have you seen Kate lately?" The question was so self-consciously casual it caught even Abby's wandering mind.

"I had lunch with her last week," she said.

"How did she seem?"

Abby took her time about answering, studying his face, trying to read what he was thinking.

"Why do you want to know? She told me the two of you aren't seeing each other anymore."

"That was her choice. Not mine. Not that I hadn't been expecting it," he added, staring down into his coffee broodingly.

"Why were you expecting it?"

"Well, hell, who wouldn't expect it?" His laugh held a bitter edge. "I'm just amazed that it lasted as long as it did. What would a woman like Kate see in someone like me?"

"You think she broke it off because she'd realized you weren't good enough for her?" Abby asked in surprise.

"Well, I wouldn't phrase it as 'not good enough.' But it's pretty obvious that I don't have a lot to offer a woman like Kate Bixby. She's been all over the world. She could go anywhere. Do anything."

"Why didn't you ever take her out to the farm?"

Dillon blinked at her in surprise. "The farm? Why would I take her out there?"

"Because you loved her. Because you wanted to share your life with her," Abby suggested.

"Of course I love her, but she'd never want to go to the farm."

"Did you ask her?"

"No." He stared at her, working her words over in his mind. "Did Kate tell you she wanted to go to the farm?"

"I couldn't break a confidence. But it seems to me that if you love Kate, you might want to include her in your life instead of treating her like a mistress."

"A mistress?" Dillon set his cup down with a thud. "Is that what she thinks?"

"Why wouldn't she? That's how you've treated her for five years. You haven't included her in your life, Dillon."

"Only because I didn't think she wanted more than what we had. Hell, I was willing to take what she could give. I wasn't going to rock the boat by pushing for more."

"You should have more faith in Kate," she scolded him. "She's not a porcelain doll."

"Does she love me?" There was such a blaze of hope in his eyes that Abby felt a twinge of envy for her friend. It must be wonderful to be loved like that.

"Ask her," was all she said but she didn't doubt that he could read the answer in her eyes.

The sound of the bedroom door closing banished the momentary distraction she'd found in talking about Kate and Dillon's problems. She hurried into the living room.

"How is he?" She pounced on the elderly doctor the moment he stepped into the room.

"Well, he says he's okay. Seemed rather put out that you'd called me in." Dr. Martin shrugged. "I can't really tell you what's wrong. A form of malaria, maybe. I'm afraid I haven't had much call to diagnose that sort of thing in Beaumont."

When Abby didn't give even a perfunctory smile at his mild joke, he sighed. He reached out to pat her on the shoulder, with the familiarity of someone who'd seen her through diaper rash and measles.

"He's running a nasty fever and I don't doubt that he feels like hell, though I don't suppose he'll admit as much. But he was pretty coherent. Fading in and out a bit, but not delirious. He tells me the fever will run its course in two or three days, and I'm inclined to take his word for it. Said all he needs is to be left alone. Got pretty adamant about it. In fact, if he'd had the strength, I suspect he might have pitched me out on my ear."

This time Abby returned his smile, though her response was weak at best. It was reassuring to hear that Dr. Martin wasn't particularly worried. But it would have been more reassuring if someone besides the patient knew just what was wrong.

"He didn't tell you what's wrong?" she asked, trailing after the doctor as he headed for the door.

"I don't think he thought it was any of my business. Something he picked up in the tropics, maybe. He spend any time there?"

"I . . . don't know." Abby pushed her hair back, realizing again just how little she did know.

"He was in Vietnam," Dillon offered.

"Well, there were all sorts of nasty things he could have picked up there," Dr. Martin said comfortably.

John had been in Vietnam?

The question kept repeating itself in her mind as she saw the doctor off. Dillon left soon after, saying that he'd be back later to see if she needed anything. Abby didn't doubt that he was on his way to see Kate and she hoped that the two of them were going to work out their problems.

As soon as he was gone, she went to the bedroom, easing the door open. In the weeks they'd been married, she'd found that John was generally alert to the smallest movement. The fact that he didn't stir at her approach made his illness all the more apparent.

She stood looking down at him, wondering about the man she'd married. Just who was he? Was he the man who was so gentle with the children? Or the passionate lover who left her breathless and more alive than she'd ever felt before? Or the man who told her nothing of himself? Not his past or his dreams for the future; not what he'd done or what he hoped to do.

Abby sighed and reached down to brush a lock of hair back from his forehead. She'd married them all—the man who held her at night and the man with the secrets. And she loved them all, every frustrating, fascinating side of him.

He stirred at her touch, muttering in a language she didn't recognize. Yet another thing she didn't know, Abby thought with a sigh. Just who had he been? What had he done before he'd walked into her life?

Not that it really mattered. All she really cared about was where they were going from here. But he had to be willing to open himself up, to take the risks that went along with making a commitment to someone—the emotional risks that went along with building a marriage.

She brushed a kiss over his forehead, feeling the unnatural warmth of his skin. John's eyes flickered open at the touch. He stared at her warily for a moment as if he didn't recognize her, his eyes smoky gray with suspicion.

"Abby," he murmured.

"Yes." She eased down onto the bed beside him, stroking her hand over his hair. "How are you feeling?"

"Like hell." He closed his eyes, seeming to gather his strength before opening them again. "Sorry."

"For what? Getting sick?" She shook her head. "You don't have to apologize for that."

"Don't want to be trouble. Just leave me alone. I'll be okay."

"We're married, John. Remember, in sickness and in health? I'll take care of you." She smiled, hoping he was too sick to notice that her eyes were overly bright.

"Supposed to take care of you," he said, his voice slurred.

"We're supposed to take care of each other. Now go back to sleep. I'll bring you some broth later. With this fever, you're going to be burning up a lot of fluids."

"Don't like broth," he mumbled, already three-quarters asleep.

Abby smiled. He sounded so much like Jason did when he was sick. Jason didn't like broth, either. But Jason, like most children, enjoyed the fussing that made being ill almost tolerable.

John obviously didn't expect to be fussed over. How long had it been since someone had taken care of him when he was ill, she wondered. When he was a child, perhaps. Had his mother been the sort to bring him soup and play games with him to keep him occupied?

Had there been anyone since then? She eased off the bed, careful not to disturb his fevered sleep. She had the feeling that it had been a very long time since anyone had taken care of him.

JOHN COULDN'T ever remember anyone fussing over him the way Abby did the next three days. Normally, when the fever swept over him, he found a place to hole up until the illness subsided and he could regain his strength. He'd been lucky in the fifteen years since the first bout that it had never struck at a critical point where his disappearance for a few days would be a problem.

This time, there'd been no warning. He'd awakened in the middle of the night, alternately shaking with chills and burning up with fever. In between delirium and consciousness, he'd cursed the fact that he was too weak to drag himself to a motel.

It didn't occur to him that married men did not go to motels when they were sick. His instinct, like a wild animal's, was to hide somewhere until he'd healed. But it was too late for that.

Nothing in his life had prepared him for Abby's reaction to his illness. He'd been a robustly healthy child, so he had few memories of being ill. But he did remember that his mother had generally done her best to avoid spending much time with him. Illness frightened her so, she'd tell him when he had recovered, and she'd buy him a toy.

John realized that it had been his father who'd generally taken over the sickroom duties. Offering soup and barking out orders like a bizarre combination of drill sergeant and nurse. Yet another thing he'd remembered too late for it to help mend fences with Mike Lonigan.

The only resemblance between Abby and his father was their determination to pour large quantities of liquids down his throat. After that, all similarities ceased. Mike's gruff and awkward concern was a far cry from Abby's loving pampering.

In the interludes of awareness that punctuated feverish sleep, he was aware that Abby seemed to be always there. Sometimes she was bathing his hot forehead with a damp washcloth that felt like pure heaven. Other times, she was gently insisting that he drink something cool that momentarily quenched the fire in his body.

Somewhere in the back of his mind was the thought that he shouldn't be letting her get so close. There was safety in distance, he'd told himself. But his protests and occasional orders were ignored and he was simply too sick to fight it.

THE FEVER BROKE thirty-six hours after it started. John woke in the gray predawn hours, drenched in sweat. The worst was over but it would be another day, at least, before he was approaching normal.

Abby slept next to him, curled on her side facing him. It took a frightening amount of strength to turn his head to look at her. In sleep, she reminded him of Mara. There was the same sweet curve to her mouth, the gentle tangle of honey-colored hair.

Looking at her in the odd half light, John felt a twinge of some emotion he couldn't quite put a name to. Closing his eyes, he let his mind go blank. He was in no condition to be analyzing his feelings.

As he drifted off to sleep, his hand crossed the short distance that separated him from Abby and his fingers tangled in the soft cotton of her nightgown.

ONCE BEGUN, John's recovery was rapid, but not rapid enough to suit him. Unreasonably, he wanted to resume his normal activities as soon as the fever was broken. His body flat refused and Abby agreed. He'd never realized what a tyrant she could be.

She'd taken sick leave from her job to take care of him. John was uneasy with the idea of her disarranging her life for him, but she dismissed his cares. He was her husband, she said. They were family now, and family took care of each other.

With barely the strength to make it from the bed to the sofa, he couldn't put much force behind his arguments. Abby ignored his frowns, propping his feet up, providing him lunch on a tray and generally making sure he wanted for nothing.

Her fussing stirred up an odd mixture of emotions in John. Pleasure and uneasiness. A hunger he couldn't quite define. Mostly it left him off balance, a position for which he had no particular fondness.

His first day out of bed, he was surprised to have visitors. Bill came by first. John wasn't too surprised by that— after all, he worked for the man. The two of them had become friends, or as close to it as he'd had in a long time.

Reassured that he wasn't at death's door, Bill gave him an ear-rattling slap on the shoulder, told him to take it easy and took his leave. John relaxed back onto the sofa, giving in to the weakness he'd felt obliged to minimize while the other man was there.

Not long after Bill left, Kate showed up, inspected him in her usual breezy fashion, told him he looked lousy and left. Half an hour later, it was Mrs. O'Leary from across the street. She arrived with a plate of cookies and a package of herbal tea she swore would have him back on his feet in no time.

By the time Dillon dropped in—he just happened to be in town, he said—John was beyond surprise. He and Dillon made arrangements to start work on the roof in a week.

It hadn't occurred to him that anyone would know he'd been sick—nor that they'd particularly care if they did know. Since leaving home at eighteen, he'd had plenty of associates and one or two people he might have called friends. But he couldn't imagine any of them driving twenty miles to see if he was feeling better, as Dillon had done. Or taking time off from work as Kate and Bill had. And he knew, with certainty, that none of them would have baked him cookies.

But the final shock was yet to come.

Abby left to pick up the children at school only after making absolutely sure that John couldn't possibly need anything in the twenty minutes she'd be gone. Despite his self-conscious protests, John dozed off on the sofa, waking only when he heard the front door open.

Mara came in first, studying him solemnly for a moment before trotting over to the sofa.

"You sick?" She frowned anxiously, her forehead wrinkled in such serious concern that John found his arm circling her small body, drawing her into a reassuring hug.

"I'm getting better, little one."

"I drew you a picture," she told him, holding up a sheet of rather luridly colored paper. It still seemed like a miracle every time she spoke.

John admired the picture, relieved when she didn't require him to identify the subject. She leaned confidingly against him, bringing a sweet feeling of responsibility and affection.

"You okay?" John lifted his eyes from Mara's picture to where Jason stood at the end of the sofa. His hands were stuffed into the pockets of his jeans, and he watched John warily.

"I've been better," John admitted with a rueful smile. Things had improved between them since they'd talked, but they hadn't yet regained the easy friendship they'd built before his marriage to Abby. "Your aunt is taking care of me."

"She bug you to drink all sorts of icky stuff?" Jason asked.

"Now that you mention it, some of it has been pretty awful," John said.

"Does she take your temperature every five minutes?" Jason pursued.

"At least that often." John met Abby's eyes over the boy's head. "She handles a thermometer like a weapon."

"Yeah. And she sticks it in your mouth when you aren't looking." Jason hesitated a moment longer, his dark brows hooking together in a frown. "I'm glad you're feeling better," he said at last, the words abrupt.

He left before John could offer a response.

All he could do was stare out the window at the peaceful street—and think. Deep inside he could feel long-held barriers threatening to crumble. Sitting here in this little house, still as weak as a kitten from the fever, he was beginning to see that the whole concept of home was more complicated than he'd thought.

It was not a comfortable feeling.

DILLON WIPED HIS HAND nervously on the leg of his pants. The fingers of the other hand were wrapped so firmly around a bouquet of flowers, the stems were in danger of being hopelessly crushed. The walkway that led up to Kate's apartment looked a mile long, as if it had grown in the few short weeks since he'd last been here.

What if Abby was wrong? What if Kate really didn't love him? It had taken him nearly twenty-four hours to convince himself to come and see Kate again since Abby had told him she really did care.

He glowered at the small apartment building, as if he could read something in its blank facade. It didn't seem possible that Abby was right. Kate couldn't have believed that he saw her strictly as mistress material. It was simply too ridiculous. Good grief, he loved the woman to distraction. Hadn't that been obvious?

Drawing a deep breath, Dillon started up the walkway. He was probably about to make a complete fool of himself but he loved Kate enough to do it. The weeks since she'd said she didn't want to see him anymore had been the longest, most miserable weeks of his life.

He marched up to the door and knocked on it without giving himself a chance to change his mind. If he was about to humiliate himself, he might as well get it over with. He'd tell her he loved her, give her the stupid flowers and leave. He'd have made a fool of himself but at least he'd have tried.

But when Kate opened the door, he forgot everything but the wonder of seeing her again. Was it possible she'd gotten even more beautiful since he last saw her? She was wearing a pair of those ridiculous silk lounging pajamas that never looked ridiculous on her. Her hair was loose, swinging around her face in a dark cloud that made him long to run his fingers through it.

Her eyes widened in surprise when she saw him. Was it his desperately hopeful imagination or was there a flash of pleasure there before she glanced away from him?

"Dillon." There was certainly no joy in her voice, no emotion at all that he could read.

"Kate." He drank in the sight of her. Did she look a little pale or was that only wishful thinking on his part, hoping that she'd suffered at least a fraction of what he had. "Can I come in?"

"I don't think we have anything to—" She broke off when he lifted the flowers he'd been holding beside his leg.

"Please?"

She hesitated, her eyes flicking from the flowers to his face and then away before he could read anything in her expression. "All right."

It wasn't exactly the open-armed welcome he'd hoped for, but it was a start. Dillon followed her into the living room, breathing in the familiar scent of the potpourri she always had in a crystal bowl on an end table. She stopped in the middle of the floor and turned to face him.

"I thought we'd agreed not to see each other again," she said abruptly.

"Actually, I think you told me you didn't want to see me anymore," he corrected. He thrust the flowers at her, wanting to distract her. "I remembered you liked pink roses."

"Yes." She bent her head over the bouquet. "They're my favorite. Thank you." Dillon took heart from the softness of her tone. But when she lifted her head, there was nothing particularly soft in her expression. "Why are you here?"

"I talked to Abby."

"Abby?" Color crept into her pale cheeks. "Abby?" she repeated. "She had no right!"

Dillon felt relief well up inside. She wouldn't be so upset if she hadn't told Abby something she didn't want him to know. Like maybe that she loved him? It was all he could do to keep from grinning.

"I don't know what she told you but whatever it was, you shouldn't have come here because nothing has changed." She turned to set the flowers on a table and when she turned back, Dillon was only inches away. "Oh."

The breathy little exclamation was all she could manage. He had her neatly caught between the table and his large frame. Smiling into her startled eyes, he leaned forward to put his hands on the table, trapping her completely.

"Why did you send me away, Kate?"

"I told you. We discussed it." Her eyes darted to his and then away, settling on his shirt collar.

"No, we didn't. You told me you didn't want to see me anymore and I accepted that."

"You seemed glad to have an excuse to leave," she flared. "Would you please move?"

"No." The blunt refusal brought her eyes to his face, wide and startled. "I'm not going to move until you tell me why you said you didn't want to see me anymore."

"It's none of your business," she said, resorting to childish illogic. She lifted her hands as if to push him out of the way and then changed her mind. This time Dillon's grin could not be contained. It wasn't often that he saw his stubborn, practical Kate at a loss.

"Do you know why I didn't argue with you? Why I just walked out when you asked me to go?"

"I'm sure you were relieved to have an excuse to go out and . . . and cat around again."

"Cat around? Is that what you think I've been doing?"

"How should I know?" She took advantage of his startled withdrawal to slip to the side, putting several feet between them. "It's no concern of mine if you want to become the Don Juan of the county again."

"Don Juan?" Dillon stared at her incredulously.

"Well, you dated every woman in a fifty-mile radius," she snapped, tugging at the hem of her loose silk top.

"You're jealous!"

"Of you?" She put a truly magnificent amount of contempt into the words. "Don't be ridiculous."

"Don't deny it. I love you when you're jealous. As a matter of fact, I love you when you're not jealous. Actually, I can't think of a time I don't love you."

"Why should I care if you— What?" She broke off as his words registered. "What did you say?"

"I said I love you." He took advantage of her stunned surprise to catch hold of her hands and draw her toward him. "I love you and these past weeks without you have been hell."

"You love me?" The vulnerability in her dark eyes tugged at his heart.

"With all my heart, Kate." All the teasing was gone from his voice. He reached up to brush her hair back from her face. "I should have said it years ago."

"Why didn't you?" Her fingers clung to his.

"I guess I thought you knew."

"Never. I thought I was just . . . convenient."

"Convenient?" Dillon was torn between laughter and regret that he'd ever let her doubt his feelings. "Kate, you're many things but convenient isn't one of them. Did you think it was convenience that made me drive into town after spending the day working in the fields getting so damn tired I could hardly see straight?''

"But you didn't argue. You just left."

"Oh, Kate." He drew her close, savoring the feel of having her in his arms again. "I didn't argue because I'd been half expecting you to tell me to get lost ever since we started seeing each other."

"You had? Why?" She pushed back until she could see his face.

"What have I got to offer a woman like you? You've traveled all over the world. You spend more on clothes than the farm clears in a year. I'm nothing but a farmer, Kate. I don't have much to offer."

"Stop that." Her eyes flashed with anger. "Don't you dare say another word or I'll hit you. Just how shallow do you think I am? Sure, I'm used to money but it isn't the be-all and end-all of my life. I don't have to have it to be happy."

"What do you need, Kate?" He suddenly realized that he needed to hear the words as much as she had. It wasn't enough that he could see the love in her eyes, feel it in the way her hands clung to him. He needed to hear her say the words.

"I need you, Dillon. Just you. I love you. And these past few weeks have been miserable."

"Good," he said heartlessly, dragging her close. "I'm glad I wasn't the only one who was miserable." His mouth crushed the smile from her lips.

"TURN HERE," Abby directed, and John turned the Gullwing onto the rough dirt road.

Abby glanced at him, wondering if she was crazy to be doing this. The days she'd taken off work to nurse him through his fever had given her time to think. They'd gone into this marriage for reasons more practical than romantic. Those reasons were still valid but they weren't enough anymore—not for her.

She wanted more than a practical marriage. She wanted a marriage with love and a strong emotional commitment. And if she couldn't have that, then she'd rather have nothing at all.

"There. You can park in front of the house."

John pulled the car to a halt in front of a worn old farmhouse. As soon as he shut off the engine, the quiet was a third presence.

"Needs a touch of paint," he said, in a masterpiece of understatement.

Abby slanted him a quick glance, wishing she could read more from his expression. He'd been so quiet these past few days and she didn't think it was a lingering effect of the fever.

His illness seemed to have thrown him off balance in some odd way. Maybe it was just that he wasn't accustomed to being vulnerable. Or maybe he hadn't been expecting so many people to care. She'd watched his face when Bill or Kate would drop by and she'd seen surprise and pleasure along with a certain wariness, as if he'd almost prefer they didn't care.

She watched John as he got out of the car and came around to open her door. He lifted the picnic basket off her lap and then offered her his hand.

Setting her fingers in his, Abby felt the familiar awareness shiver through her. It reminded her of the risk she was taking and of the reasons. She couldn't go on pretending that a marriage based on a vaguely defined regard for each other was enough.

THEY SPREAD the old army blanket beneath the soft shade of an ancient apple tree, part of the orchard that extended from the back of the house. Neither of them spoke much as they unloaded the basket, setting the containers of food out on the blanket.

The cold fried chicken and potato salad were delicious, but Abby doubted that either of them tasted it. She was too nervous to eat and John didn't seem to have much of an appetite, either. He must have known that there was more to this excursion than a simple picnic but, as usual, she couldn't read anything in his expression.

He waited until after the barely touched food had been put away before saying anything.

"So, why have we driven twenty-five miles from town to eat lunch at an abandoned farm?"

"See that house?" Abby nodded toward the old farmhouse.

"It's a little hard to miss," John said dryly, looking at the sprawling building.

"The old man who owns this place was a friend of my grandfather's. I can remember coming out here with my grandparents when I was a little girl. I'd climb in these apple trees and try to skip rocks in the pond at the bottom of the orchard."

"Sounds nice." He picked up the basket and set it to one side, leaning back on one elbow on the blanket, his eyes on the old house.

"It was. After Steve and Diane died and I moved back to Beaumont, I found out old Mr. Lindsay was in a nursing home. This place just stands here empty."

"Too bad."

"Sometimes I lay awake at night and think how great it would be to buy this place and restore it."

"It would be a lot of work." His tone was noncommittal though the look he slanted her was questioning.

"Yes, but it would be rewarding. The orchards could be restored and replanted. And there's a couple of old greenhouses on the other side of the barn where you could raise perennials for sale. People are starting to use perennials more in their gardens. There's always a market for good plants. Some unusual things—native stuff, maybe."

John tried to look at the rundown property through her eyes. The house was old and worn but it looked solid. The trees were gnarled with age and even his untrained eye could see that they were badly in need of pruning. But they were putting forth a brave show of shiny green leaves. When they bloomed, the orchard must be a cloud of white blossoms. The house would sport a fresh coat of paint—white, of course, with contrasting trim.

He shook his head, the image fading. A gentleman farmer he was not. But before he could dismiss the hazy images from his mind, he looked at Abby's face. She was still wrapped in the fantasies of what the property could be, her eyes all soft brown and dreamy.

And suddenly he wanted more than anything in the world to make her dreams come true.

"Is the old man willing to sell?"

Abby shook herself out of her dream, turning to look at him. "Yes. But I didn't bring you out here to talk you into buying the place."

"Then why did you bring me out here?" He sensed that they were finally getting to the point of the whole day and he didn't think it had much to do with apple orchards or greenhouses.

He'd never dreamed that acquiring a family was such a complex thing. Or that the price it extracted was so high. He'd thought it was simply a matter of moving into a house, doing his share and roots would simply grow of their own accord.

And grow they had, much deeper and stronger than he'd ever imagined they could. And somehow, all those roots, all the vague dreams he'd been having for the future, were tangled around this one woman. If she asked him to leave...

"I wanted to show you my dreams," she said softly, without looking at him. "I wanted to show you something that's a part of me."

John looked around the neglected property, piecing together her meaning. It wasn't the house or the land she was showing him. It was something important to her, a part of herself she probably didn't share with many people. He felt at once touched and uneasy.

"Why?" he asked simply.

"Because you're my husband. And being married means you share things." She lifted her eyes to his face. "You share things like being sick and you share dreams and you share plans for the future. Good times and bad. We promised to share those things, John."

"Yes," he agreed cautiously.

"You don't share things, John." There was no anger in her words, no reproach. Just a statement of fact. "Not real things. You don't tell me where you've been or where you want to go. You don't tell me what you dream of for the future. I had to find out from Dillon that you'd been in Vietnam. Why didn't you tell me that?"

"Why would you want to know?"

"Because it's part of what makes you who you are. I don't expect you to tell me every little detail of your past but you don't tell my anything at all."

"I guess I don't see any reason to talk about the past," he said, shrugging.

"The past is part of who you are. I think you don't talk about your past because you don't want anyone to get too close. You don't want to be vulnerable."

"Most people put up a few walls, Abby." He sat up, wishing he could shut out her words.

"Not like yours." She looked at him, her eyes pleading. "You said you wanted to have a family. That was why you married me. But you can't be part of a family without being willing to lay it all on the line.

"You go through the motions, John, but you're not taking any chances. When you got sick, you expected me to just leave you alone to recover. I bet if you hadn't been too sick to drive, you would have found a motel room somewhere and not come back until the fever was gone."

The way his eyes flickered revealed the accuracy of her guess. "There was no reason to bother you," he muttered.

"No reason? I'm your wife."

John stared at the old house as if he could find the right words written in the peeling paint. How could he possibly make her understand?

"When I was growing up, my parents fought constantly," he said abruptly. "They loved each other, at least at first but they were hopelessly incompatible and by the time I was old enough to understand what was going on, they'd come to hate each other at least as passionately as they'd loved."

He plucked a fluffy dandelion out of the grass, spinning it between his fingers, his eyes on the motion. "All my life I listened to them fight. My mother would scream that my father was destroying her. I could never hear what he said in reply but I could hear the tone of his voice. And then he'd leave and I was never quite sure he was coming back.

"They said they stayed together because of me, but I think the real reason is that neither could bear to leave the other, even though they were destroying each other.

"I can remember promising myself that I'd never let myself be that vulnerable to someone else's moods. I'd never tie myself into somebody else's life like that."

Abby looked at his profile, feeling her heart ache for the scared little boy he must have been. He'd learned to lock his feelings up inside and he'd never let them out.

"Not every love is that destructive, John."

"I guess." He opened his hand, staring at the crushed flower a moment before tossing it away. "If I don't tell you things, Abby, it's because I'm not used to anyone wanting to know. I've spent a lot of years alone and you get into some bad habits that way. And my work hasn't encouraged me to be talkative."

And that was probably all he'd ever tell her about his job, she realized. She could guess some of it from the way he moved, the fact that he handled a gun as comfortably as he did a hammer. Well, she could live with whatever secrets he kept about his work. That wasn't important to her. What was important was what was in his heart.

"I love you, John."

The words fell between them, creating ripples in the quiet air. The look of shock that crossed his face would have been funny if she hadn't been gambling with her heart.

"Abby...I... We didn't— Hell." He ran his fingers through his hair, ruffling it into thick dark waves. He swallowed against a wave of something that could have been panic. She was moving too fast, dragging him into waters he didn't want to swim.

"I don't expect you to vow your undying love," she told him, struggling to keep a note of humor in her voice.

"We didn't go into this talking about love," he said, a vague indignation in his voice.

"I know. It was unfair of me to fall in love with you."

"That's not what I meant." He thrust his fingers through his hair again. He didn't look at her—couldn't look at her. His gut churned with emotions he couldn't put a name to— was afraid to put a name to.

"I'm not the kind of man who falls in love," he said at last, unsure even as he said it that it was still true.

"What kind of man falls in love?"

"I don't know. I just never thought . . . There was some-one once but she died and I—" He broke off, shaking his head. No, he couldn't throw Eileen into this. It wasn't honest.

"Did you love her very much?" He heard the catch in Abby's question and his chest ached.

"I thought I did." John looked at her, seeing the way the sun caught in her hair the soft curve of her cheek. Had he loved Eileen? It was so long ago now. Somehow her image had grown distant, like a fondly remembered photograph.

No, it wasn't her memory that stood between them. It was— What? His own fear, he admitted silently. All his life, his one rule had been to always be in control of himself and of as much of his environment as possible. It was safer that way, personally and professionally.

But what he felt for Abby wasn't safe. Whatever it was, it wasn't safe at all. She'd opened herself up to him, made herself vulnerable. Because she loved him. He shied away from the thought even as he drew it to him hungrily.

What could he say to her?

"It's all right, John. I didn't expect you to say you loved me." She must have read the conflict in his eyes. "I just thought I should give you fair warning that I want more from this marriage than practicalities. I want passion and laughter. I want to be able to argue with you and know that we're going to make up because we love each other too much not to. In a few years, I think I might like to have children of our own."

John closed his eyes, trying to shut out the image of her carrying his child. This wasn't the way he'd planned it, he thought, feeling something close to panic. This wasn't the way it was supposed to go at all.

"Abby, I don't know that I can give you what you want," he said at last, aware that he wanted nothing more in the world than to make her happy.

"Is it this woman you loved?" she asked, her eyes dropping to where her fingers plucked at the blanket.

For a moment, he wished he could seize on that as an excuse but it wouldn't be fair, either to Abby or to what he'd once felt for Eileen. He reached out and caught her restless hand.

"No. What I felt for her was a long time ago. It's me, Abby. I don't think I'm capable of giving you what you want."

"Oh, I think you are." She reached up to set her free hand against his face. "I think you're capable of a great deal more than you give yourself credit for, John Michael Lonigan."

John closed his eyes, not wanting to see the vulnerability in her expression. How could she open herself up to him like that? Didn't she know he wasn't worth the risk?

With a groan, he pulled her across the blanket and into his arms. She met his kiss with all the warmth and passion a man could ever dream of having. This was a woman who deserved more than he could offer.

But, God, how he wanted to be able to give her what she asked.

Chapter Fourteen

There were no miraculous overnight changes. Abby hadn't expected there to be. But she'd gained some insight into the man she'd married. She understood his reserve, his caution about emotional commitment.

He might think he couldn't give her what she wanted but she knew he could if only he could bring himself to trust her enough. Only time could build that trust. She was willing to give him the time he needed as long as she could believe she'd gain his love with her patience.

She couldn't be sure it wasn't her imagination, but it seemed as if there were something different about the way he looked at her after their picnic at the farm, a sort of puzzled expression, as if he were seeking some reason to doubt her.

Abby didn't tell him she loved him again, though there were moments when the words nearly spilled out. She'd told him how she felt; now it was up to him and patience to prove the truth of it.

JOHN'S THINKING wasn't quite so clear. But then, he was trying to work his way through a lifetime of distrust. To Abby, life was straightforward and simple, if not easy. She opened her arms to it, accepting that you had to take the bad in order to get the good. In John's experience, the bad had generally far outweighed the good.

Life came without guarantees and he wasn't fool enough to expect one, but he wasn't sure he was ready to throw out forty years of caution and reach for what Abby had to offer.

But was he willing to lose her?

God, no. The answer came fast enough to knock the breath from him. In the few weeks they'd been married, she'd managed to wrap herself so firmly around his heart that he couldn't imagine tearing her loose.

John swung his feet off the bed, careful not to wake Abby. Grabbing his jeans, he pulled them on before slipping out into the hallway. One thing he'd learned was that when you lived with children, you never assumed they were going to be sleeping when they should be, and he was in no mood to encounter Mara without his pants on.

He flipped a light on in the kitchen and set water on to heat for coffee. Frowning at the gaping hole in the cabinets that would soon hold a dishwasher, he wondered if they should have just replaced all the cabinets while they were at it.

God, there he was, thinking like a typical suburban husband.

But that's what he was.

With a curse, he turned off the water and slipped out the back door. Gravel crunched beneath his bare feet as he walked to where the Gullwing sat, gleaming ebony in the moonlight. He rested his hand on one fender.

The car was woefully out of place in Beaumont, Washington. Even more out of place in his current life-style. It was a car that begged to unwind on the open road, not sit next to a slightly scruffy little house in a small town.

But he'd left the open road behind him, hadn't he?

He shoved his hands into the pockets of his jeans, frowning down at the car. Was he holding on to the Gullwing because he still had some vague idea of leaving? If his oh-so-practical marriage didn't work out, he could just throw his duffel into the car and take off?

The thought held no appeal. He'd spent two years seeing what lay over the next hill and it was nothing but more hills. The call of the open road that he'd once thought so irresistible wasn't even a faint whisper in his ear anymore. He was done with traveling.

He'd come home.

The thought slipped in unbidden, bringing peace with it. He'd married Abby to have a home but he'd been looking in the wrong place. Home wasn't a house or a town or even staying in one place. Home was in a pair of warm brown eyes, in a soft smile, in the words, I love you.

He tilted his head back, staring up at the full moon, feeling a peace he'd never known pouring through him. Loving Abby was taking a chance, but he couldn't pretend anymore. He loved her, risks and all. He grinned up at the moon. He loved her.

And he knew just how to prove it to her.

"I'LL BE BACK in a week. Maybe a little more."

Abby nodded in answer to John's words, trying to look as if her heart weren't cracking into a thousand pieces. He thrust a handful of underwear into his duffel and zipped it shut. Glancing around to see if he'd forgotten anything, his eyes settled on her face.

She immediately forced a smile. "I guess we can rub along without you for a little while."

She trailed after him to the front door. He'd told her about this trip yesterday and she'd had plenty of time to convince herself that he was never coming back, despite what he said.

"Abby, I'm coming back."

"Of course you are." But her agreement was a little too bright to be believable. One corner of John's mouth rose.

"Even if you think I'd lie to *you* about it, do you really think I'd lie to Jason and Mara? I told them I was coming back, remember?"

"I know." She lowered her eyes, not wanting him to see the tears that threatened to spill over. "I'm just being silly. I always hated goodbyes."

"Then don't say one." His hand cupped her cheek, lifting her face to his. "I've just got a few things to straighten out. And when I come home, I have some things I want to tell you."

"What kind of things?" Her eyes searched his face but there was nothing to be read there.

"When I get home," he said again. "Have a little faith."

She swallowed hard. She wanted to have faith, wanted to believe he was coming back. Seeing that half smile, she could almost believe.

"I've never lied to you, Abby," he said quietly, his eyes meeting hers.

No, he'd never lied, she thought, feeling some of her fears ease. He might not be the most forthcoming of men but he'd never lied to her.

"I'll see you next week, then," she said, forcing a note of confidence she didn't quite feel.

If John heard the doubt in her voice, he chose to ignore it. He bent to kiss her, his mouth slanting hungrily over hers. *As if he'd never kiss her again?* she wondered frantically. When he lifted his head, her cheeks were flushed, her breathing uneven. His gaze was searching, but she couldn't begin to guess just what he was looking for.

"I'll be back before you know it. I promise."

"Okay." Abby's smile was even shakier than her agreement. She watched him walk out the door, the duffel carried easily in one hand. She shut the door before he got to
the curb where the Gullwing sat waiting, all sleek and black.
If she'd thought it would do any good, she would have gone
out the night before and slashed the tires on the damn car,
she thought savagely, leaning back against the door.

Where was her pride? she chided herself. If he didn't
want to stay, then she certainly didn't want to hold him.
Not even if it killed her to let him go. Besides, he'd said he
was coming back and she believed him.

Didn't she?

IT WAS INCREDIBLE how empty the house seemed once he
was gone. Admittedly he was a rather large presence, but it
was more than just the physical absence. In the few weeks
they'd been married, he'd become such an integral part of
her life that now there was a hole where he should have
been.

The children missed him, too. Mara's demands to know
when John was coming home were so persistent that Abby
had a fleeting moment of remembering how quiet it had
been when her niece didn't talk. Not that she wanted *that*
back again, of course, but wasn't there a **happy** medium
between silence and harassment?

Even Jason missed him, mentioning that he'd been hoping to get John's advice on a model car he was building and
when did Abby think he was coming back?

Oddly enough, the children's questions made her worries that John might not be back at all seem foolish. As he'd
pointed out, even if she thought he'd lie to *her,* she had to
know he wouldn't lie to the children. He'd told them he was

coming back and they believed him. Their only concern was the when of it.

Abby fended off their questions and tried to keep up her flagging spirits. Had she been wrong to tell John she loved him? He seemed to believe he couldn't give her what she wanted. What if he was right? Not that he couldn't love *anyone*—she didn't believe that for a minute—but what if he couldn't love *her?*

"What are you looking so glum about?" Kate's cheerful voice broke into her increasingly gloomy thoughts.

Abby looked up from the menu she'd been frowning at, grateful for the interruption.

"Sorry. I didn't mean to go into a funk on you." She set aside the menu. "I suppose I could ask you what you're looking so cheerful about but I suspect I already know. When's the wedding?"

"Spoilsport. The least you could do is look surprised." But Kate's radiant smile made it clear that she didn't need Abby's surprise to make her happy.

"If you wanted me to be surprised, you shouldn't go around looking all bridal. I can practically smell the orange blossom. So when's the wedding?"

"Next month." Kate stuck out her hand so Abby could admire the small diamond she was wearing. "Dillon asked me last night. That's why I asked you to lunch today. You will be my matron of honor, won't you?"

"Of course. Didn't I promise when we were eight?"

"Oh, Abby, I'm so happy."

"No one would ever guess," Abby said teasingly, seeing her friend's slightly teary smile.

"Go ahead and make fun of me," Kate said, putting on a martyred air.

"I really am happy for you, Katie." Abby reached across the table to squeeze her hand. "You and Dillon are going to be madly happy. I just know it. I'll bet you have the hog pen swathed in silk and the chickens paper-trained a month after you move out to the farm.''

"Do you think it will take me a whole month?" Kate asked anxiously, and then they both laughed.

The waitress arrived just then to take their orders. After she was gone, Kate reached for a bread stick, crunching into it with obvious relish. Her appetite had deserted her in the weeks she and Dillon were apart. Now that he was back in her life, she'd rediscovered food.

"You should be over your gloomy mood now that John's home," she said between nibbles.

"Excuse me?" Abby raised her brows. "John isn't home."

Kate stopped chewing and stared at her. "Sure he is. I saw him yesterday."

"Where?"

"At the liquor store." Kate set down the half-eaten bread stick. "I'm sure it was him. He was getting out of a car."

"The Gullwing?"

"No. It was a rather scruffy Corvette—old, I think. I don't know the models." She shrugged her indifference to automotive design.

"What would John be doing driving an old Corvette?"

"I don't know. Maybe it wasn't him after all. I mean, I was driving down the street and how good a look at a person can you really get when you're driving by at thirty miles an hour." Concerned that she might have upset Abby, Kate tried to smooth the moment over.

Privately Abby thought you could probably get a pretty good look at someone but she didn't say as much. If Kate was wrong and it hadn't been John, then there was no reason to get upset. But if Kate was right and John had been back in town since yesterday and hadn't bothered to come home, then that was something else again.

"John?" Bill frowned as if trying to remember someone by that name. He'd looked uneasy the moment Abby came into the store, his eyes skittering around as if looking for a way to avoid her.

"My husband," she reminded him, with a patient smile. "He works for you."

"Of course he does." Bill chuckled as if someone had made a joke. Abby kept her smile in place but her eyes remained steady on his.

"*Did* he mention to you when he might be back?" She'd already asked the question but Bill still hadn't managed to come up with an answer.

"Back?" Bill frowned down at the counter, polishing an invisible smear out of it with the dust rag he held. "No. No, can't say he did. Mention it, that is." He looked up at Abby. "Problem? I'd be glad to help if there's something you need."

It was the first completely honest thing he'd said since she'd come in, Abby thought. Her smile relaxed around the edges, became more genuine.

"There's nothing you can do, Bill. But I appreciate the offer."

"Well, you keep it in mind, Abby."

She left the store with the answer she'd sought and hoped she wouldn't get. Bill didn't have to tell her that John was already back in town, she could read it in the way he avoided her eyes.

She slammed her car door shut and then sat staring broodingly out the windshield. Just what had John been doing back in town yesterday—and why hadn't he come home?

SHE HAD ANOTHER twenty-four hours to contemplate questions to which she had no answers. The only person who could provide the answers was John, and the longer he stayed out of sight the more Abby found anxiety turning into anger.

Who did he think he was? No matter how uneasy he was about making an emotional commitment, he *had* made a commitment when he'd married her. Their wedding vows might not have included "thou shalt not sneak back into town without telling your wife" but that should have been self-evident, even to John.

All the worrying she'd done, wondering where he'd gone, if he was all right, wondering if anyone would know to call her if something happened to him. And he hadn't even bothered to tell her when he did come back.

Twenty-four hours gave her plenty of time to stew. If she were honest with herself, she would have been forced to admit that the anger was more a defense than anything else. Deep inside, she'd never really believed that John would come back. Now, he apparently *had* come back. But not to her.

IT WAS LATE AFTERNOON the day after she talked to Bill when John finally put in an appearance. Abby had been home just long enough to change into jeans and a T-shirt and tie her hair back with a ribbon. Her mood had fluctuated from hurt to anger to confusion and she'd decided to match her activity to her mood and clean out the linen closet, which contained more junk than linens.

She had her head buried in the back of the closet, struggling with a box of empty bottles she couldn't remember why she'd saved, when she heard the front door bang shut.

"Abby?" At the sound of John's voice, she jerked back, banging the back of her head against a shelf. But it wasn't pain that made her heart start to pound.

"Abby?"

He was home.

She stared into the closet, panic emptying her mind of thought. What was she supposed to say to him? Was he going to pretend he'd just gotten back from wherever he'd been? Did he think he could leave for a week and a half, worry her half out of her mind and then just waltz back in as if nothing had happened?

She wanted to run out and throw herself at him, feel his arms close around her, the reassuring solidity of him against her. He'd come home. Despite all her doubts, he'd come home.

She wanted to confront him, preferably opening the conversation with a good right cross to his damned, uncommunicative jaw. Get his attention before she told him what an inconsiderate beast he was.

And most of all, she wanted to pull the closet door shut behind her and pretend she wasn't here at all.

"Abby?" His shadow blocked the light as he stopped in front of the open closet door. It was too late to pretend she wasn't here, and pride wouldn't let her throw herself at him like a mindless ninny. Abby drew a deep breath and turned toward him.

"John." She managed to put a note of surprise in the name, as if she'd just been so absorbed in the fascinating contents of the closet that she hadn't realized he was there.

There was an awkward pause. John seemed to be waiting for her to say something more. Abby couldn't have said another word to save her soul.

"Are you in the middle of something you can't leave?" he asked finally.

"No, of course not." She didn't think he was likely to believe that there was toxic waste lurking among the towels that needed immediate disposal. He stepped back and she was forced to leave the dubious shelter of the closet.

"Where are Jason and Mara?" he asked as he followed her into the living room.

"They both went home with friends. If we'd known when to expect you, I'm sure they would have been here."

He didn't seem to hear the edge to her voice. "That's okay. My schedule was unpredictable."

Abby stopped in the middle of the living room and turned to look at him, startled to find him so close behind her. She was struck yet again by the solidity of him, the feeling he gave of being even larger than he was.

He was too close. It was difficult to think, to remember why she had every right to be angry with him, when he was so close. It was even more difficult to think when he reached out to cup the back of her head with one large hand, tilting her face up for his kiss.

As much out of uncertainty as anything else, Abby remained unresponsive. She didn't know why he'd left, didn't know why he'd come back. She loved him and she'd thought she could give him time and room to develop feelings for her. Now she wasn't so sure.

John drew back, his eyes searching her face, questioning. "Is something wrong?"

"When did you get back?" Abby stepped back out of reach.

Hearing the chill in her voice, John's eyes were suddenly shuttered. "Why do you ask?"

"Kate saw you two days ago. *Two days.*"

"And?"

"And? And? Why didn't you call? Why didn't you come home?" Abby waved her hands to emphasize the questions, feeling all the hurt anger welling up in her throat. "We went into this marriage for practical reasons. You never made any promises of undying love and devotion and I've accepted that. But you can't just waltz in and out of my life—our lives," she amended, including the children.

"Is that what you think I've done? Waltzed in and out?"

"How should I know?" she cried. "You don't tell me where you're going or why or when you'll be back. 'I've got things to clear up,' you say and off you go. And then, when you do come back, you don't even bother to tell me. How do you think I felt when Kate said she'd seen you and it was perfectly obvious I had no idea you were even in the state?"

"It didn't occur to me that there would be any problem," John said, without expression. "I had some business to attend to and—"

"There you go again." Abby's hands clenched into fists at her sides. "I told you I could live with you not talking about your past and I meant it. You can be as close-mouthed about your work as you want. But I can't live with all the secrets you seem to like to keep.

"You told me once that you didn't think you were capable of giving me what I wanted, what I needed in this marriage, and I said you were wrong. But I'm beginning to wonder if you were right after all. Maybe you aren't capable of giving me the kind of trust and love I need. Maybe you aren't capable of making this something more than a practical marriage."

Abby caught her breath, staring at him, waiting for his reaction. John stared at her, his eyes dark and unreadable. *Say something. Tell me you want to make this marriage work. Tell me you care.*

"Maybe you're right," he said slowly. He pushed his hands into his pockets and then pulled them out again, staring at them uncertainly. "Maybe I can't give you what you need."

Without another word, he turned and walked out the door, closing it quietly behind him. Abby stared after him, horrified. He couldn't just walk out. They had to talk this out.

She had a sudden memory of him telling her about his parents—how he'd listened while they fought, how his father would leave. It hit her suddenly that he was probably dealing with her attack in the only way he knew how, just as his father had dealt with his mother's attacks all those years ago.

She couldn't let him go. Not like this. She was angry but that didn't mean they couldn't work things out. They could talk—she'd talk, if he didn't know what to say. They'd work it out.

Her breath catching on something perilously close to a sob, she rushed to the door and snatched it open. She had to catch him before he simply drove out of her life.

She nearly fell into his arms. Clutching his shoulders as if she'd never let him go, she pressed her face against his chest.

"I'm sorry for jumping all over you. I had no right."

"You had every right." John's arms closed around her, sure and strong. "I should have explained everything. I shouldn't have walked out."

Abby didn't care what he was saying, just as long as he kept holding her as if he'd never let go. He picked her up and carried her back into the house. He sat down on the sofa, cradling her in his lap.

"I got halfway across the lawn and realized I was doing just what I've done all my life," he murmured. "I was running away. And I promised myself I wasn't going to do that anymore."

"I shouldn't have jumped all over you without waiting for an explanation," she said, lifting her head to look at him. "When Kate said she'd seen you, I was so hurt and angry. I acted like a shrew."

"A bit." His smile took any sting out of the agreement. He reached up to brush a lock of pale hair back from her face, his expression tender. "But I deserved it. I should have explained everything instead of keeping it to myself. Old habits die hard, I guess. Forgive me, sweetheart?"

Forgive him? If he called her sweetheart and continued to look at her as . . . as if he loved her, she'd forgive him anything. She nodded, afraid to believe what she thought she saw in his eyes.

"I brought you something." He pulled a folded stack of papers out of his shirt pocket, handing them to her. Abby took them, her eyes leaving his face reluctantly. But she couldn't seem to focus on the printed lines well enough to make sense of them. She didn't really care what was on a piece of paper, all she cared about was what was in his eyes.

Sensing that her attention was less than caught by his gift, John took the papers back. "It's a preliminary agreement to buy the farm."

"Farm?"

"Your perennial business? The orchards? That monster of a house you seem to like so much?" he prodded her flagging memory.

"You bought it?" she asked incredulously.

"Subject to your approval. I thought, if you wanted, you could quit work at the market and go to work full-time on those greenhouses you seemed to like so much."

"For me? You bought it for me?" She snatched the papers back, staring at the word that made her dream a possibility.

"You're also looking at Bill's new partner in the liquo store."

"Partner?" Abby couldn't seem to grasp everything h was telling her.

"Eventually, I'll be able to buy him out."

"How did you do all this?" she asked, looking from hir to the papers.

"I sold the Gullwing. I went to L.A. and sold it to a col lector I knew of."

"You sold your car? Oh, no."

"I didn't think you particularly liked it," he said frowning.

"You loved that car." She hated the thought that he'o sold it to buy her farm.

"No, I didn't. It was a great car but I didn't need it any more. It was my escape hatch, my way out, and I don't nee a way out anymore."

"You don't?" she whispered. There it was again. Tha look in his eyes that she could almost believe was love.

"When I married you, I was looking for a home, a plac to sink roots. But I didn't really believe it would happen and the car was a way to run away when it became obviou that our 'practical' marriage couldn't work."

"And you think maybe it could work now?" she asked swallowing hard.

"I think it has to. When two people love each other a much as we do, it's bound to work."

"Two people?" She closed her eyes, crumpling th agreement on the farm between her fingers. "Two peo ple," she said again, savoring the words.

"I...love you, Abby." The words didn't come easily bu they came from his heart.

Opening her eyes, Abby looked at him, all her love in he eyes. The words might never come easy for him but it didn' matter if he didn't say it often, as long as he looked at her the way he did right now. And she had the feeling that secrecy might always come a little easier to him than openness. But she could live with that, as long as he shared the important things.

"I love you, John."

His mouth smothered the last of her words and Abby threw her arms around his neck.

They'd gone into this marriage with all kinds of practical reasons. But maybe love was the most practical reason of all.

PENNY JORDAN

Sins and infidelities . . .
Dreams and obsessions . . .
Shattering secrets
unfold in . . .

THE HIDDEN YEARS

SAGE — stunning, sensual and vibrant, she spent a lifetime distancing herself from a past too painful to confront . . . the mother who seemed to hold her at bay, the father who resented her and the heartache of unfulfilled love. To the world, Sage was independent and invulnerable— but it was a mask she cultivated to hide a desperation she herself couldn't quite understand . . . until an unforeseen turn of events drew her into the discovery of the hidden years, finally allowing Sage to open her heart to a passion denied for so long.

The Hidden Years—a compelling novel of truth and passion that will unlock the heart and soul of every woman.

AVAILABLE IN OCTOBER!
Watch for your opportunity to complete your Penny Jordan set. POWER PLAY and SILVER will also be available in October.

HARLEQUIN®
OFFICIAL SWEEPSTAKES
RULES

NO PURCHASE NECESSARY

1. To enter, complete an Official Entry Form or 3"× 5" index card by hand-printing, in plain block letters, your complete name, address, phone number and age, and mailing it to: Harlequin Fashion A Whole New You Sweepstakes, P.O. Box 9056, Buffalo, NY 14269-9056.

   No responsibility is assumed for lost, late or misdirected mail. Entries must be sent separately with first class postage affixed, and be received no later than December 31, 1991 for eligibility.

2. Winners will be selected by D.L. Blair, Inc., an independent judging organization whose decisions are final, in random drawings to be held on January 30, 1992 in Blair, NE at 10:00 a.m. from among all eligible entries received.

3. The prizes to be awarded and their approximate retail values are as follows: Grand Prize — A brand-new Mercury Sable LS plus a trip for two (2) to Paris, including round-trip air transportation, six (6) nights hotel accommodation, a $1,400 meal/spending money stipend and $2,000 cash toward a new fashion wardrobe (approximate value: $28,000) or $15,000 cash; two (2) Second Prizes — A trip to Paris, including round-trip air transportation, six (6) nights hotel accommodation, a $1,400 meal/spending money stipend and $2,000 cash toward a new fashion wardrobe (approximate value: $11,000) or $5,000 cash; three (3) Third Prizes — $2,000 cash toward a new fashion wardrobe. All prizes are valued in U.S. currency. Travel award air transportation is from the commercial airport nearest winner's home. Travel is subject to space and accommodation availability, and must be completed by June 30, 1993. Sweepstakes offer is open to residents of the U.S. and Canada who are 21 years of age or older as of December 31, 1991, except residents of Puerto Rico, employees and immediate family members of Torstar Corp., its affiliates, subsidiaries, and all agencies, entities and persons connected with the use, marketing, or conduct of this sweepstakes. All federal, state, provincial, municipal and local laws apply. Offer void wherever prohibited by law. Taxes and/or duties, applicable registration and licensing fees, are the sole responsibility of the winners. Any litigation within the province of Quebec respecting the conduct and awarding of a prize may be submitted to the Régie des loteries et courses du Québec. All prizes will be awarded; winners will be notified by mail. No substitution of prizes is permitted.

4. Potential winners must sign and return any required Affidavit of Eligibility/Release of Liability within 30 days of notification. In the event of noncompliance within this time period, the prize may be awarded to an alternate winner. Any prize or prize notification returned as undeliverable may result in the awarding of that prize to an alternate winner. By acceptance of their prize, winners consent to use of their names, photographs or their likenesses for purposes of advertising, trade and promotion on behalf of Torstar Corp. without further compensation. Canadian winners must correctly answer a time-limited arithmetical question in order to be awarded a prize.

5. For a list of winners (available after 3/31/92), send a separate stamped, self-addressed envelope to: Harlequin Fashion A Whole New You Sweepstakes, P.O. Box 4694, Blair, NE 68009.

PREMIUM OFFER TERMS

To receive your gift, complete the Offer Certificate according to directions. Be certain to enclose the required number of "Fashion A Whole New You" proofs of product purchase (which are found on the last page of every specially marked "Fashion A Whole New You" Harlequin or Silhouette romance novel). Requests must be received no later than December 31, 1991. Limit: four (4) gifts per name, family, group, organization or address. Items depicted are for illustrative purposes only and may not be exactly as shown. Please allow 6 to 8 weeks for receipt of order. Offer good while quantities of gifts last. In the event an ordered gift is no longer available, you will receive a free, previously unpublished Harlequin or Silhouette book for every proof of purchase you have submitted with your request, plus a refund of the postage and handling charge you have included. Offer good in the U.S. and Canada only.

HQFW-SWPR

HARLEQUIN® OFFICIAL SWEEPSTAKES ENTRY FORM

4-FWARS-3

Complete and return this Entry Form immediately – the more entries you submit, the better your chances of winning!

- Entries must be received by **December 31, 1991**.
- A Random draw will take place on **January 30, 1992**.
- No purchase necessary.

Yes, I want to win a FASHION A WHOLE NEW YOU Classic and Romantic prize from Harlequin:

Name _____ Telephone _____ Age _____

Address _____

City _____ State _____ Zip _____

Return Entries to: **Harlequin FASHION A WHOLE NEW YOU,**
P.O. Box 9056, Buffalo, NY 14269-9056   © 1991 Harlequin Enterprises Limited

PREMIUM OFFER

To receive your free gift, send us the required number of proofs-of-purchase from any specially marked FASHION A WHOLE NEW YOU Harlequin or Silhouette Book with the Offer Certificate properly completed, plus a check or money order (do not send cash) to cover postage and handling payable to Harlequin FASHION A WHOLE NEW YOU Offer. We will send you the specified gift.

OFFER CERTIFICATE

Item	A. ROMANTIC COLLECTOR'S DOLL (Suggested Retail Price $60.00)	B. CLASSIC PICTURE FRAME (Suggested Retail Price $25.00)
# of proofs-of-purchase	18	12
Postage and Handling	$3.50	$2.95
Check one	☐	☐

Name _____

Address _____

City _____ State _____ Zip _____

Mail this certificate, designated number of proofs-of-purchase and check or money order for postage and handling to: **Harlequin FASHION A WHOLE NEW YOU Gift Offer,** P.O. Box 9057, Buffalo, NY 14269-9057. Requests must be received by December 31, 1991.

ONE PROOF-OF-PURCHASE

4-FWARP-3

To collect your fabulous free gift you must include the necessary number of proofs-of-purchase with a properly completed Offer Certificate.

© 1991 Harlequin Enterprises Limited

See previous page for details.